THE DISCOVERY

Jill was angry when she saw what looked like a trash pile somebody had dumped in the mud on the shore. Stink Lake was bad enough without people helping it along.

But when she got closer, she saw it wasn't a trash pile at all. It was white and fleshy in parts; other parts looked like raw hamburger mixed with mud; it was wrapped in ropelike strands of algae reddened with blood and tangled in bone.

Jill gasped, for the trash that littered the shore had kissed her the night before....

THE DOUBLE READ
4233 N. DIXIE
ODESSA, TX 79762

More Chilling Tales of Horror from Avon Books

EXCAVATION
by Steve Rasnic Tem

THE FAIR RULES OF EVIL
by David C. Smith

THE HUNGER
by Whitley Strieber

MIND BENDER
by William Saxon

SATAN'S SPAWN
by Richard Jay Silverthorn

THE WOLFEN
by Whitley Strieber

Avon Books are available at special quantity discounts for bulk purchases for sales promotions, premiums, fund raising or educational use. Special books, or book excerpts, can also be created to fit specific needs.

For details write or telephone the office of the Director of Special Markets, Avon Books, Dept. FP, 105 Madison Avenue, New York, New York 10016, 212-481-5653.

JOHN PEYTON COOKE

AVON BOOKS NEW YORK

THE LAKE is an original publication of Avon Books. This work has never before appeared in book form. This work is a novel. Any similarity to actual persons or events is purely coincidental.

AVON BOOKS
A division of
The Hearst Corporation
105 Madison Avenue
New York, New York 10016

Copyright © 1989 by John Peyton Cooke
Front cover illustration by James Warren
Published by arrangement with the author
Library of Congress Catalog Card Number: 88-92970
ISBN: 0-380-75768-0

All rights reserved, which includes the right to reproduce this book or portions thereof in any form whatsoever except as provided by the U.S. Copyright Law. For information address William Morris Agency, Inc., 1350 Avenue of the Americas, New York, New York 10019.

First Avon Books Printing: August 1989

AVON TRADEMARK REG. U.S. PAT. OFF. AND IN OTHER COUNTRIES, MARCA REGISTRADA, HECHO EN U.S.A.

Printed in the U.S.A.

K-R   10 9 8 7 6 5 4 3 2 1

This book is for:

Tamara Temsik-Sniffin
Julie Keown
Joe Martin
Luis "Alex" Brocksen

PROLOGUE:
Forty Years Ago

Wolf Lesch grabbed the silver sugar bowl and opened his car door, stepping out into the storm. He tossed his fedora onto the seat of the coupe, knowing it would get blown off anyway if he were to wear it, and slammed the door with a solid *thunk*. As he turned to face the rain, he clutched the sugar bowl against his stomach with both hands, like a football. Although Wolf had left his lights on and pointing toward Burroughs Lake, he could already see they were going to be of little use; no light could penetrate a storm as thick as this, much less at night. Wolf had also, absentmindedly, left the radio on, and could still hear the muffled Benny Goodman rendition of "Blue Skies," which was more than inappropriate. Rain cascaded down the folds of his trench coat. His face was drenched.

Wolf started running across Burroughs Park, unable to see the shore of the lake. He knew it lay some yards ahead.

A huge gust of wind blew Wolf off his feet, into soggy earth, and at the same time he heard a loud crash. He looked behind and saw his car had been knocked onto its side in the street, its headlights glowing dimly in the darkness.

It had started raining only an hour ago, and already it had become a deluge. Funnel clouds had been reported in the vicinity, and the entire town had gone running for cover in cellars and church basements, wherever a safe haven could be found. But Wolf could think of no place in Sherman that was safe, because he knew something the townspeople didn't: this was no ordinary storm they were dealing with, it was a witch's curse set forth to destroy them.

Wolf struggled to his feet in the mud, and was glad he'd worn his combat boots, which he hadn't touched since the end of the war. The sugar bowl remained tightly in his clutch. The witch's storm was getting as bad as the tropical storms Wolf had experienced in the Pacific, and he knew it was going to get worse.

Up ahead an eerie glow appeared, a dull orange through streaks of gray. It was a fire at the lake, right in the midst of the rain. Around the shore it spread, quickly encircling Burroughs Lake in a ring of flames. The rain began to thin, and the park was now slightly illumined. Squinting his eyes, Wolf could make out a large funnel cloud directly above the lake, swirling in a frenzy, like a coiled cobra about to strike.

The storm howled on all sides, and Wolf fought the wind with every step, trying as hard as he could to reach the shore.

According to what he knew, the witch's curse would turn Burroughs Lake into a trap for human souls. Once it had found and killed everyone in Sherman, their souls would be sucked into the lake, never to escape. This would augment the witch's power tenfold, and after that there would be no stopping her.

Wolf, on the other hand, had no proof people even had souls to begin with, so he was skeptical of the curse's eventual outcome, but there was no doubt in his mind that everyone was going to be killed.

All this, because the witch wanted revenge.

Wolf was determined to see that she failed. If he didn't stop the curse, by tomorrow morning Sherman would look like Truman had dropped an atom bomb on it, with one important difference—at least if the bomb hit you'd go to meet your maker instead of being consigned to the shallow, murky waters of Burroughs Lake, without chance of parole.

Wolf saw now the source of all the flames. Emerging from the lake were hundreds of salamanders, the firelight reflecting off their slimy hides as they crawled about in the grass. Wherever they stepped, fire sprang up like magic. Of course, it *was* magic, of the blackest kind, and Wolf couldn't believe he had nearly married the woman that was causing all this. The witch. *The bitch*.

But if he hadn't been engaged to her, he would never have found out about the curse, or stolen a page from her notebooks to find out how to stop it. Wolf had had to slice open a salamander from the lake up its ventral side, stuff it into a silver sugar bowl, add a few drops of his own blood, and weld the thing shut. Then all he had to do was throw it in the lake once the curse was under way, and even then it wouldn't truly stop the curse, it would only suppress it for as long as the sugar bowl remained there. According to the witch's own instructions, Wolf would have to "forfeit" his soul to make it work. He figured that was a small price to pay, because he was pretty sure that if he'd ever had a soul, he'd already gotten rid of it back on Guadalcanal. For all he knew, the damned sugar bowl might not even work, anyway.

Wolf tried to get good footing in the mud as he made his way, but twice he tripped and fell flat on his back. Yet he never lost grip of the sugar bowl; it was supposed to protect him.

The salamanders were spreading fire amazingly fast across the grass, which only minutes ago had been drenched by torrents of rain. Wolf crossed their perimeter, but the creatures paid him no heed, while flames shot up on all sides of him. He wasn't even singed, though he could certainly feel the heat. He kept the sugar bowl clutched in one hand and shaded his eyes with the other, trying to make out the edge of the shore.

The funnel cloud overhead had turned into a cloud of flame. Wolf could see the lake water swirling like a vast whirlpool, and the flames all around it turned into a firestorm, rolling outward from the lake on all sides.

Wolf emerged through this unscathed, and finally made it to the shore. With the wind the way it was, he couldn't chance throwing the sugar bowl in from farther inland. He had to make sure it went far out into the lake.

Planting his feet firmly on the banks, Wolf brought the sugar bowl behind his head and hurled it with great strength toward the center of the lake.

But when he did this, something else happened.

Wolf could see himself from outside his body. He drifted up into the air, but his body remained standing by the lake, until suddenly the salamanders were upon it, setting it aflame. His body went up like kindling, and collapsed in a heap on the shore, while the salamanders crawled all over it.

Then the sugar bowl plunged into Burroughs Lake, and Wolf could feel himself (or his spirit, or his soul, or whatever the fuck it was) getting sucked in as well. The storm had ceased utterly. The firestorm was gone. The funnel cloud was gone, and the rain, and the wind. The salamanders, benign once more, were crawling back into the water. The curse had been vanquished.

But Wolf's soul was being drawn down into the brackish water, past the algae growths, past the sludge and the silt, down at last to the sugar bowl that rested on the bottom of the lake.

ONE

A calm came to Burroughs Park in September. The summer was drawing to a close, and there were few days warm enough for people to sunbathe on the grassy banks of the lake. School had begun; weekdays, children were scarce until the afternoon, and disappeared once more at supper time. The Little League season was coming to an end; the baseball diamonds would soon be vacant. The parks crew would no longer come to mow the lawn or set the sprinklers, for the first frost was on its way. People took fewer evening walks as well, choosing instead to watch the new fall shows on TV or help their children with their homework. This time of year, the lake was not only calm, it was lonely.

Jill Beaumont stared west toward the lake from the foyer of the high school, where she stood slumped against a cold stone wall, waiting. Outside, beyond the smudged and streaked plate glass of the front doors, pine trees bent reluctantly in the wind. The American flag fluttered madly atop the flagpole on the high school lawn, as did the Wyoming flag beneath it, with its white ghost of a buffalo upon a stark, blue background. Telephone lines swayed to and fro between their weathered poles. Cumulus clouds rolled swiftly across the glaring afternoon sky, as if they had a pressing engagement elsewhere—or perhaps Jill's time perception was off. She had been waiting for a long time, with her daily headache, for nothing at all.

No one was coming to pick her up, no one was coming to meet her, and the building was empty, aside from the janitors and Jill. She had stayed after school to take a French test, missed when she had been home with a cold two days before. After she had finished the test, she had come down the cement stairs slowly, each step echoing through the deserted lobby, and then stopped short of leaving the building. She had almost wished she could stay longer without feeling it was a waste of time.

On any other day, Jill would have rushed out of the school promptly at three with everyone else and walked home hurriedly across the park. Today, however, while walking the empty locker halls after the test, that had suddenly seemed completely irrational. Of course she hated school— it had a stifling atmosphere about it, more akin to a mausoleum than to a pillar of wisdom. But that afternoon, Jill had thought: *What am I rushing home to?*

After all this waiting, she had finally admitted to herself the answer, which she had known all along: *Nothing*.

A memory of a cool summer night, ten years before, tried to take hold. It came not as a whole, but in isolated fragments: sleeping above the covers because Mom wasn't there to tuck her in; dreaming of horses prancing on a distant island beach; Aunt Celia turning on the bright bedside lamp and scaring the wonderful dream away; and then learning, amid her aunt's tears, that Mom and Dad had died in an automobile accident on their way home. Every time the memory returned, it seemed less real, so by now it felt as if her parents had never even existed, as if they were mere characters on television or mannequins in a department store window.

Jill was disturbed at her own distance from the death of her parents. But she had also come to realize it was their death that had trapped her in Sherman. For the past ten years, she had lived with Celia, gone to school, and seen everything there was to see in the town. Today, worse than ever before, she was feeling the pangs of desperation.

Please, somebody let me out!

"You waiting for someone, Jill?"

A gust of wind rattled the nearest door, and Jill suddenly returned to awareness. Mr. Prenez, her French teacher, was standing before her. He was clearly on his way out, although he didn't have his briefcase with him. His white hair was receding, and the wrinkles and patches of discoloration on his face made him look older than he probably was, but he dressed sharply—today with a tweed jacket over a brown ski sweater and gray slacks. He had kept himself trim; Jill saw him walking his dog every day at Burroughs Park.

"Oh! I didn't know you were still here," she said, trying to transform what she knew was a grim expression to one of surprise.

"I stayed a while to grade some papers so I wouldn't have to do them over the weekend. Got them all finished, too, including your test. You got an A, of course," he said, and smiled pleasantly. "I'd offer you a ride somewhere, but as usual I'm walking."

"That's all right. I wasn't waiting for anyone. Just—a bad headache, that's all. I was just leaving. See you Monday, Mr. Prenez." She gathered her stuff off the floor: a backpack and a warm Cherry Coke.

"Bye, Jill. Have a sober weekend," he said, and walked out the door. A strong burst of wind rushed in, as if there were a helicopter right outside. Students' discarded papers swirled around the tiled lobby before the door closed, then glided to rest on the floor.

What a strange thing to say, Jill thought. *Does he think I go home and get sloshed every day like Celia? Or was he just joking? God! I've got to get out of here.*

Jill threw her backpack over one shoulder, her pop in the trash can, and opened the door. It swung wide and banged against the brick wall on the outside before the pneumatic door-closer could react. It finally shut behind her, but the sound was lost in the gusty wind.

She felt no better now that she was walking home. She had traded the desolation of Sherman High for the loneliness of Burroughs Park. Nothing for nothing—a fair trade. Thinking about all this made her headache worse. With her hand, she shielded her face from the wind, the afternoon sun, and the stink, but it did little to help.

She needed to talk to Maggie, Curtis, or Sam. One of them would be able to cheer her up.

Jill had always hated Burroughs Park, but today she hated it even more, simply for its being there. Sandwiched, like the high school, in the three-block space between Fremont and Grant streets, it stretched four blocks before meeting Third Street and the backside of the new shopping plaza. The lake took up half that space, but it was dead; it had been stillborn from the first. Ever since its construction, it had been too shallow to turn over annually as a lake should. No fish had ever lived in it because there was too little oxygen, and every year, the lake worsened, freezing, thawing, and rotting in cycle. Algae grew with greater abundance every summer, giving the lake a rotten-egg smell. All that existed there were microscopic animals, insects, sea gulls in the air, and salamanders along the banks. In winter, people ice-skated on the lake's cold, stiff skin. Its name had died, too, long ago; now it seemed as if it had always been known as Stink Lake.

The grass along its shoreline grew over the edge of the earthen banks in long tufts the lawn mowers couldn't reach. The Douglas fir and blue spruce trees grew at sparse intervals, and none were more than forty feet in height, so there was no windbreak. Floating on top of the water, a wreath of slimy algae encircled the lake. When the wind picked up, Jill could see green in the tips of the tiny blue waves. Even if it didn't stink, she still wouldn't have liked it.

At least this year the city was doing something about Stink Lake's condition. At the beginning of the summer, they had installed an aeration device, a metal tube spewing white water in the middle of the lake. It operated day and night, a nondecorative fountain bringing dead water to the top for oxygenation. Jill could notice the difference it had made; the lake didn't smell quite so bad this year as before.

Three men from the parks department in hip-waders

were standing in the water, scooping the algae out with rakes and depositing it on the shore. It seemed a hopeless task; the algae easily reached thirty feet into the lake at any given point.

Jill passed the playground equipment on her left; there were no children, but the wind took their place, pushing the swings back and forth, swirling down the twisted slide, and rocking the strange, fiberglass spring-horses—on which children seldom played anyway.

The people frequenting Burroughs Park were generally those seeking more privacy and open space. Jill had often seen loners sitting by themselves on separate benches at the park, staring for hours. Apparently, the park offered nothing anyone wanted, except loneliness—which made Stink Lake seem even more desolate when all the people were gone.

On Grant Street to her right, Jill saw Mr. Prenez entering his small, white house with its immense flower garden out front. His Labrador, Claude, greeted him at the door. Claude was nice, but Jill didn't think she herself would be able to put up with a dog who wanted nothing more out of life than to fetch sticks.

When Jill was halfway across the park, she saw that one of the men in the water was not from the parks department at all, but Curtis Bowles. His brown, spiked haircut and tanned, gaunt face made him easily recognizable even at a distance. The suspendered hip-waders he stood in absurdly enveloped his tall, lean figure, making him look like a clown with baggy pants. Jill hurried over to the shore, close to where he was working shin-high in algae and muck.

"Hey, Jill," said Curtis as she approached. "Want to join me? It's real fun."

"No thanks."

"You coming to my party tomorrow night?" he asked, bringing the rake out of the water and dumping a load of slime at her feet.

"I'd like to, but—"

"C'mon, it'll be your first chance to do some legitimate slam-dancing. You'll never be able to slam at someone else's party." He paused, extending the rake over the water to reach a far clump of algae. "And besides, my parents never go out of town. This'll be my only chance all year to have a party, so it'll be the last chance you'll ever get to slam-dance in Sherman."

"Not if I'm stuck here forever," she said, moving out of the way of another load.

"Hey, you're not upset about that again, are you?"

She nodded. Curtis was used to this. It seemed all they ever talked about anymore was what a pit Sherman was. They both hated it. But Curtis's parents had money, so he would be able to go to any university he wanted after graduation, while Jill would have to hope for financial aid of some kind.

"I don't really feel up to a party right now," she said.

"Well, it's not right now, anyway, it's tomorrow." He pointed at the piles of algae upon the banks. "Look at this wonderful job they gave me. I've only been here a couple hours, and I've cleared off maybe twenty feet of shoreline. And now we're almost through for the day."

She wondered why he was there, and asked him.

"My good deed for the day." He showed off a toothy, Boy Scout smile. "Not really. Oh shit, that's right! I've hardly seen you the last couple of days. You mean Miz Becky didn't tell you about my 'incident'?"

Jill shook her head. She had no idea what he was talking about, and she tried to avoid schizoid bitches like Becky Roth. Whatever it was, it was probably all over the school if Becky had gotten onto it. Then Jill figured it out. "Aha —you're doing time for the city."

"Right-o, Kemo Sabe. The cops nabbed me coming home from Sam's Wednesday night. DWI, MIP, all that crap. So I've got some big-time hours to work off now, since my dad wouldn't pay the fine—"

"—of course," she finished for him.

"And at the time I didn't have any cash."

"Of course. Why didn't you tell me about this?"

"I haven't had the chance. Yesterday I was at Sam's track meet in Rawlins."

"You could have told me during French today."

"Yeah, but you were busy studying for your makeup exam. If I had told you, you would have just been upset and then screwed up your test." Curtis seemed to have forgotten about cleaning up the algae; he was leaning on his rake.

"You're right, I would have. But still . . . DWI is pretty bad. You must be in deep trouble."

"Not really. Judge let me off easy, and I'm supposedly grounded, but since my parents are taking off for the weekend, how are they going to keep tabs?" He smiled.

"That's real smart to have a party right now," she said lightly. She wasn't worried—she knew Curtis would come through this unscathed. "Look, about the party, I think Sam and I are probably going out tomorrow."

"I thought you guys were going out tonight."

"We are. Both nights. Otherwise, I'd come. Honest."

Curtis grabbed his rake and gathered some more algae, scowling at the water.

"You haven't even told Sam about your party, have you?" Jill asked. "What's this great silence between you two all of the sudden?"

"It's nothing."

Jesus! Curtis was her oldest friend, but when he didn't want to talk about something, not even she could reach him. Curtis and Sam had both been gone on Thursday, to Sam's track meet. They were best friends, usually inseparable, but suddenly today they were ignoring each other. Whenever they had an argument, it was blatantly obvious, and Jill usually got caught in the middle.

Curtis's supervisor called to him, saying it was time to quit. Curtis waved back at him, acknowledging.

"So you're through with the slave labor for the day, huh?"

Curtis brightened with the change of subject. "That's

the wildest thing. Being a slave paid off." He reached down underneath the hip-waders, pulled out a hundred-dollar bill, and flashed it to Jill before replacing it again in his pocket.

"Where did that come from?"

"You know that old lady you spend so much time with?"

"Maggie."

"Yeah, her. She came over to the lake, and said she'd pay me if I could find this old, silver sugar bowl for her. On my break, I went out there, where she told me to look —about halfway to the center—raked up a ton of weeds, until finally I heard this *clink*, dug around something, and pulled it up out of the silt. Sure enough, there it was—the fucking sugar bowl!"

"And she gave you a hundred dollars for it?" Jill couldn't believe it.

"Yeah. Weird, huh? So tomorrow I'm going to pay off the rest of my fine and I won't have to do this shit anymore." Curtis threw his rake on the shore and climbed out onto the bank, dripping dirty water. "Well, I've got to go now. Off with 'the boys' so they can clock me out. If you don't go out with Sam tomorrow—for any reason—please come by my party, all right?"

"OK, Curtis. I'll see you later."

"Yeah, bye." He grabbed his rake and trudged off toward the other two men, who were throwing their equipment into the back of a battered pickup truck.

Jill suddenly realized it must have been nearly five, and she had to get some coffee ready before Celia woke up. She jogged the rest of the way across the park, not worrying about the coffee, and not thinking about Curtis and Sam's latest fight, but wondering why Maggie had just spent a hundred dollars on an old sugar bowl, and how she had known where it was to begin with.

➣ TWO

She crossed Grant Street and came to her and Celia's trailer house in the Lucky Z Trailer Court. The trailer court looked across at the northwest corner of Burroughs Park. All the trailers in this half-block space dated from the fifties and sixties, and their age showed. Jill's trailer was a washed-out blue with a once silver-looking wing design tacked onto its sides. It had a small yard of thick grass, but only because Jill kept it up. Weeds sprang up all the time, blown in from neighboring plots. Jill tried to keep up with them, but sometimes it seemed pointless.

The only other nice front yard at the trailer court was Maggie's, right next door, but it was a garden. Maggie grew her own vegetables and herbs.

Jill opened the gate. The peeling white paint came off in her hand. She went up the cinder-block steps slowly, unlocked the door, and went inside. The trailer was immaculate, as usual. Somehow, Celia always managed to clean up the tremendous messes she made, even when she was drunk. The only things out of place were in the kitchen: Jill's own mess from breakfast, still there because she had been in a rush that morning before school.

She shut the door behind her, went to the kitchen, took two aspirin, and started a pot of coffee. Then she cleaned up her breakfast dishes and tried to straighten up the kitchen.

Celia worked the graveyard shift as an orderly at Wells Memorial Hospital on the other side of town. A co-worker picked her up every evening. When she was dropped off from work around three-thirty every morning she usually drank in front of the TV, then went to bed until five in the afternoon.

The alarm clock went off in Celia's bedroom at the back of the trailer, followed by a low, rumbling moan before the ringing stopped, and then the sound of the alarm clock striking the carpet with a *ding*. It would be a long time before Celia emerged down the narrow hallway and disappeared into the bathroom.

It was five o'clock now, an hour since Jill had finished taking her French test. How long *had* she stood there, tucked away inside the entrance like that? And how long had Mr. Prenez been standing, watching her, before he had spoken?

Jill scribbled a note to Celia, tossed her backpack in her bedroom, and left the trailer to go over to Maggie's.

Maggie set Jill's stuffed zucchini in front of her, garnished with parsley, with two deviled eggs beside it. Jill couldn't believe such a dish could be whipped up so fast, but she had watched it being prepared with her own eyes, so she had to.

"Do you ever eat anything normal?" Jill asked, unfolding her napkin and looking with anticipation at the food.

"Not if you mean Big Macs and french fries," said Maggie. She sat down across the table from Jill, unfolding her cloth napkin. "Do you know that if you keep eating that garbage, when you die you won't have to be embalmed?"

"Maggie, get serious."

"You'll resemble a wax statue, perfectly preserved with BHA and BHT, for eternity." Maggie took a bite, and added, "Chemicals are bad for the soul."

Dinner was mostly small talk. Jill didn't want to spoil the food by bringing up the sugar bowl or her own after-school depression. But afterwards, while Jill washed the dishes and Maggie dried, the timing seemed right and Jill asked about the sugar bowl.

"That was Curtis?" Maggie asked, surprised. "Somehow I didn't recognize him."

"Forget that. What did you give him a hundred dollars for?"

"Sentimental reasons," Maggie said, putting a plate away in the cupboard. "That sugar bowl has been lost for years."

"Maggie," said Jill calmly, and pointed at the shelf of plates. "That plate is still wet."

"Oh, cob!" Maggie pulled the dripping plate off the shelf, dried it, and after first wiping off the plate beneath, put it back.

"Still, a hundred dollars!"

"An old maid's folly. If you were as old as I, perhaps you would understand." Maggie's moist eyes glistened. "Here, let's sit down. I want to show you something."

Jill had always liked the cluttered decor of Maggie's trailer. The atmosphere it created was much more comfortable than the one back at her own trailer. There was no consistency or order to the interior. The living room walls were shelves filled with worthless artifacts from gift shops, antique stores, junk piles, and who knew where else. Maggie seldom dusted them, and they were arranged in clumps rather than orderly rows. There was a maroon recliner from the seventies; a braided oval rug from the sixties; a wooden couch with gray, speckled cushions from the fifties; a coffee table with peeling varnish that looked like it pre-dated World War II; and an old-fashioned rolltop desk against the far wall that was older than any of them.

Sometimes Jill came over to Maggie's just to study, because it stimulated her brain better than the sterile trailer she had lived in for the past ten years. Often just being in the same room with Maggie while studying made a difference in her comprehension. Whenever Jill studied, Maggie knitted, crocheted, or did needlework, the end products of which she sold at craft shows at the senior center. Over the last few months, Jill had been spending a greater amount of time around Maggie than ever before, although they had been friends most of Jill's life.

Jill sat in the living room on the couch, while Maggie poked around in one of the drawers of her rolltop desk.

"Ah, here it is," Maggie said, pulling an old photograph out into the light. She set it on the coffee table, in front of Jill, and sat down in the recliner with a sigh.

Jill looked at the yellowed photo with interest, and picked it up; it was stiff, brittle, delicate. A handsome young man stared back at her from the paper. His short, neatly cut black hair matched the color of his penetrating eyes. Standing out against his deeply tanned skin was a broad, ivory smile. Jill smiled herself, unable to turn away from the old, almost timeless image.

"Looks like a young Cary Grant," Jill said.

"No, he doesn't. You're just projecting."

"Well, who is he?"

"He was my fiancé. But he died a long time ago."

"In the war?"

Maggie paused. "I'm afraid this will sound silly, but you see, that sugar bowl belonged to him. It's really all I have left of him now. Thank goodness Curtis found it for me! It's been such a very long time...." She seemed on the verge of tears.

"Oh, Maggie, I'm sorry."

"Don't worry yourself about me, Jill. I've been like this all afternoon—reminiscing, nostalgic, thinking of things I haven't thought about in years. But I'm over it now. I'll be all right." Maggie spoke distantly, as though she were telling herself as well. Although Maggie was very old, Jill imagined the beauty she had once had, now hiding beneath the surface. Maggie had rounded, plucked eyebrows, part of which had been penciled in. The wrinkles on her face were small. If anything, her skin had grown taut with age, accentuating her cheekbones and jaw, and drawing back across her temples. She had lost some of her hairline. Nevertheless, Maggie had a healthy appearance, partly due to the color she showed from working in her garden all summer. She had aged like an old movie star: definitely old, but somehow larger than life.

"Still, it's sad," Jill said, setting the photograph back down on the coffee table. "He was gorgeous. Reminds me a little of Sam."

"Yes, how are you and Sam getting on these days?" Maggie had dabbed her eyes with a tissue and was now smiling politely.

"Just great. We're going to a movie at nine, and then I have a romantic evening planned."

"Jill, you're seventeen. You're too young to have a romantic evening," Maggie said. She reached into a bag near her chair and pulled out a crocheted pillowcase she had been working on. She began adding stitches to a half-finished design on its front.

"I don't feel seventeen. I feel more like forty. I don't know what my problem is. Everyone tells me my high school years are supposed to be the best of my life."

"It's not true."

"I hope not! So far, this year has been lousy. Every day, by the end of sixth period, I have a headache." Jill stretched back and stared up at the light fixture hanging from the ceiling. It was a yellowed ring of flowery designs with six decorative light bulbs poking up, meant to resemble candle flames. Even if this were bad taste, Jill liked it.

She went on to tell Maggie everything that had been plaguing her mind that day. She told her how she couldn't relate to the idiots at the high school, and how all her classes were boring; how she only had three "true friends," and how all the rest were mere "acquaintances"; how she was going to scream if she had to live one more day with Celia, yet there were still eight months left until graduation. But college was what was really bothering her.

"Will you be going to UW?" Maggie asked.

"Most likely. But I hope not. I don't have the money to go anywhere else, unless I get some kind of miracle scholarship."

"Which you will, so stop worrying."

"I'm not worrying," Jill said slowly. "I'm... stagnating, like that stupid lake."

Maggie stiffened in midstitch, then composed herself and continued her work, saying, "But even if you do end up going to UW, that will be a change of pace. Laramie's different. Believe me, there are many interesting people, and there is certainly more to do."

"I've been there a lot, Maggie. It doesn't seem that different to me. Sherman is just a cow town: Laramie is a bigger one with a university, that's all. I have to get out of Wyoming."

"I bet you'll get a scholarship to another university, if you try. Just wait. You'll see."

"I almost think my life depends on it. Sam will definitely be getting a track scholarship to some out-of-state college that I can't afford, and then Curtis will probably go wherever Sam is going. And if I go to UW, you'll still be in Sherman. Next year I'll be completely deserted."

"All you have to do is make new friends. It's that simple."

Jill wasn't so sure, however. She was worried that she might never again talk to Curtis, Sam, or Maggie after high school was over, as if there were a law against it.

Maggie sighed. "You know, you shouldn't be thinking about all these things. Seventeen-year-old girls aren't supposed to have this kind of pressure. Why don't you and Sam skip the romantic evening and go roller-skating?"

"We can't. We're both neurotic. Honestly, Maggie, if anything can relieve this pressure, it'll be a romantic evening with Sam."

Maggie rose, set her crocheting down in the chair, picked up the photograph from the coffee table, and replaced it in the rolltop desk. "You'd better be going now, so you can get ready for your date," she said.

"Yeah, I guess you're right. Thanks for the stuffed zucchini, Maggie, it was terrific. Sometime I ought to bring Sam and Curtis over and we can have a big dinner, the four of us."

"Perhaps," Maggie muttered. "Have a good time, and don't do anything... foolish. I was about to tell you not to do anything I wouldn't do, but that would mean you'd have to sit around all evening doing needlework alone."

"Don't worry, Maggie. Sam's no rapist, and I can take care of myself. But thanks anyhow. See ya!" She opened the door and went down the steps, past Maggie's garden, and shut the gate. The sun had already set. Elk Mountain was a mere silhouette looming above the lake, the sky behind it a darkening purple.

That was strange, Jill thought. Maggie should have been delighted to have guests over for dinner, and she had always said that Sam and Curtis were "swell." It must have been her nostalgic mood. Maybe there were too many memories clogging her thinking. After all, she had put that plate away when it was still soaking wet, and a hundred dollars was too much money to pay for a lost memento— or whatever it was—even if it was made out of silver. Or it could have been senility, although Maggie had never shown signs before.

Jill suddenly realized that Maggie had avoided showing her the sugar bowl. She had given her the explanation, and shown her the old photograph, but not the sugar bowl itself—and it hadn't been on Maggie's shelves. Maggie had deliberately hidden it from her, but *why?*

Maybe the old woman was growing senile after all.

The streets were quiet. The parks crew had left hours before, and everyone in the neighborhood was probably eating dinner. Jill thought she should have seen Mr. Prenez walking Claude around the lake at that time, but there was no one at the park. The only sound in the air was that of the aeration-tube fountain, busily trying to save the lake. The wind was dead, the water still.

Suddenly the aeration tube burped and hiccuped, spewing water erratically. Then, quickly, the tube was pulled under, and there came to the surface a large, bubbly foam where the fountain had been a few seconds before. The bubbles dissipated, flattened, and disappeared, until the dark surface was again smooth and undisturbed.

Jill gasped and looked around, searching for anyone else who might have seen, but there was no one. She headed for Maggie's door, but noticed all her lights were off. *Had she already gone to bed?* And perhaps it wasn't such a good idea to tell Maggie anyway, at least not this evening, with the peculiar mood she was in.

Jill couldn't shake the image from her mind: as if something had pulled the tube under from below. The neighborhood was silent except for, every now and then, a distant *bubbling* from Stink Lake.

THREE

Norbert Prenez woke with a start in his living room. He was seated in his favorite chair, an open book in his lap. Outside, it was dark. He hated September, when night started falling noticeably earlier. Every year it ruined his schedule; he sometimes forgot to take Claude for his walk until the sky was in the late stages of dusk. That, he figured, was what had allowed him to fall asleep; and now— he looked at his watch—*damn*, it was eleven-thirty. Sometimes it seemed as if the sun did not actually set earlier, but that the mountains to the west rose slightly higher every evening. That would make more sense. All the same, he would still go for the walk, because he owed it to Claude.

Before dropping off, Norbert had been reading *Nouvelles Histoires Extraordinaires,* an edition of Baudelaire's translations into French of some of Poe's stories. Madeline had given this to him on their last anniversary before her death. It was now priceless to him, and he read from it often. Poe's tales had taken on an extra element of horror when told in the delicacy of the French language. Somehow the degree of desperation in them was heightened:

—*Pour l'amour de dieu, Montresor!*

But Norbert did not allow the loneliness and despair of Poe's characters any farther than the bindings of the book. Although Madeline was gone forever, he had Claude, his hobbies, his books, and his students. In five years he had grown as close to these as he had ever been to his wife. Life had to go on, of course. Claude was an excellent companion, and when Norbert was away from his dog, he was with his students. The French classes still managed to enlighten him occasionally, even as bizarre as some of the kids had become. Spiked hairdos, guys with earrings, and girls made up like prostitutes were certainly more "grotesque" than anything Poe had ever dreamed of.

Like that kid Curtis Bowles—Norbert had never known a more arrogant student in all his years of teaching. The way he dressed, the way he acted, he was nothing more than a punk. Yet he made good grades, even though he obviously hated school. It seemed whenever there was a disruption in class or in the halls, Curtis was found close by, as if his mere presence set people off balance. Norbert could never fathom how a person like that could breeze through his studies, as Curtis apparently did. But Norbert had a theory that Curtis simply intimidated his teachers, and was pulling the wool over everybody's eyes. Oh well, he thought, it'll hurt him more than it will me!

Jill Beaumont was another mystery—probably the best student he had ever had, yet she was Curtis's best friend. She admittedly disliked school as well (*Moi, je déteste les études*... she had written in one of her papers), but she was nothing like Curtis in any other respect. Jill at least looked *normal,* and was far more mature, but if she were to hang out with Curtis all year long, she might never amount to anything.

Norbert had stopped trying to figure out these kids a long time ago, but his life as a teacher was seldom dull. And never lonely. Norbert liked his students, even the "different" ones.

He slid the Poe volume into its space on the large oaken bookcase filled with row after row of well-used books. The front picture window showed his reflection against a pool of darkness. The only light in the room came from the small reading lamp beside his padded chair. From below, the warm glow cast deep shadows across his wrinkled face, making him look very, very old.

It was a silly time for him to be walking his dog. Not that it worried him; there was little crime in Sherman, and although the park wasn't lighted at night he had never encountered a mugger there; but this was going to make a mess of his weekend. After walking Claude, he would have to prepare some supper—for both of them—and then he would feel like staying up and reading all night, would have to sleep late in the morning, and so on, and so on. It would be Monday before his inner clock was finally back on its proper track.

"Claude," he called. *"Viens!"*

The large black dog got out from behind the chair Norbert had been sitting in. He, too, had been asleep. He pranced over to Norbert's side. He was smiling, his long tongue hanging, limp, out of the side of his mouth. His tail wagged furiously; he knew what was coming.

"Ready for a walk?"

At mention of the word *walk,* Claude's ears pricked up reflexively, making him look like a puppy again.

Norbert grabbed his red-and-black checkered wool coat from the closet and pulled it on. He put his hunting cap on; it fit his head snugly, the flaps dangling over his ears. With the wind howling outside and the sun gone, even in September the cold could be bracing.

He opened the door, and Claude bounded outside ahead of him and ran across the street. His limber black figure was engulfed by the darkness of Burroughs Park.

"Now don't you go jumping in that lake, you hear me?" Norbert called, more as a friend than a master. "I don't want you stinking up the house when we get back."

He stepped out into the night, straining his eyes to locate his dog, and noticed in the harsh light from the porch that his flowers were dying.

➤ FOUR

The familiar red Porsche 911 roared up to the self-service island at the 7-Eleven, behind the parking space where Jill and Sam Taylor sat talking in the backseat of Rick McAlister's Vega.

"There's Curtis," Jill said, looking over her shoulder.

"Shit," said Sam.

Rick and his girlfriend, Deb Zografi, were inside hanging out with some fellow jocks they had run into, and seemed to have forgotten they were dropping off Jill and Sam at Jill's trailer. For now at least, they were stuck near Green Hill Estates, on the other side of town from the Lucky Z Trailer Court. Jill was anxious to get home; there were only four more hours until Celia got off work.

"Who is that riding shotgun?" Jill asked. She could only see the back of the person's head, but it could have been anyone; the only people with whom Curtis hung out were her and Sam.

Sam craned his neck to see. "Can't tell. I hope Curtis doesn't see us."

"Why?"

Curtis, in black leather jacket and worn jeans, started pumping gas. The other guy, dressed in a loose-fitting white jacket with black pinstripes, pleated black leather pants, a black mesh T-shirt, and a dangling white leather tie, headed inside to pay. His closely cropped blond hair was moussed to perfection, and he had a long, silver earring hanging from one ear.

"Erik Mürer," Jill said, surprised.

"Mr. Style," Sam added dryly.

Jill noticed Rick whispering something into Deb's ear when Erik walked into the store. Deb laughed and then nudged a friend of hers, who was wearing a cap that read: "Wyoming Shit Kickers." The jocks were huddled together, talking, laughing, and glancing over at Erik while he waited at the counter to pay for Curtis's gas. Erik was ignoring them, something Jill knew he was very good at.

"Curtis doesn't know this car, though," Sam said. "I don't think he spotted us."

"So what if he did? What's the big deal?"

Sam looked at her for a moment, as if to say, *Don't bring it up, OK?* His stare was always very intense. It was the way he looked at everybody, although it seemed very intimate. He had an all-American look about him—a rugged, stern face with prominent cheekbones, coupled with a gentleness that emanated from his probing gaze. Some people avoided eye contact with him, as if to prevent getting trapped, but Jill locked her eyes on Sam's whenever the two of them were talking.

"What's with you and Curtis all of a sudden?" she asked, eager to stay on the subject.

"It's nothing important."

Jesus! He wasn't going to tell her anything, either. "C'mon, you guys are my best friends. This is driving me crazy. You've got to tell me—does it have anything to do with me and you going out?"

Sam laughed. "Of course not."

"You're sure?"

"Positive. It's got nothing to do with that."

Jill sighed; she was getting nowhere. Turning her gaze, she saw Erik walking back to the Porsche. Erik shouted to Curtis across the gas pumps, "All set. Let's go, guy."

"OK," Curtis yelled back. "My house?"

"Sounds cool."

Erik was still getting into the car as Curtis revved up the engine; Jill found herself hoping they hadn't been drinking. Then the car peeled out, made a tight "U-ie" in the parking lot, and sped past Elk Mountain Golf Course at well over the speed limit.

Sam stared after the car a while.

"They're back," said Jill.

"Huh?"

"Rick and Deb."

"Oh yeah."

Rick sank into the driver's seat, carrying a six-pack of Mountain Dew. Deb slinked in beside him. "Hey, dudes," said Rick, and tossed them each a can. "Here you go."

"Did you guys see that Mürer fag?" Deb wanted to know.

"Looks like a moth chewed up his shirt," said Rick.

"Yeah, you could see his bra," said Deb, who then couldn't stop laughing.

Jill had always thought Deb was screwy, but she knew it probably wasn't her fault. Her whole family was strange. They lived only slightly outside the city limits, and Deb's father, who worked on the railroad, was seldom home. Her mom's entire function seemed little more than to produce a new baby every nine months. Jill didn't know how many Zografis there were, all told, but she knew Mrs. Zografi was currently pregnant again. Deb was the oldest, and in all the years Jill had known her, she'd seen her grow ever more obnoxious. Jill's image of Deb's father was monstrous; she pictured him coming home drunk and beating the first kid he could get his hands on. But that was only speculation. All she knew was, the Zografi kids who were old enough stayed away from home as much as possible, especially Deb's next oldest brother, Troy, who Jill liked somewhat. Troy was a burgeoning juvenile delinquent and the leader of a gang of kids who called themselves the Skunks. Jill had met Troy a couple of times at parties, where he had been hanging out with kids much older than himself; in fact, she recalled once sharing a joint with him (contributing to the delinquency of a fellow minor) and having a long, animated discussion that waxed both philosophical and sexual. Troy's brain was miles ahead of

Deb's; Jill couldn't imagine Troy making the same sort of ignorant comments his sister had just made about Erik Mürer. Jill was about to come to Erik's defense, but to her surprise, Sam beat her to it.

"Have you ever talked to him?" he asked. "I bet you haven't even met the guy."

"Fuck, no, man." Rick started his car.

"Are you kidding?" Deb sneered. "That weirdo?"

"I have," said Sam. "He's a real nice guy, too, so why don't you keep your bullshit to yourselves? You two can be real assholes sometimes. Now, are you going to take Jill and me over to her place or not?"

"Yeah . . . sure, bud," said Rick. He turned the key in the ignition, the starter whined, and the engine rattled to life.

No one spoke the rest of the way.

~~ FIVE

Swift gray clouds with wispy borders drifted like spectres over the park, backlighted by the glow of the gibbous moon.

Claude was waiting for Norbert at the edge of Stink Lake. His shiny coat glistened in the moonlight whenever there came a break in the clouds. He was gorgeous—the best dog Norbert had ever had. He was untrained, but then Norbert had always thought too much discipline took all the life out of a pet.

As precarious as things were for Norbert these days, Claude was the only truly stable thing he could count on. His life was in constant transition: every year he had a new crop of students to teach; he watched the older ones graduate and run off to seek fame and money; old friends in the faculty retired or moved away; new faculty members arrived with whom he found it increasingly difficult to get along; toward the end of each year he felt the ever-growing pressure from the administration to "take advantage" of an early retirement; and he definitely wasn't getting any younger while these things were going on.

Claude was special: something in Norbert's life that no one else could touch. Not only were their daily walks good exercise, they were good therapy.

"Claude, *viens!*" They set out on the foot-trodden path encircling the lake. Claude pranced out in front while Norbert walked at a calm, leisurely pace.

Empty shadows skimmed over the grass like wraiths.

At times, the path brought Norbert and Claude next to the dark, waiting bulk of a spruce tree or a caragana bush

—or their shadows—and Norbert felt ill at ease. Since he was used to taking Claude on his walk in the late afternoon, when there was always some noise, the silence at the lake was disconcerting, as was the absence of sea gulls. Norbert felt as if he stood out from his surroundings with every step, every breath, every *whiff* of his hunting jacket's arms as he walked.

Claude would be little protection against an attacker; he would probably fight by instinct, but poorly. Norbert had never thought the training necessary.

A *bubbling* came from the lake. Norbert stopped suddenly in his tracks and listened carefully, his eyes wide and staring at nothing. But he heard only silence.

He wondered then if the Skunks were about.

The thought made his heart skip a beat, which made him laugh at himself. Surely, the Skunks were harmless; they were all younger than fourteen. The worst thing they had ever done was sneak into the high school and leave a rotting skunk carcass in one of the empty lockers—thus their name. Aside from that, they rode around on their bicycles and called people obscene names. They were an annoyance, but certainly nothing to be afraid of. Norbert knew this; however, with age he had developed a great fear of youth, for what seemed no apparent reason. He could handle the high school students well, being around them constantly. It was the younger ones, the junior-high-aged kids who bothered—no, scared him. He knew his fear was ridiculous, but there was nothing he could do about it.

"Claude," he called. He was careful not to be too loud. "Why don't we call it a night, huh boy?"

As he spoke, though, he saw Claude lunge ahead to a boggy, mud-caked portion of shoreline, and return dancing with excitement, holding a large stick in his jaws.

All of a sudden everything was back to normal, and a sense of relief settled over Norbert. He laughed.

"So you want a game of stick?"

Claude wagged his tail. His coat abruptly ceased to glisten. Looking up, Norbert saw that the clouds were covering the sky with a sheet of blackness, though he could still perceive the faint glow wherein the moon was hiding. His eyes took a moment to adjust to the quick change of lighting. But he could still clearly see the lake beside them, the grass surrounding them, all the houses along Fremont and Grant streets, and the high school.

He grasped an end of the stick and said, "Drop it." After getting the stick from Claude, he told him to sit. The dog complied quickly, his tail brushing back and forth in the grass while he panted excitedly.

Norbert threw the stick as far inland as he could and nearly pulled a muscle in his shoulder. "Get it," he said.

Claude raced off after the stick, into the shadowed areas near the playground equipment.

Norbert was surprised at how dark it was without a flashlight. Already the high school across the street was but a hollow black form without detail. He had lost sight of Claude among the bushes, slides, swings, and shadows. He heard him scampering for the stick. He squinted his eyes.

The lake water lapped at his shoes, startling him.

"Goddamn!" He spun around and saw that he was standing in the mud at the edge of the shoreline. *How did I manage that?* He figured he must have unconsciously backed up while straining his eyes to see Claude.

Norbert glanced at the sky, but could no longer find the gray glow of the hidden moon; the clouds were thickening.

Where was Claude? All Norbert could hear was the water rippling, and the blood rushing through his veins— the sound of the ocean in a seashell. But he was not at the ocean—he hated the ocean, especially the filthy Mediterranean—he was walking his dog at Stink Lake.

Out of nowhere, Claude appeared, running swiftly toward Norbert. The stick, naturally, was in his mouth.

"Here, boy!" Norbert called, relieved. "Atta boy!"

Claude ran past him, as he always did, and into the water for a moment, but then he circled back in front of him, dropping the stick at his feet. Claude sat, waiting for his master to throw it once again.

Norbert scratched the top of his dog's head. "No, Claude, no more stick tonight. You just stay with me—thatta boy! Let's go back home. I promise I'll take you for an extra-long walk tomorrow. What do you say?"

They started back. Right away, Norbert had to stop. Beyond the park all he could see was blackness. The night had grown darker. Something about it was strange, and he found himself wondering exactly how far they had gone around the lake, so he could remember in which direction their home lay. There were no discernible landmarks—no visible houses along the lengths of the park, no high school at one end, no backside to the shopping plaza at the other. There was nothing but the lake, grass, and trees; and in the gathering darkness the shadows remained.

Norbert was getting scared. Was it possible for night to become so *black?* He knew he hadn't had an eye examination in many years. Perhaps his eyesight was worsening. Or perhaps he was going blind.

Claude tugged on his master's coat sleeve; he wanted to chase another stick.

"Hold on a sec."

Claude tugged again, harder.

"I said hold it!" Norbert snapped. He looked away from the blackness surrounding him, into his dog's face. At least at this distance Norbert could see. Claude stared at him with watery, cold, sad eyes. Against the smooth sides of his head lay his ears, twitching slightly in the midnight breeze. Claude's hanging jowls began to quiver. He was whimpering.

"I'm sorry, Claude. I didn't mean to get angry."

There was only one way for Norbert to reconcile with Claude; but the stick he had thrown before was nowhere to be found.

Suddenly Claude looked toward the water. He pricked up his ears and trotted out into the lake. Another stick came floating in between a break in the colorless algae, and Claude snapped it up immediately.

That's twice he's gone in the lake this evening, Norbert

thought. *I'll have to give him a bath when we get home.*

Claude dropped the stick at Norbert's feet.

The lake's stench was growing worse. Norbert was taken aback, had to turn aside to search for some fresher air before he could do anything else.

He told Claude to sit, and the dog did so, right in the mucky water. Norbert grabbed the stick. Claude's tail flung water on both sides of him, but he didn't seem to care; his eyes were on the stick. Norbert raised it slowly. Claude's eyes followed it, unblinking. Norbert took a deep breath, hoping for some pure air, but instead breathing the pungent air. Testing Claude's intensity, he twitched the stick slightly and the dog flinched, ready to chase it. Claude licked his chops. Norbert brought the stick behind his head, shifted his weight, stepped forward, and hurled the stick far into the field of grass.

Or so he thought.

Claude was gone like a bullet before Norbert realized he had had his directions reversed, and had thrown the stick out into Stink Lake.

Impossible! He knew he had thrown it toward the grass; he had aimed at a fixed point on the field. There was no way in hell he could have thrown it into the lake.

But there was Claude now, barely discernible as he splashed his way out into the brackish water at a sluggish rate, looking for his stick.

My God, Norbert thought, *he's going to get parasites, worms, diseases . . .*

Just then a black wave rose in the water, several feet high, and broke exactly where Norbert had last seen Claude's bobbing head.

but this isn't the ocean

The wave rolled in slowly and splashed at Norbert's feet, spraying him with algae and stagnant water. It was followed by another, and a third, until waves were springing up everywhere, rolling, breaking into white froth, and disappearing. They splashed the grassy banks whenever they made it that far, and they all came in Norbert's direction.

Claude was still out in the water, somewhere.

"Claude!" Norbert screamed. "Claude!"

Within moments, the waves began drawing away from the shore, pulling out Stink Lake's tide.

but I hate the ocean

Norbert felt the urge to swim out into the water, find Claude, and pull him in to safety, but he didn't know how to swim. He felt like a fool, at sixty-two, unable to swim.

"Claude!" he called at the top of his voice.

He closed his eyes to block out everything he was seeing, but it made it worse by enabling him to think: *This is really happening. I am not home in my bed dreaming, I am here, awake, right now, standing on the banks of Stink Lake, and the waves are crashing, and now the tide for Chrissakes is going out, and Claude is out there drowning, and there is not one damned thing I can do about it.*

Norbert heard Claude yelp and his eyes sprang open. Unfolding before him was the exposed lake bottom as the shoreline came to rest fifty feet from where he stood. But it wasn't a white sandy beach; it was nothing but slime settling in heaps in the open night air. Norbert saw no trace of Claude, either among the algae clumps or out in the distant, now calm water. He began to cry.

Claude is gone. The damned lake tricked me into throwing his stick in the water, and now it's taken him.

The darkness surrounding the park was coming closer, too quickly. Norbert saw only out to where the new shoreline sat lapping quietly and . . . waiting.

it knows I can't swim

Norbert turned and broke into a run across the grassy field when he saw the waves begin to roll rapidly toward him, followed close behind by the enveloping blackness. He wasn't about to let the water get him. He would go home and lock his doors and go up into the attic to hide. But his foot plunged into a hole in the grass and he fell headlong. His ankle was twisted, and it would be harder to outrun the tide. Norbert winced at the sharp pain.

When he tried to get up he fell again; his ankle was

caught in the hole—the grass had closed over it. He heard the rushing, sweeping sound of the water getting nearer—and then nothing but a faint *rippling*. He craned his head to look behind him, and now everything was exactly as it had been before, for as far as he could see, which was to the shore of the lake. The water had returned to its former level, and there were no longer any waves crashing the banks. It looked perfectly ordinary.

What is it waiting for? I'm trapped now—why doesn't it finish me off?

it knows I can't swim

Norbert heard, for a moment, complete silence. Then, as he tried to pull his foot out of its trap, a great wind blasted his ears and the blackness came upon him. He could no longer see anything, and screamed.

Something shook his foot from below. He felt a tug. Suddenly his legs were pulled under the grass. He reached with his arms, trying to pull himself out, but the blades of grass slipped between his fingers as if they had been greased. Inch by inch, he went under, sucked by the rippling, shifting mass. Norbert felt a dizziness take hold. The ground swirled as it reached his armpits, and he realized he was caught in a whirlpool of dirt, grass, and worms, and it was devouring him. He kept his arms high, hoping someone would see his waving and pull him out. The dirt piled over his shoulders. The grass yanked at his out-thrust arms, trying to pull them under along with the rest of him. The cool, moist earth rose over his mouth and shut it fast, ending his screams. It filled his nostrils as he held onto his final breath, scratched at his eyes as he went deeper, and finally enveloped his head. Norbert was cold, and all was dark. His lungs gasped for air and the dirt, worms, and bugs entered his mouth.

As he choked, he was aware that the whirlpool had stopped, and that his hand was still exposed above ground.

Something wet fumbled around his fingers.

It was Claude, alive, trying to put his stick back in his master's hand.

SIX

"Well, well, well," said Sam as Jill brought the wine bottle and the plastic Mini-Mart cups to the center of the living room carpet. "And you're sure Celia isn't coming home soon?"

"About three and a half hours."

"Must be nice. My parents are always home."

Jill sat cross-legged next to Sam, and filled their cups equally. She felt sorry for him, since his parents hadn't let him borrow their car. She knew he would have preferred picking her up himself in his own car, instead of catching a ride with Rick and Deb, but the Falcon had been out of commission for months. This meant he was also going to have to walk home, later, in the cold.

Sam drank some wine and said, "Mmm."

"No, no, no—wait. Let's toast something," Jill said.

He gave her a quizzical look. "OK—to the Stink Lake Monster." He raised his glass and took a gulp.

Jill lowered hers without drinking from it. "It was *not* a monster. Oh . . . forget it."

Sam grinned playfully. "No, c'mon, I want to know more about this 'thing' you saw."

"Look, Sam, it was nothing. Really." She forced a smile. "Really." She sighed, and downed some of her wine. "I'm not sure just what I saw. I called the police right away—you wouldn't believe what a jerk that officer was!"

"Sherman cops. I believe it."

"I told him about the tube thing being pulled under the water, and it was like, 'Right. Uh-huh. Sure.' Then he said it was the parks department's problem, not his. He didn't want to mess with it, but I kept pestering him, so he took my name and address and all that, and sent a squad car over to 'check it out.' Then, the officers who came over told me there had probably been a malfunction with the pump—it wasn't anything to worry about—and it still wasn't the police department's problem. They were humoring me the whole time. I think I told them that I saw it being 'pulled under by something.'"

"That's what you told me."

"It must have set them off. They think I'm nuts." Jill took another sip. "But I did not see any monster, I swear. I guess the pump could have malfunctioned or something, like they said."

"I think you're right," said Sam, wielding an empty cup. "It couldn't have been anything else."

That's true, Jill thought. *It couldn't have been.*

Sam unfolded his legs and stretched out on his side, propping his head up with his arms. "Too bad no one else saw it."

"Why don't you just forget about it, huh? I mean, what does it have to do with us, anyway?" Jill asked.

"OK, forget I brought it up." Sam smiled and brushed a lock of hair from Jill's forehead.

Jill wanted to get the image of the drowning aeration tube out of her head. After finishing off the rest of her cup, she realized how she could . . .

"I liked the movie," Sam said. "I thought the—"

Sam's thought was cut off as Jill kissed him, her tongue intruding into his mouth. Her arms held him tightly, she uncrossed her legs, lay down, and whispered, "Hold me."

Sam's body was a dead weight against her, with one arm draped loosely over her back. His slow, steady breathing warmed and tickled her neck. She opened her eyes, and saw that Sam's were still closed. "Sam," she whispered. "Sam." There was no response, just a soft, relaxed whistle.

Jill sighed and thought of waking him up, then realized

she had to go to the bathroom. She rolled him onto his back, and his arm fell away from her, landing across his chest, where it looked comfortable.

When she returned from the toilet, she lay back down on her side, staring at Sam. There was a slight smile on his face; he looked content. Jill decided he belonged in this room, where the immaculate carpet met polished wood paneling on which hung beautiful prints of rugged mountain landscapes. No speck of dust could be found, nothing old and atrophying. Sam fit the room well, but Jill felt out of place.

She looked at the clock, saw that it was twelve-twenty, and wondered if Sam was going to wake up. The room was growing warmer. Her back itched, and her arm was falling asleep from propping up her head. Her nostrils flared, and she noticed the carpet was getting stale. She had a compelling urge to vacuum the place. If nothing else, it would bring Sam back from the dead.

He snorted, still asleep, and rolled over onto his stomach, his limbs sprawling. Jill reached out her hand and touched his, which was lying in a loose fist. "Sam?" she whispered softly. "Are you really asleep?" She worked her first finger into his grip, hoping he might grasp it. When he didn't, she moved her hand away. She wanted to touch him—not his hand, but his entire body. Her hand traveled down his back, skimming within a centimeter of his shirt without actually touching. She pretended to stroke his right buttock, then did the same along his muscular legs, to his feet, as if she were stroking his aura. She felt her own heart beating faster. Sam's feet were bare, and looked cold.

"Stop teasing," said Sam, in a monotone.

Jill jumped. "I thought you were out—cold as custard, as Maggie would say."

"Just playin' possum."

"You're a rat." She tickled his feet; they flinched and squirmed under her attack.

"Stop! . . . Please," he said.

She did, and moved closer, until she was nearly on top of him. She goosed his ass.

"Hey! Not fair."

"You asked for it." Jill licked his ear and said, "What do you want to do?"

Sam grinned. "I don't know. What do you want to do?"

She stroked his short, bristly hair. "I want to do what we did last week, you know?"

"Me no comprendo."

"Samuel . . ." She reached around his front and unbuttoned his shirt slowly, with respect; it was like unveiling a marble statue. She kissed his neck while smoothing her hands across his taut pectorals, then slid his shirt off his chest and over his back. He turned over and faced her in the warm light from the nearby table lamp. The hours he had spent each week at track practice had produced a classically lean, athletic build. Jill kissed the few dark hairs sprouting on his chest, and around his nipples.

"Oh, you mean *have sex*," said Sam. "I thought you wanted to go swimming." He stretched, folded his arms behind his head, and smiled. "Now you can have your custard, and eat it, too."

Jill laughed. "Don't be gross."

She unzipped his pants, and reached inside briefly, to stroke him. Then she pulled his pants down over his legs, admiring them as she did so; Sam being the star runner on the track team, his thighs were solid, his calves tight, his legs a dark brown. Aside from his ass, which was incredibly cute, his legs were Jill's favorite part of his body.

She straddled him, and he removed her clothing with care, exposing the breasts she thought too small, the hips she thought too wide, the skin she thought too pale. Sam embraced her, his biceps and pectorals tensing against her skin, his rough hands gently caressing her back—as if she were something as perfect as he.

Her hand roamed down to his crotch and found him soft; she stroked him while they kissed, but nothing happened.

"Give it time," Sam whispered. His arms were trembling.

"You're too tense. Loosen up," said Jill.

"Maybe if you . . ." Sam began. "Naw. Forget it."

"What?"

"Maybe," said Sam, and hesitated. Then his eyes brightened. "How about just a massage."

"Yeah, that might do it. Your muscles are hard as a rock."

He laughed uncomfortably. "But not the rest of me."

Jill massaged him all over until he was like jelly; still nothing happened. She was turned on herself, yet he remained half-erect, and that was as far as he was going to get.

"I don't know what's wrong," he said. He kissed her on the lips and pulled away, muttering, "Damn, I'm sorry."

Jill had no idea what to do or to say. The stirrings inside her were left hanging. "It . . . it really doesn't matter," she tried.

"It's not you, Jill. I mean, it isn't you at all; it's me. It's all my fault." Dark rings encircled his eyes; his entire expression was weary.

She thought of telling him *it happens to everyone* like they did in the movies, but Sam wasn't like everyone and this sort of thing shouldn't have been happening to him. "I understand. Really, you'll be all right. Don't worry about it." She tried to smile at him warmly, but failed; she knew it betrayed her nervousness.

For a few minutes, Sam was lost in thought, his eyes glassy. When a tear made its way down his cheek he quickly came back to awareness, hopped up, and began to dress with his back turned to Jill.

"I'd better go," he said softly.

"No, Sam, don't. Please stay."

"I have to. I'm sorry." He sniffed.

"Are you going to be OK?"

"Yeah." He finished dressing, then turned back around to face Jill, pressing his eyes. "I'm tired, that's all. The walk will do me good. By the time I get home I'll be all straightened out." Sam zipped up his jacket and grabbed the small tape deck and earphones he always carried with him. He bent over, gave Jill a long, deep kiss and said, "I'll call you tomorrow, OK?"

Jill put on her bathrobe, and they said good-bye. Sam left listening to a David Bowie tape over his earphones. Jill could hear the tinny sound from where she stood at the front door, while Sam went out the gate. Music was his way of blocking out the rest of the world, and he always kept the volume at maximum.

It wasn't until Sam's silhouette had crossed Grant Street and was starting across the darkness of Burroughs Park that Jill realized she could have done something more. She could have held him, made him stay, talked to him for a while. She could have told him that she loved him. Now it was too late.

Depressed, she went back inside and straight to bed.

Scary Monsters by David Bowie was playing over Sam's headphones, but sounded as if it were emanating from the center of his head. He'd hoped listening to it would keep his mind off his problems, but instead Bowie had become mere background music to the three-ring circus of his addled brain. He knew that tonight he'd let Jill down.

Sam watched the asphalt turn to sidewalk turn to grass beneath the treads of his new sneakers. He felt the cool ground through his soles, and could feel a noticeable give in the earth, as if it had just rained, which of course it hadn't. The grass had last been mowed a week or more ago, and was thick and matted like an uncombed head of hair—at least where it hadn't been overtaken by weeds. Sam flipped up the collar of his jacket against the chilly night breeze, and kept his head down. There was nothing to see, anyway. Streetlights shone around the perimeter, but the park itself lacked any sort of lighting. The field of grass surrounding Sam was a dark, murky gray, and the lake was black.

What Sam *didn't* see at the lake confirmed Jill's story about the aeration tube. Whatever the reason, it certainly wasn't there anymore. Sam didn't really care what had happened to it, if he were perfectly honest with himself. Still, it had truly bothered Jill. He hoped he hadn't been too condescending about it toward her. Why was it he never had these concerns until after the fact? *Maybe*, he thought, *maybe I'm just a jerk*.

Sam's shoes were getting muddy. He supposed the sprinklers must have been set up earlier in the evening, otherwise the ground couldn't possibly have gotten so damp. No rain had fallen in days, and Sherman wasn't known for excessive humidity. Hell, it was practically a desert.

Sam couldn't figure out what was wrong with his penis. All he knew was it had something to do with Curtis. Somehow Sam had to make up with Curtis, or he'd continue to feel guilty spending so much time with Jill. Jill and Curtis had been friends since childhood, while Sam had come along much later. The last thing he needed was to cause any sort of rift between Jill and Curtis, simply because he and Curtis couldn't work out a few little problems. Besides that, Sam knew it was all his fault. He had done much thinking in the last few days and realized he himself was the cause of their falling-out.

Sam was going to call Curtis first thing when he woke up, and see if Curtis was willing to get together and talk. If Sam didn't even try to patch things up, he knew the situation with Jill would get worse and worse. *Christ!* That wasn't the only reason—he also wanted Curtis back as a friend again, as long as they could work it out, as long as Curtis would forgive him.

When Sam reached the path around the lakeshore, he tripped in the mud and fell flat on his face. His headphones popped off his ears and hung themselves around his neck. Sam had come within inches of tumbling into Stink Lake.

I must be falling asleep, he thought, rising to his feet. *It must be after two o'clock.*

Sam bent over, squinting in the darkness, trying to see what he'd tripped over.

"Fucking—" he began, trying to figure out what *exactly* it was. It was a stick, he could see that much.

He leaned over to touch it, and then saw that the stick lay clutched in a human hand half-buried in the ground.

"Shit!"

The earth around the hand was squishy and soft, as if the thing had been freshly buried. Sam couldn't help but stare at it in morbid fascination. *What the hell is it doing here?*

Unexpectedly, bile rose in his throat and Sam found himself vomiting the remnants of movie popcorn and Jill's wine. No more than two feet from the hand, he doubled over and fell on his knees. While he sat there trying to finish, he began to realize *someone* had *put* the hand there, and this someone might still be around.

Sam wiped his mouth with his sleeve and stumbled to his feet, keeping his eyes on the hand. He backed up and stepped carefully up the small rise behind him, then finally turned and ran away along the lake path. *It's OK,* he thought, *I'll go home and call the cops. I'll just call them when I get there, and everything will be all right. Fucking shit!*

Sam kept sliding in the mud as he ran, but managed to keep his balance. All he wanted was to make it to the street, where he'd be in the light, where he could see if anyone was following him.

On the lake's southern shore, he landed on something slippery and fell again. This time his tape deck flew out of his hand and disconnected itself from his headphones. Sam tasted mud in his mouth, along with the vomit he'd finally gotten rid of. His hand was scraped up from landing on a rock when he'd tried to catch himself. He placed his hands against the ground and tried to get up.

Then something slimy wrapped itself around his wrist.

"What the—"

Sam tried to yank himself free as a long, thick strand of seaweed coiled around his arm and began to squeeze. It was more like a slimy rope or a vine than anything else. Another one like the first grabbed hold of his ankle, and started slithering up his leg. Sam pushed and kicked with his unencumbered limbs, but it did no good. He was caught.

Sam wondered who was doing this to him. Looking around, though, he couldn't see anyone else at the lake.

He screamed and tried yelling for help, but then another vine whipped itself around his neck and started tightening. Sam could barely make a sound. Everyone in the neighborhood was in bed, and he probably hadn't managed to wake anyone up with his brief screams.

The seaweed was dragging Sam toward the lake. He struggled and fought all he could manage, but the vine around his neck continued to cut off his air.

Out of the lake, several vines were suddenly coming at him. Sam cringed before they struck. They whipped him. They tore at his clothes and drew blood. They cut into his skin, leaving long gashes.

They're shredding me, Sam thought, whimpering. His body was being dragged down into the mud.

A cold, wet strand of algae stroked Sam's bleeding face before he finally lost consciousness.

SEVEN

More than anything else, she wanted sleep. Her mind was a jumble of thoughts bouncing against the walls of her skull, keeping her awake. The images went around in her head and kept coming back, like horses on a carousel. Sticking clearly in her mind were Curtis's striking face, begging her to come to his party; Sam's loving hands, exploring her sensitive skin; the aeration fountain disappearing beneath the surface of the lake; the hundred-dollar bill Curtis had shown her; Sam crying and being ashamed to do so; Maggie showing her the old photograph, and *not* the sugar bowl she so valued; and Mr. Prenez, staring at her. She tried not to think at all, but her head kept spinning. The wine had probably caused it, or perhaps the stuffed zucchini Maggie had made.

Jill finally found sleep, sometime before Celia got home from work.

A noise woke her a few hours later, and it took great effort to open her eyes. Her alarm clock read 4:15 a.m. She wondered vaguely what she was doing awake, and felt a minor headache pulling at the base of her brain. In the darkness, her bedroom had the look of a grainy black-and-white photograph.

Mr. Prenez was staring at her from the foot of her bed, dressed in his hunting jacket and hat. His mouth was hanging open, and he seemed to flicker as if he were in an old, silent movie.

Jill was still only half-conscious—too tired to be

alarmed. "Mr. Prenez, what are you doing here?" Her voice slurred lazily when she spoke.

"I don't know," he said in a shallow whisper that drilled deep into Jill's ears, like a blast from an organ pipe, and echoed aimlessly around the room. "Something—"

Jill yawned and tried to keep her eyes from closing. "What are you talking about?"

Mr. Prenez stood there flickering, searching for words.

Jill blinked, and decided his flickering was merely an effect of the dim, grainy light. She sat back a little, propping herself on her elbows. "And what are you doing in my bedroom?" Awareness was returning slowly, and with it a feeling of apprehension. Of course, Celia was home by now—Jill could always scream if Mr. Prenez tried anything, and everything would be okay.

"I've lost my dog. I remember now, that's why I came. I want you to find Claude."

"Do you know what time it is?"

"Please, Jill, find Claude and take care of him. I can't any longer. I can't even touch him. Find him, and keep him. He needs love."

"Mr. Prenez, why don't we talk about this tomorrow, huh? I can't think straight right now."

"Claude doesn't know how to survive on his own. You have to find him and take care of him."

"Did Celia let you in?"

Mr. Prenez flickered quietly. He looked desperate, and all Jill could figure out was it had something to do with Claude. *Christ!* He wakes her up in the middle of the night to talk to her about his dog! He had to be out of his mind. More likely, he was drunk.

have a sober weekend

"Celia!" Jill screamed.

Celia was there in an instant, in her terry-cloth robe, and suddenly Mr. Prenez was . . . *gone*. Celia had let down her dark hair and looked as gray as Mr. Prenez had, only she wasn't flickering. She hadn't been drinking, either. Jill could always tell, and tonight Celia was obviously straight. "What's the matter?"

Jill said, "Mr. Prenez—" and pointed toward the foot of her bed. "Did . . . you let Mr. Prenez in?"

"What the hell are you talking about, Jill? Mister who?"

"Prenez! You know, my French teacher. He was just . . . in here . . . a moment ago—" Confused, she looked at Celia, who was standing with her hands on her hips.

There was no sign of Mr. Prenez anywhere.

"Jill, are you stoned?" Celia asked, exasperated.

"No, I—Sam and I had a little wine, but not very much. Hardly any, really. Not enough to make me see—" Jill's racing heart calmed down, and she laughed. "God, I'm such an idiot! It must have been a dream."

"I'm sure it was. I've been watching a movie on TV and the front door is locked. No one could have come into your bedroom without my knowing it. And where could the guy have gone? Of course it was a dream." Celia shook her head back and forth.

"Yeah," Jill said, smiling now. "He was just standing there and he said something about his dog, about wanting me to find his dog. It didn't make any sense. I've had a pretty weird day, though. I made up a French test in the afternoon—I guess these things have a way of creeping up on you."

"Probably something you ate."

"Yeah, maybe Maggie's stuffed zucchini."

"Yuck. I can't eat that stuff. No wonder you dreamed about your French teacher. Is he cute?"

"Celia, he's about sixty years old."

"Oh. Well, if you're okay now, I'll get back to my movie. You go back to sleep." Celia began to leave, then turned back around and asked Jill, "Do you have some dirty clothes hiding somewhere, or something?"

"I don't think so."

Celia crinkled up her nose. "You'd better clean your room, then. Something in here really stinks." She left, closing the door softly.

"Good night, Celia." Jill yawned and fell back against her pillow, laughing at herself for producing such a strange dream.

Just before falling asleep, she noticed Celia was right; her bedroom smelled like fucking Stink Lake.

➤ EIGHT

Jill's alarm clock rang at six-thirty, the same as every weekday morning, but it wasn't until after her shower that she remembered it was Saturday. By then she had already woken up, so she decided to go jogging instead of back to bed. The sky was overcast outside her bedroom window, and it would be too cold to wear shorts and a T-shirt; so she put on her black sweat suit.

As she started down the hallway, the first thing she heard was the droning buzz of the TV, then a few snatches of dialogue from whatever movie Celia was watching. The living room curtains were still drawn, so the room was illuminated only by the dim, flashing glow of the TV screen. The air was stale.

Celia was still awake, as usual, although she didn't notice Jill had entered the room. She never went to bed until eight or nine o'clock, except on the occasions when she got too drunk and fell asleep comfortably during one of her late movies.

Jill recognized John Wayne on the screen, but not the other guy, a young, skinny man with dark hair and intense eyes. The print of the black-and-white film was poor; scratches, lines, and dust specks passed in front of the two men's faces.

"John Wayne, right?" Jill asked.

"Right."

"Who's the other guy?"

"Montgomery Clift. *Red River,* Howard Hawks, 1948."

"Good morning, too." Jill smiled at the back of Celia's

head, which still faced the screen. Her aunt didn't seem terribly drunk this morning, but she had clearly had enough booze to make her inattentive. Jill opened the curtains in the living room and kitchen, letting the dull morning light into the trailer.

"When I was your age," Celia mumbled, "I was in love with Montgomery Clift. All us girls were. Sue—I mean, your mother and I used to scream whenever his face appeared on the screen. What do you think?"

"Yeah, he's cute. Celia?" No response. "Celia?"

"Uh-huh?"

"I'm going jogging, OK? See you in a bit."

"OK."

Jill left.

Jill and Celia didn't live together, they coexisted. During the few hours when their paths crossed each day, Jill found it almost impossible to communicate with her aunt. Celia was three times as old, but Jill doubted that was the problem. After all, Maggie was four times as old—as far as Jill could tell—and they got along splendidly. Jill blamed her situation with Celia on the alcohol, even though Celia wasn't a chronic drunk—she was just more active than the average social drinker. Jill and Celia had never taken the time to sit down and figure out what their impasse was all about, and Jill doubted they ever would.

She walked over to Burroughs Park and, when she reached the grass, began her stretching exercises. The grass was cold, still wet with dew. The lake smelled worse than it had the day before, but that was probably because there was no wind.

No one else was at the park. Saturday mornings in Sherman were not known for their liveliness. Since there was little entertainment in town, people got drunk on Friday evenings and slept late the next morning. Liquor sold well there, and drinking was still the preferred method for getting "fucked up" among Jill's fellow students. But no matter what form of drug they took to have fun Friday evening, nobody jogged at the park Saturday morning, usually not even Jill, although many did on the weekdays.

Jill contorted herself into a hurdler's stride and stretched, grabbing her toes. The muscles on the underside of her legs grew painfully taut.

She remembered Sam had said he was going to call her, and she figured he would around noon. If he didn't call her by then, she would call him herself and find out how he was feeling. Jill sighed in exasperation; now that she was up so early, she would have to come up with something to do to keep her mind off Sam until noon.

She finished stretching and jogged over to the lake path. There were places along the shore where she had to stray from the path because the banks had eroded and portions of the path had crumbled into the slime-coated water. Because of Stink Lake's small size, she always had to do several laps around the lake before the jogging did any good.

A long line of sea gulls stood squawking on the eastern shore. When Jill went past, they fluttered their wings and flew away gracefully one after the other, the way bathing beauties dove into Hollywood swimming pools.

Halfway through her first lap, on the southern shore, Jill got angry when she saw from a distance what appeared to be a large pile of trash someone had dumped in the mud. It was bad enough Stink Lake was an ecological disaster without the residents helping it along.

As she neared the thing, however, she saw it was not a trash pile at all. Protruding from the algae and mud of the shore, it was white and fleshy, tinted blue, like a beached albino whale, only smaller, the size of a man. Jill slid down the muddy bank to get a closer look. Some parts of the thing looked like raw steak, and some like hamburger. Jill's running shoes sank deep in the mud. She gasped; the musculature of the thing's outstretched arm showed it *was* a man, but the body itself was a ragged mess of deep, long lacerations through firm muscle and skin, and wrapped tightly with thick, rope-like strands of algae that had once been green, but were now red and soaking with the man's blood. Jill had mud up to her ankles. She shifted ground, searching for a better place to stand. The man's face was hidden from view, yet through the blood streaks and deep cuts, she could visualize what his body should have looked like: young, muscular, agile. He looked as if he had been whipped to the bone. Jill shook and gasped for air. Near her feet lay a smashed cassette player and an ejected cassette. She bent over and picked them up, listening to the thump of her own heart. She stared puzzledly at the tape for a moment; it was David Bowie's *Scary Monsters*.

Then she screamed.

The cassette fell from her hand and was promptly sucked into the mud, along with the shattered tape deck.

She tried to back away, but lost her balance and fell into the muddy bank. "No! NO!" she shrieked as she saw the torn, mangled body *(it couldn't be Sam)* begin to sink slowly into the mud, and felt something pulling at her feet from below. She tried to pull herself back onto the grass, and jerked her feet out of the mud, but her shoes stayed behind and disappeared into the ground. Her breath was short. In sock feet, she tried to get up the bank to safety, but she had no traction and kept sliding farther down.

"Oh God!"

Sam's body sank deeper, the mud gurgling and bubbling.

Her feet only managed to push more mud down from the bank with each step. Finally, she threw herself on her stomach, arms outstretched, and managed, somehow, to grab onto the grass. The mud sucked at her feet from one end while she hung on tightly at the other. The force pulling at her was strong. Suddenly, her socks were pulled off her feet and she was released. She lurched forward onto the grass. Feeling she was safe, she glanced back briefly and saw Sam's body as it went under, enveloped by brown ooze.

murdered

Jill tried to catch her breath while her eyes welled up with tears, but her chest was convulsing, and the more she gasped, the less air she seemed to get. All she breathed was the rank smell of Stink Lake. She could barely see through her watery eyes, and she felt dizzy, as if she were about to black out and faint. "Oh... Sam," she muttered feebly.

The grass felt soft beneath her bare feet. Then the ground itself softened and started to ripple, like a water bed. Jill screamed again, and *ran*, faster than she had ever run before, heading blindly for Maggie's trailer.

She ran across Grant Street and fell over Maggie's gate. She got back up quickly, and looked back at Burroughs Park. Now the lake was still, the grass was no longer rippling, and the sea gulls had returned to the banks. Everything appeared just as it should have.

Jill dashed up the steps and pounded on Maggie's black aluminum screen door, which produced a noisy, hollow rattle rather than a knock. She was wheezing in rapid, shallow breaths, and the wind blowing against her sweat-drenched face felt terribly cold.

"Maggie! Wake up! Wake up!" She pounded some more. "Oh, God, Maggie, please! Wake up! Mag—"

"I'm up," came the loud, grumbling voice from inside. Then the door opened and Maggie was standing before her in a nightgown, with bags under her eyes and tissues rolled in her hair. "Jill?"

Jill came in hurriedly, unable to see straight, her limbs shaking. She dripped mud all over the carpet. "Oh, God ...oh, Maggie...it...it was...he...murdered... oh..."

"What's the matter, Jill? Slow down," said Maggie, closing the door and then turning the dead bolt.

Jill collapsed against Maggie and buried her face on the older woman's shoulder. "It's awful," she sobbed, shivering.

"Gracious, girl! I think you're in shock."

NINE

Jill pulled back the brown speckled kitchen curtains and looked out across the lake to see if any progress was being made. The sky was now clear, and darkening fast. The paramedical unit had joined the two police cars, and a commotion had erupted between several of the men digging along the bank. Jill let fall the curtains, and returned to Maggie's comfortable couch in the living room to lie down.

A fresh mug of hot cocoa was waiting for her on the coffee table, complete with three marshmallows slowly dissolving.

Maggie was sitting in her chair doing needlework. "Is anything happening out there?" she asked.

"Yeah—something," Jill said as she lay down. "There's a lot of people making a lot of noise. I think they've found the . . . him." She took a timid sip of cocoa, but found it had already cooled.

"How are you feeling now?"

"I don't know. I feel wretched, but I guess that's better than before. I'm trying not to think—just waiting. God, I hope I'm wrong. I don't care who it was, as long as it wasn't Sam."

"It's getting dark," Maggie said, a nervous twinge in her voice. "The police will be coming soon, whether or not they've found anything. Do you think you're up to it?"

Jill smiled as best she could. "I think so. I would have gone over the edge if it hadn't been for you. Everything you've done for me today—"

"Come now, Jill. Don't worry about it."

Maggie turned her gaze and glared at her needlework. She looked disconcerted, as if she had been pulling her thread too tight. She must have been equally distressed about talking with the police again.

Jill couldn't think of anything else to say; she drank the rest of her cocoa. The only thing left to do was wait.

Maggie invited the officers to sit. They took the couch while Jill sat in Maggie's chair, which Maggie chose to stand behind, her hand on Jill's shoulder. The two men had dour expressions, as if wishing they were someplace else.

Jill frowned, discouraged by their faces.

"I'm Detective Martin," said the one sitting across the coffee table from Jill. He was near fifty and sported a hefty, flabby torso. His face looked as if it had been carved in an apple and left to dry in the sun. "And I believe you met Officer Warren earlier today."

Indeed they had. Jill had disliked Officer Warren; his voice had seemed filled with insinuations. He was about twenty years younger than the detective and looked like what, to Jill's mind, was the typical Sherman cop. They seemed to wear their mirrored sunglasses constantly, even at night, went to the same barber, had similar military haircuts, similar bushy mustaches, similar paunches from their all-cop beer parties, and did everything by the book, which they had obviously gleaned from watching *Adam 12* and *T.J. Hooker* on TV. Something about Officer Warren, and the other cops like him, made Jill's skin crawl.

On the other hand, Jill's skin didn't react one way or the other to Detective Martin, who was different from what she had expected, and perhaps—though she couldn't be too sure—of a sympathetic nature.

"I think we need to have a serious talk," said Martin carefully. He leaned forward in his seat, resting elbows on knees, and looked straight at Jill. Warren sat back leisurely, looking bored, withdrew pad and pen from his jacket pocket, and waited.

"Was it Sam?" asked Jill anxiously, hoping he would promptly say *No, it was someone else.* "Can you tell us who it was yet?"

Warren glanced expectantly at Martin and sighed noticeably. Martin's gaze shifted momentarily to the floor, then came back to Jill.

"It wasn't anybody," he said. "What I mean is, there was no *body*. At least we didn't find anything."

Jill gasped.

"For now, you can rest easy about Sam Taylor, I think, although he has been reported missing—"

"W-what," Jill said, looking up briefly at Maggie for strength, "what in the world are you talking about?"

"He is missing, yes," explained Warren, while Martin blew his nose in a rumpled, stained handkerchief. "But until we have a body, we don't have a murder, or a death. There's nothing at Stink Lake but mud and mudpuppies."

Jill's eyes were stinging. *The body was gone?*

"Now, I wish this weren't such a delicate situation, Miss Beaumont," said the detective, "but under the circumstances I'm afraid I'm going to have to ask you if this is all—how else can I put it—some sort of hoax?"

"I wasn't lying, if that's what you mean," Jill said, her voice quavering. "I saw his . . . I saw it myself."

Warren was writing everything down.

"You're sure about that?" asked Martin. "You still want to stick to your original story?"

"It's the truth," she said with difficulty. Either she had all her wits, and Sam was dead; or Sam was alive, and she was down to her last remaining one.

"I'm sorry. I just wanted to make sure. But you should appreciate the odd predicament I'm in here, with this investigation. The only fact any of us knows for certain is that Sam is nowhere to be found. I've come up with what I feel is a simple, reasonable solution to his disappearance, and I'd like to share it with you, and see what you think."

"All right," Jill said. Despite his pleasant demeanor, he was playing a game.

"You were the last person Sam Taylor was with before he disappeared. You were his girlfriend. I think Sam wanted to hide, or run off for a while—"

"Why would he want to—"

"Please let me finish. Then you can talk. Anyway, he came to you for help, and together you and he concocted a plan. You would report finding his dead body in the morning, murdered, at Stink Lake, and that it got sucked up in the mud. The amount of time it would take us to find a body that didn't exist would give him an ample head start before a serious search could begin, once we found he wasn't actually dead. You would admit it was a lie, and probably get off easy—depending, that is, on what it was Sam did that made him run away. Now, please, for the last time, I'm asking you to level with me and tell the real story."

He acted sincere, but he was so damned wrong he didn't deserve an answer.

"Do it for Sam's sake," he added. "I would frankly like to clear this whole mess up and find that kid, before some actual harm does come to him."

"I don't believe this," Jill said. "You're not taking me seriously. You just think I'm some stupid 'kid.' I've given you the real story already. Sam is *dead*." She began to sob. "I saw him with my own eyes!"

"Did anyone else see him?" Warren asked rhetorically. He shifted his position on the couch, his billy club clattering on his belt. "We were willing to believe you up until now, but the fact is—"

"Cut it, Warren!" snapped Martin sharply, like a drill sergeant. Then he continued, to Jill, in a fatherly, understanding tone: "The fact is, there is no body. And until I have a body, I can't assume anyone's dead, can I?"

"Maybe you didn't dig deep enough," Jill said. Maggie tightly clutched Jill's shoulder, meaning: *Easy, easy.*

"No," stated Warren. "We dug all the way down to the gypsum. Two of our men weren't paying attention to what they were doing—got stuck in the mud. We had to call the paramedics to get them out. But there was no quicksand, no sinkhole of any kind."

"Jesus," Jill mumbled. "And you're blaming this all on me? You aren't kidding—you really think I made the whole thing up?"

Maggie interjected, "She was in shock when she reached my place. She didn't fake that."

Detective Martin said, "Technically, Miss Aldrich, she could have. It could have been psychosomatic."

"I was in shock," protested Jill. "I was treated at Wells Memorial."

"Yes," conceded Martin. "I'm afraid that's the biggest hole in my theory. Even if it were psychosomatic, it's doubtful you could have conjured it up at will. Which leaves me with the second theory. Like I said, I think you can rest easy about Sam, but if my second theory is correct, I can't rest easy about you."

Oh shit, here it was. She was crazy. That was his second theory.

"If I take your word that you're telling the truth," he went on, "then I'm forced to think that you truly believed you saw a dead body, convinced yourself it was your boyfriend, and this induced the condition of shock. I know from your blood test at the hospital that you weren't on any hallucinogens."

"I'm not crazy."

"And that's not for me to decide. But even if this second theory is correct, it still hints that you knew something of Sam's disappearance, and its probable cause."

"You're wrong," said Jill. Her brain was getting muddled. The detective had almost convinced her Sam was still alive, which she knew was untrue. But maybe, just maybe, there had never been a dead body. Perhaps she had seen something that wasn't there. She could have been going crazy. No—*no!*—definitely not. She knew what she had seen. And she knew, now more than ever, that it had been Sam. After all, he was "missing." *The body had to be there!* These cops were inept. They were too lazy to continue the search. Surely they would find Sam's body if they looked long enough.

"Why would Sam want to disappear?" she asked. "Give me one good reason."

Warren sighed again and said, "Well, we're working on one theory..."

Fuck them and their stupid theories.

"At two a.m. this morning, we found the body of Norbert Prenez in Burroughs Park. We believe he was murdered, although we haven't yet seen the autopsy."

"Oh no!" shouted Maggie. "Oh no, it can't be! Not our Mr. Prenez? Oh goodness." She cried stiffly, and muttered, "Poor man, poor man," as if to herself.

"We haven't found the killer, either," continued Warren. "Time of death was sometime between midnight and one a.m., or about the same time you claim to have last seen Sam Taylor."

"Are you trying to say that Sam killed Mr. Prenez?" Jill felt dizzy, but caught herself on the arm of the chair.

"Not necessarily," explained Martin. "He may have just been a witness, and gotten scared. But it *is* our only lead."

"Why don't you believe me? He hasn't gone off anywhere—he's dead!" She yelled it at them. There seemed nothing she could possibly say that they would understand.

The two policemen were both impatient and ambivalent. They didn't seem to know what they were doing, nor did they seem to care. Suddenly, Martin seemed to be no different from Warren; he spoke friendlier and more compassionately, perhaps, but he was driving at the same conclusions: Jill was either a liar, or crazy, or both.

"Let's set aside the whole body business for a moment," said the detective. "I'm looking into Sam's disappearance. For the purposes of my investigation I must get the whole story of what took place last night between you and him."

Jill stared at him viciously. A horrible suspicion had crept into her mind, that they were back to the first theory, and trying to get a confession out of her. They wanted her to admit she had made the whole thing up, that she was covering for Sam. They didn't want two such perplexing cases, so they were looking for an easy way out of both. First, they were faced with a mystery killer. Then, they had a missing person, a report of his dead body, and the embarrassing fact that they couldn't find it. Sam had probably been killed by whomever had killed Prenez, but it was much easier for them to say Jill's report was a bald-faced lie. Sam would forever be a missing person, and they could blame Prenez's murder on him. Open-and-shut case. One for the books. Everybody would be happy. Sherman could keep its false image of being completely safe. All Jill had to do was confess to a lie. In other countries they tortured people for this. In Sherman, well...

Jill's adrenaline was flowing.

"You want the whole story?" she shouted, wrenching her shoulder away from Maggie's grip. "I'll give you the whole story." She wiped her face dry and threw back her hair. "Last night, Sam Taylor and I went to a movie. Are you getting this down, Officer Warren? Then we came back to my trailer to fuck, only we had to have some of his friends drop us off because Sam's fucking parents—"

"Jill!" said Maggie.

"—wouldn't let him use their fucking car. Then we got naked and tried to screw, except he couldn't get a hard-on no matter how much I played with his cock, because he was confused about something. And I asked him to stay and he said he'd rather go home. Then he started walking home across the park, and that was the last I saw of him until this morning, when I found his body ripped to shreds, lying in the mud. Then the mud swallowed him up and tried to swallow me, too."

She paused to catch her breath, and watched the look of shock on the officers' faces as Warren scribbled down every word.

"Those are the facts I know," she said gravely. "Sorry to burst your bubble, guys."

"Fine," said Martin heavily. "I'm afraid I'm going to have to recommend to your aunt—Celia Parker, is it?—

that you undergo some psychiatric evaluations, as part of my investigation. We can have Dr. Benson perform them at your school, if you like, sometime in the early part of next week."

"I think that's a good idea," said Maggie, who had probably been mortally offended at Jill's frank language. Jill was already realizing herself that she'd made a gigantic mistake, even if it was the truth. But how could Maggie agree with the police? Didn't she trust her?

"May I go home now?" Jill asked. "I want to be left alone for a while."

TEN

Simon Taylor strode jauntily across the packed, busy parking lot of the shopping plaza. He was proud of the way he walked. Having been born with one leg slightly shorter than the other, he had compensated by turning what used to be an awkward hobble into a cool, cocky gait. He always walked quickly and with a noticeable bounce that made him look, he thought, like a real stud.

In front of the pizza parlor, he ran into a couple of girls he knew from Math. "Hey, Suzanne, Kelly," he said, stopping before them. He hitched his thumbs in his pockets and tried to act calm; Suzanne was real cute.

"Hi, Simon," said Suzanne, smiling. Kelly didn't speak. Both were wearing designer jeans, Esprit sweatshirts, ponytails, and braces. Suzanne's chest was already large, but Kelly's still looked like a boy's.

Simon suddenly realized the particular pair of 501s he had on were too small, and incredibly tight. He wondered if he was bulging too much. *Don't look down, though, idiot!* The crease in the denim at his crotch rubbed him uncomfortably, and there was an itch down there, too, that he had to scratch...

"What're you guys doing?" he asked the girls. He decided he would make a quick exit.

"Nothing."

He should have let his mother throw these jeans away when she had wanted to, instead of simply promising her he wouldn't wear them to school. They had always been his favorite pair of pants, but as his mother had said, he was growing "like a cornstalk," and there were some clothes that he just couldn't wear anymore. His thighs felt as if they were going to split the seams, and he couldn't even lift the pants legs high enough to pull up his socks. The jeans had been old from the start for him, being hand-me-downs from Sam; they were supposedly "shrink-to-fit," but they had shrunk to fit Sam, so they had never fit Simon properly, even when he had been smaller. He had held onto them as long as possible, however, hoping they would someday fit him perfectly. But now, when the waist, the crotch, and the thighs were too small, the bottom of the legs were still turned up in cuffs. He had to admit it was finally time to throw them away, but he couldn't right now, not in front of the pizza parlor.

"Well, see you 'round," said Simon.

"Bye," said the girls in unison. "Where are you going?" asked Suzanne. Kelly was staring at his crotch—*shit!*

"Around back. I'm going to go talk to the Skunks for a while."

He walked away, down past the row of shops, and *knew* Suzanne and Kelly were staring at his ass, and giggling, as girls will do. He turned the corner, out of their sight.

Whew! He stuck his hand in his pants and scratched down there, where that mass of hairs was still growing. He hiked his underwear up a bit so the crease in his inseam wouldn't pinch so much. Then he felt better, as he went back behind the shopping plaza.

Overhead, the stars were coming out. The back of the building was very dark, compared to the brightly lit parking lot and store facades; here there were only single light bulbs, shielded by metal guards, perched above the back entrances, with flies and moths swirling about them incessantly.

Stink Lake lay flat, silent, and dark across the street, fading with the twilight, on the verge of becoming black. The police cars that had been there all day were leaving.

The four Skunks were standing around at the back door of the pizza parlor, beside a large green garbage dumpster, sharing a large combo pizza among themselves.

"What took you so long?" asked Troy Zografi, their leader, who was wearing his denim Skunks jacket and was propped leisurely against the wall eating a messy slice with his greasy fingers. When standing straight, he was a half-head taller than Simon, and he had larger arms and broader shoulders. However, he was an eighth-grader. Perhaps in another year Simon would look like that, too. He wondered how much hair Troy had growing in his crotch, and if he also had any growing up his crack.

"I had to find the right time to escape from my parents," Simon said. "They didn't want to let me out of the house today. They're all weirded out, you know?"

"Yeah," said Clint, a short, skinny creep who was in Simon's grade, "your big brother ran off, didn't he?"

"Shut up," said Troy, his mouth full of pizza.

But Clint continued, "That's why the cops have been looking around the lake all day, isn't it? That's why they keep going and talking to Sam's girlfriend. Maybe she shot him or something, huh?"

"No way, man." Troy always spoke as if he knew all the answers. "Jill's cool, and anyway, who ever said anyone was shot?"

"My dad."

"Your dad's a wuss. And I thought I told you to shut up, Clit!" Troy snapped.

"Hey!" said Clint in objection.

"Hey, what, Clit? What's the matter, Clit? That's all you are, is a clit, so shut up." Then, to Simon, casually: "What a clit! Don't you think so?"

"Yeah, sure." Simon ignored what Clint had said. He knew Jill would never have killed his brother or anything dumb like that.

"Have some pizza, Simon." Troy offered him a gooey slice.

"Thanks. I'm starving."

"We get the pizza from Stewart," explained Kraig, another eighth-grader and Troy's best friend. "He makes one just for us and sneaks it out the back door. We get 'em every Saturday night, 'cause if he don't, we'll tell his boss about all the other pizzas he's made for us."

"Under the thumb," said Troy with glee.

The fourth Skunk was Jeff, an average-looking guy Simon's age, who sat quietly devouring his food. Simon had P.E. with him, had seen him in the showers, and knew he didn't have any crotch hair, and his dick was puny.

He wondered how big Troy's was, and Kraig's, and if Clint had one.

"So," said Troy, when he had consumed his last slice. "What did you want to talk to us about?"

And suddenly Simon was brought back to reality, having nearly forgotten why he had called Troy in the first place.

At Simon's home, it had been a madhouse all day.

First, he had woken up at eleven-thirty that morning to find his mother sitting slumped at the dining room table, her wide, bloodshot eyes staring into the middle distance. The bags under her eyes hung purple and heavy. She had obviously been awake all night—probably with one of her migraines.

"What's the matter, Mom?" he asked, sitting down at the table, beside her. An unwelcome yawn escaped his lips; he had only been awake for two minutes. "You look like someone punched you in the face."

"Do I?" she asked blandly, as if she weren't surprised. "It's Sam. He's missing. He's run away." Tears flowed from her bloated eyes. Her hands came up to rub her face dry. She was dressed in her maroon bathrobe, and her long, wavy blond hair was a mess of tangles. "Your father and I have been up all night."

For a moment, Simon was struck speechless. His brain wasn't in gear yet, but he also couldn't believe what he was hearing.

"I'm worried sick," she continued, her voice verging on a sob. "He hasn't called, he didn't leave a note, no one has seen him since last night. We called the police and reported him as missing..."

Christ! They had called the *cops?* Sam was going to be in big trouble this time!

"I just know something's happened to him. I know it!"

"Oh, Mom, I'm sure nothing's hap—"

"I know it," she repeated.

Simon couldn't say anything. How could his parents have let him sleep late? How come they hadn't woken him and told him what was going on?

He knew he couldn't get through to his mother. When she was like this there was nothing he could say. Time would take care of it... or when Sam came back.

"He's been out all night before," Simon offered, thinking, *She lets him stay out all night, but never me*.

"But he's always called!" was her retort.

Silence fell, long and uncomfortable. Simon wished his mom would cheer up.

"Maybe he forgot," he said, in an effort to say *something*.

"No."

"Maybe he spent the night over at Curtis's... and forgot to call you. Didn't he do that once before?"

"No, Simon!" she exploded. "We did call over there, and—" she paused, looking awkward "—Curtis hasn't seen him. Just like everyone else." She looked hard at him. "And I don't ever want to hear you mention Curtis Bowles again.... This is all his fault."

"What's wrong with Curtis, Mom?" Simon couldn't understand this one bit; he *liked* Curtis.

"Everything!" she snapped. "It's his fault. Let's leave it at that."

"Where's Dad?"

"He's out looking for him in the pickup."

"For Curtis?"

"No! For Sam, for Sam!... Dammit, Simon!"

"Sorry."

He wanted to go out looking for Sam, too. How come

Dad had left him behind, *asleep,* here, where the only thing he could do was make his mother angry?

"How long's he been gone?" he asked quietly. "Dad, I mean."

"I don't know. A couple hours."

Simon went into his room and got dressed. When he came out, he headed for the front door.

"Where do you think you're going, young man?" yelled his mother.

He stopped, turned. "I was just—"

She got up from the table and stomped toward him.

"I'm going out to find Sam," he said, turning to run out the door.

"Oh no, you're not!" She grabbed his right arm and wrenched him backwards. He lost his balance momentarily, and swung back with his left, striking her hip. Reaching for his other arm, she scratched long red marks into his skin with her fingernails. Then, she spun him around by his right arm, until he was facing her.

"Don't touch me!" he said.

She shook him once, violently, and said through clenched teeth, "You're not going anywhere today. You're staying right here!"

"No, I'm not!" He struggled, trying to free himself from her clutch.

She raised her free hand high behind her, a look of fury on her weary face.

For a moment, Simon actually thought she was going to hit him. "Mom, don't!" He cringed.

Then she did. The side of his face was smacked hard by her open palm. For a brief moment his vision faded to black; then, like a flower blooming in time-lapse photography in one of those nature videos in Life Science class, his sight opened back up. He was still standing, only because of the vise-like grip she had on his arm.

Simon stared at her in horror. She had never done that before. She wasn't the hitting type.

"OK, Mom," he said meekly, trying to back away from

her. "OK, Mom. Whatever you say." She let go, and he fled to his room and locked the door and fell on his bed and cried.

She came to his room several times that afternoon, knocked on the door and said, "Honey, I'm sorry. I really am. I didn't mean to hit you..."

And he would tell her "Go away," because his mother scared him—gave him the fucking *creeps*—and he didn't like it at all.

Besides, that, he was hurting. His face was still stinging from the blow, but the pain was mostly inside, a cold numbness around his heart, from everything that was going on around him.

His brother had deserted him.

His father didn't care about him one way or the other.

His mother hated him, and had even *hit* him.

Simon stayed in his room all day. He listened to all the albums he had borrowed from Sam's record collection, tried on all the clothes Sam had handed down to him or he had stolen from Sam's closet, and stared at the photo on the wall, taken by Curtis, of Simon and Sam on a fishing trip the three of them had taken to the Twin Gap Lakes. He kept looking in the full-length mirror on his door, staring at his own face, trying to make himself look as much as possible like Sam. It was no use. Simon's hair was blond, his eyes blue, unlike Sam's brown and brown. He examined his own muscles, to see if they were ever going to be as big as Sam's; they were nice-looking, he decided, but not nearly as nice as Sam's.

He refused, through the door, to eat supper.

On the phone in his room, he called up Troy and said he had to talk to him and the Skunks. They decided to rendezvous behind the pizza parlor at eight o'clock.

Finally, at sunset, Simon sneaked out his window while his parents were talking in low, serious tones with some neighbors in the living room.

He was determined to find his brother, and he had an

idea of where to look—a place no one else would think of finding him.

"I've changed my mind," Simon said. "I want to be a Skunk, for real this time."

"You're not going to back out on us again, are you?" asked Troy in a brotherly fashion.

"No, I mean it. I really want to be a Skunk. Bad."

"Then you've got to prove it," said Kraig. "Come over here." He extended his denimed arm.

Simon went over and Kraig put his arm around his shoulders.

"We wanted you in the Skunks all summer, you know. You're quick, a real athlete, and you don't mess around with people. You tell 'em what you think of 'em."

"And that's the way to be," said Troy, who was cleaning his fingernails with a pocketknife.

"We thought you thought you were too good for us."

Simon laughed.

Troy said, "But we could really use you," and glanced over accusingly at Clint and Jeff.

"Still," continued Kraig, "if you want to be a Skunk, you got to prove yourself. I mean—"

"What can you do for us?" interrupted Troy.

Simon looked around at Jeff, Clint, and Troy, each staring at him in the warm, yellow light of the pizza parlor's back-door bulb; he looked over his shoulder at Kraig's grinning, fraternal face.

"I can show you guys how to get into the high school," Simon said with a touch of arrogance.

"Anyone can get into the high school!" Clint spoke through his nose. "Big fucking deal."

"He means after dark, shithead," said Troy. "When it's all locked up."

Clint stared at Troy, mouth agape, and said, "Oh."

Troy sneered his best Billy Idol imitation at Clint for a moment, and muttered: "Clit-lips."

Simon laughed, as did Kraig, while Jeff grinned sheepishly. Clint looked morose.

Kraig started walking, Simon still in tow beneath his arm. "C'mon, guys, let's blow."

"Yeah, c'mon," said Troy.

They all crossed Third Street.

Simon felt magnificent. Not only did these guys—or at least Troy and Kraig—truly care about him, but he was also certain that together they were going to find Sam, somewhere, in the steam tunnels beneath the high school.

Two policemen were roaming around on foot at Burroughs Park with flashlights, so the Skunks skipped the park altogether and walked down the middle of Fremont Street to the high school. The building stood two stories high, stretched long, and was *L*-shaped. Every window was dark; the janitors didn't work on Saturday nights.

In a couple of years, the Skunks would all be in high school, and then they would "rule," just as they ruled the junior high now. Simon felt good. By his senior year, he would be the toughest guy in school, just like Sam.

Simon led the Skunks to the inside corner of the *L*, behind a clump of tall pines.

"This is it, here," he said, pointing down.

A hinged, iron door sat fixed in a square slab of concrete raised six inches above the grass. It was rusty, a yard on each side, and locked with a shiny combination lock.

"Steam tunnels, you say?" asked Troy with a grin.

"It's locked," said Clint. "Tough beans, huh?"

Simon sneered at him, the way Troy had. "My brother locked it. He and his friends found the real lock missing one night and went down to explore the tunnels. Later he came back and locked it himself, so no one else could get into it."

"You know the combination?" asked Kraig.

"Sure I do. It's my bike lock." Simon crouched down close to the lock, and tried in the dark to make out the numbers. "Anyone got a flashlight?"

Kraig flicked his disposable lighter and held it near the lock so Simon could see.

"Got it," said Simon, yanking it open. He pocketed his lock. "This thing's kind of heavy." He lifted the door open himself. A thick chain on the inside kept it from banging down against the concrete, and held it open for them.

Kraig lowered his lighter near the blackness of the hole. "It's a bottomless pit," he said. "Can't see nothin'."

"It's not that far down," said Simon. "You just have to hang from the edge and drop down. It's easy."

"Nothing to it, right?" said Troy. He crawled over the edge, hung by his fingers for a moment, and dropped into the darkness, hitting bottom with a crunch that echoed around and up out of the hole. "Kraig, you're next," he called. "It's a cinch!"

Clint looked over the edge, and asked, "We have to go down *there?*"

"If you're a Skunk you do," said Kraig, as he climbed down over the side. He dropped in the manner of Troy. "No problem!"

Simon went next, then Jeff. Clint still sat up above, peering down into the hole, the stars twinkling behind his shadowed head.

Blue light filtered down from the square opening. They were standing in a gray, cement-walled room with a gritty floor that looked as if it had never, since the building's construction, been cleaned up.

"Come on, Clit!" Troy shouted. "Get your buns down here!"

Clint stared down at them, a silhouette, unmoving.

"It's easy," said Kraig, his voice shaking. "Nothing to be afraid of."

"Jesus Christ!" said Troy in anger.

Then Clint's dark figure disappeared from view.

The four of them stared up at the hole, waiting.

"What the—" Troy muttered.

Then the iron door slammed closed with a *crash* that

reverberated around the room and down the tunnels, and plunged the Skunks into total darkness.

Troy lighted his own disposable lighter and held it near his face. The flickering flame cast dancing shadows across his features and created an eerie glow in his dark, glossy eyes.

"That kid," he said, "is going to die."

 **ELEVEN**

Jill punched out the phone number and waited, letting the other end ring several times. She twirled a gnawed toothpick around in her mouth, then withdrew it and tossed it on the grimy floor of the phone booth when she realized there were small slivers of wood on her tongue. Her fingers drummed against the glass wall of the booth. She stared at the phone, then down at her Top-Siders, in which her toes were wiggling.

"Come on, dammit!" she shouted into the receiver.

One more ring sounded before the anxious answer: "Hello?" In the background buzzed the untamed, distorted, raw power of a hardcore punk record.

"Curtis! Jesus, I thought for a moment you weren't home."

"Speak up, I can't hear."

"Curtis? Hello?" she said louder than before.

"Oh, Jill! Hi!"

"I have to talk to you."

"OK, shoot."

"No, not over the phone. You've got to come pick me up."

Jill watched a large family file out of a van in the Denny's parking lot, gather themselves into a group, and head inside the restaurant, smiling and laughing.

"Great! I'll be by in a few minutes, and then you can join the party. It's just starting."

Shit! She had forgotten all about Curtis's goddamned party. She glanced about her, at the Denny's, the shopping plaza, the cars whizzing past on busy Second Street. Behind her lay the park, and darkness. The glaring light shining down upon her from the booth's low ceiling made her feel vulnerable.

"How can you still be having your party?"

"Oh c'mon, Jill. Sam will turn up. I'm sure it's no big deal. He probably wanted some time to himself. Personally, I'm not all caught up in this 'What could have happened to Sam' bullshit. That's exactly what he wants—a little attention."

"Curtis, you don't understand." She paused, and laughed nervously, the way Celia sometimes did when she was very angry. Of course, Curtis didn't know—nobody knew—that Sam was dead. She wondered how the hell she was going to explain it to him. "I'm in trouble. I need to talk to you. Celia's pissed off at me. She wanted me to stay home, and I blew my top and took off. She thinks I've flipped out. Everyone thinks I'm crazy—Celia, Maggie, the cops, everybody. It's Sam. I have to talk to you about it, and I can't over the phone. Jesus Christ, Curtis, are you going to come pick me up or not?"

"Calm down, Jill—"

"This is real fucking important."

"Hey! Hold on until I can come get you, okay?"

"I'm not kidding, this is really—"

"Shit. OK. This incredible bash won't really get under way for a few hours. I guess we can talk in my bedroom, if Carl and Pam are finished with it. I'm leaving right now. I'll be over in a couple minutes, all right? Where are you, anyway?"

"I'll wait for you just outside Denny's."

"Got it."

"And hurry, will you? Thanks, Curtis."

"I know. I'm a peach."

What little light shone in the Bowles's vast living room was coming from the kitchen, where several of Jill's and Curtis's friends were congregated. Erik, looking very serious, was manning the blender; on the Formica countertop before him, he had laid out all the necessary ingredients for his infamous alcoholic concoctions. Becky stood facing the open refrigerator, ripping open a box of Pudding Pops, while her friends Robin and Gale peered over her shoulders, trying to get at a pitcher of orange juice. Billy and Dean, two juniors Becky and Gale had brought over, were standing by the trash compactor drinking St. Pauli Girls.

"Erik!" Curtis yelled over the *whirr* of the blender.

"Yeah? Oh, you're back! Hey, Jill, glad you could make it!" Erik dropped half an orange into the machine and shifted up to *purée*.

Jill said hello to everyone and added, "I'll see you guys in a bit, all right?" She recalled that Becky still owed Sam some money, and envisioned Becky saying, "At least I'm twenty dollars richer" upon learning that Sam was dead. Jill gave Becky a vicious glare, and received in return a look of annoyed bewilderment. Curtis started to chat with Erik, but Jill tugged sharply on the sleeve of his jacket, pulling him back. All she wanted was to tell Curtis what was going on. Sam was the only important matter any longer, and Curtis had to know. Jill didn't feel like facing any of her other friends.

She remembered Sam hadn't even been invited to this party in the first place, since Curtis wasn't speaking to him. She didn't want any part of it.

"Curtis," she said, trying to snatch him out of the kitchen.

"Erik, run things for a while, OK?" asked Curtis.

"Sure, guy."

"C'mon, Jill." Curtis gestured down the dark hallway. The door to his parents' bedroom was slightly ajar. A flicker of subdued light and the buzzing of a TV screen wafted through the opening. Curtis whispered in Jill's ear: "Go in and say hello. They're all sophomores." He pointed at the door.

Jill opened it wider, poked her head in, and said, "What's up, guys?"

The eight sophomore boys in the room jumped a foot off their seats. On the TV monitor was a naked, unattractive woman sucking on an eleven-inch penis. One of the boys on the floor quickly threw a pillow over his lap while Jill stood there smiling at them. None of the boys uttered a word.

"See you later," she said, and winked.

"That should get them hot and bothered," said Curtis. "Let's go down to my room."

They descended the carpeted, circular staircase, to Curtis's room. When they opened the door and turned on the lights, they saw no one was in it.

"Good," said Curtis.

Jill wondered how many hours Curtis, Sam, and she had spent together in this room. She could see the three of them laughing, passing around Curtis's pipe, getting stoned off their asses—something that had not happened often, but had always taken place here. This was where they would inevitably end up after a night of carousing, sometimes staying up talking until dawn. Often, Sam and Jill crashed here on the floor, innocently, if the three of them had partied very hard. Curtis's room was their hideout. Once inside, they were shut off entirely from the rest of the world; it might as well have been a tree house, for the feeling of privacy it instilled and the camaraderie they felt within.

Without Sam, the room felt dead.

Yellowish light overhead filtered dimly down through the layer of camouflage netting that sagged loosely across the length of the ceiling. In the far corner, from the netting, hung, upside down, a plastic lawn-style pink flamingo. Beneath it in a large iron cage sat a real bird on its perch: a green Amazonian parrot named Dr. McCoy, who was rapidly nodding his head up and down in greeting to Curtis. Along one wall were two well-kept aquariums, one saltwater, the other fresh, as well as a small terrarium. Inside the terrarium was a salamander named Dino, splotched in olive and black, who had grown amazingly long and fat since Sam had caught him at Stink Lake and given him to Curtis the year before. He was Curtis's favorite pet.

The far wall, behind the water bed, was covered by a white sheet on which Curtis and Sam had spray-painted the names of their favorite bands (Dead Kennedys, Suicidal Tendencies, Fear, Naked Raygun, Butthole Surfers, The Minutemen, Sex Pistols, The Clash, Bauhaus, Killing Joke, 999, P.I.L.), and written song titles with permanent marking pens ("California Über Alles," "Anarchy in the U.K.," "Bela Lugosi's Dead," "Nazi Punks Fuck Off"), as well as slogans ("I'm so bored with the U.S.A.," "Ultra-Violence," "Tax religion"). The opposite wall was one long closet with sliding doors, stuffed with clothes of every imaginable style. More clothes lay in heaps on the floor. The remaining walls were plastered with posters: David Bowie from his most recent tour; Sid Vicious bare-chested with self-made razor cuts dripping blood down his front; a comparatively tame, leather-clad Billy Idol; three different faces of Sting; two Dead Kennedys posters, from the albums *Fresh Fruit for Rotting Vegetables* and *Frankenchrist;* and movie posters for *Creepshow* and *A Clockwork Orange*. Beneath the posters sat Curtis's desk, stereo system, and bookshelves. He had most of Stephen King's books, a large amount of science fiction, and a few each by Kurt Vonnegut and William S. Burroughs. Atop one bookshelf shone a lava lamp Curtis had found at a garage sale, and at the head of his bed was a tacky western lamp with bogus ranch brands all over its shade. Somehow, among the posters, Curtis had managed to find space for three mirrors, each one at his own eye level. His prized possession, an ivory-handled switchblade, was sticking out from the wooden door frame.

Jill stretched out on top of the rumpled sheets of his water bed and groaned. Curtis was still standing.

"Oh, Curtis, I feel like shit," said Jill. Why this burden had fallen upon her, she had no idea. Even though it had been the police who had kept her from telling anyone else what she thought she had seen, she felt enormous guilt having gone all day without letting Curtis in on it. Curtis deserved to know about Sam more than anyone, herself included. Yet there remained the difficult task of telling him. Jill was impatient to get it over with and get everything out in the open, although she knew she would have to lead up to it carefully. There was more to it than just Sam's death—there were also the *weird* elements for which Jill had no answers.

The light from overhead made Curtis's brow ridge, cheekbones, and jaw stand out, and glinted off the moussed spikes in his hair. Beneath his wrinkled, beige Swedish Army surplus jacket he wore a Clash T-shirt that he had bought at a concert of theirs the last time they had come to Denver. He also wore a touch of eyeliner, something he had picked up from Erik, which on a guy was unheard of in Sherman, but which Jill thought made him look sexy—in a sinister sort of way. A silver-dagger earring hung from his right ear, but there were lots of guys in Sherman with pierced ears; it didn't necessarily *mean* anything. Curtis had once told her he wanted to look "rabid." What he had meant by that wasn't totally clear.

I'm going to have to tell him everything, she thought.

"Curtis, I don't think Sam's going to be coming back at all..."

"Do you want a drink?" Curtis asked, as if he hadn't heard her. He stood up. "I'm going to go get one. Do you want one?"

Jill's head throbbed with the rage she suddenly felt toward Curtis. He was making everything far more difficult than she had hoped it would be. She wanted to yell at him and demand he show more respect for Sam's memory, demand he cancel the party to which Sam hadn't even been invited, demand he stop being such an ass, and demand he come and hold her in his arms, comfort her, protect her.... But she had to hold it back. Curtis simply didn't have any idea. It was not his fault he was being such a jerk. If she didn't manage to tell him soon, then she truly would go crazy out of anger and frustration.

She realized, resignedly, that a drink was precisely what she needed, to lose some tension as well as loosen her tongue. Her shoulders were small, hard knots sending needle-sharp feelers up into her neck, and whenever she turned her head even slightly it produced creaky noises, like the sound of snapping bones. She felt, in fact, as if she had just sat through another day of school.

"Sure," she said, attempting a smile. "What's that thing Erik makes? The one that tastes so awful."

"A DeBicardi?"

"Yeah. A tall one." Jill didn't know exactly what, besides rum, was in a DeBicardi; it was a homemade concoction Erik had learned from his older brother, who had picked it up at some raucous parties in Laramie a few years earlier. All she knew was, it packed a punch and didn't taste like anything else known to man. Her mouth watered. "And hurry up."

She couldn't bear to withhold her secret from him any longer.

Curtis said, "Gotcha," and left, closing the door behind him.

Jill closed her eyes, trying both to relax and to push Sam out of her mind. Curtis was taking a long time, probably gabbing with Erik or saying hello to new arrivals. Even though he was ignorant of what had happened, Jill couldn't help but feel he was somehow betraying Sam. She knew as well that if he didn't return soon, she might doze off right there in his bed, she was so exhausted.

Curtis's hand crept up her side, resting beneath her left breast, cupping it through her blouse.

". . . Don't, Curtis. I said, stop it." Jill scooted away from him on the vinyl car seat, resting her head against the cold, foggy window.

"But Jill!"

"I told you I didn't want to do any of that stuff. It would

wreck our friendship. I want to be just friends with you. That's all."

"I don't think it would ruin anything! Jeez, Jill, how could it? You're just scared, that's all."

"No, I'm not. Look, I love you and everything—"

"That's what I mean—"

"—as a friend. I love you as a friend. I want it to stay like that."

Curtis opened his door and started to get out of the car.

"Where are you going?" asked Jill.

"For a walk, okay?"

"Damn, damn, damn," she muttered, rubbing her eyes with her knuckles. She hated herself for having dredged up that vivid memory from ninth grade. She was supposed to be thinking of Sam, and getting help from Curtis, and instead she had drifted off into *that*. She didn't know why she couldn't simply let it rest. She had had her chance with Curtis back then, long before Sam had even appeared on the scene. Now that she found herself attracted to Curtis, it was too late. Jill had played her part too well back then, fixing it so she and Curtis would never be anything more than best friends. *Shit,* she thought, *how could I have been so stupid?*

She was disgusted with herself for thinking all these things, with Sam dead. It was shameful, and wrong, and it wouldn't do any good anyway, because Curtis no longer wanted her. Sam had wanted her, and had had her, but now he was gone and Jill felt like a traitor. She was there because of Sam, and should never have been thinking of anything else. Jill thought, *I'm pathetic*.

"I'm back!" announced Curtis, wielding two tall, sweating DeBicardis.

"Oh God, thanks!" said Jill.

"My friends call me Curtis." Curtis forced one of the drinks toward her, reminding Jill of a murderer in a mystery movie, trying to make sure his wife received the glass with the arsenic in it. She sat up on the bed and took it from him. Curtis sat down beside her. For a while, they simply sipped their drinks, without talking.

Jill knew she would have to lead up to it, and tell Curtis everything that had happened to her in the last two days. It would be a delicate conversation, and she would have to be careful.

"Curtis, do you remember, when we were kids, the stories your father used to tell us about an evil wizard who lived at Stink Lake?"

"Yeah."

"Did you ever wonder if any of that was true?"

"When I was a kid, I was scared to death."

"I mean now."

"No, of course not."

Jill gulped too much of her drink; it had a strong bite; she winced. "Your father said there was an evil wizard. He hid in the lake during the day, and if you went swimming, he would make the weeds grab you and pull you under, or he'd make sure you left the lake carrying about five deadly diseases. He was the one who made the lake stink. He also stole Frisbees and kites and dogs, when he could get his hands on them. In the winter, just as the water was beginning to freeze, he would grab you from below if you walked out on the ice. He supposedly grabbed a bulldozer, too, that one year when they tried to smooth off the skating rink a little too early. Then at night, of course, he would come out of the lake and prowl the park, looking for tasty little children to eat."

"C'mon, Jill," said Curtis. "He just told us that stuff to keep us from ever doing anything stupid in the park. He made it all up. You know that."

"And if anyone ever stole anything that belonged to the wizard, he would come and get them."

"My parents didn't want any salamanders in our house."

"Didn't your dad tell you once about a skeleton that was found along the lakeshore?" asked Jill, after downing the rest of her drink.

"Yeah, some German professor from Laramie, Wolf

somebody or other—but that was ages ago, in the forties, after the war. It was spontaneous combustion. The man burned to death instantaneously. They found his skeleton the next day, and some charred bits of clothing. But that had nothing to do with an evil wizard."

"But doesn't it make you wonder?"

"Jill, you're not making any sense. I thought you wanted to talk about Sam."

"Nothing makes any sense," she said. "Strange things have been going on, Curtis. I need your help. I can't do this alone."

"Whatever you want—just tell me what you're talking about."

"OK," she said. The DeBicardi was starting to kick in; she felt light-headed.

She told him about the aeration tube, how it had been pulled beneath the surface of Stink Lake by something unknown. All the while, she paid close attention to his face, which stayed rigid. He seemed to be listening, but was probably anticipating his chance to speak.

"Something about it was completely wrong," she explained, her hands making as many motions in the air as her voice made nervous inflections. "I mean, it looked like it was swallowed up, by a shark or something." Oh, that sounded swell. The closest she had ever been to an ocean was Utah, and even then there were no man-eating sharks in the Great Salt Lake. The moment she mentioned a "shark," Curtis must have thought she was crazy.

"Accidents happen," said Curtis calmly. "Things go wrong. Like that time your toilet erupted all over me, remember that? And we couldn't figure out how to turn the water off."

A smile tugged at the corners of her mouth, but she held it back. This was no time to be reminiscing. It couldn't wait any longer; Curtis had to know about Sam.

"This thing with the aerator," he continued, "it's just like that. There wasn't any monster in Stink Lake, any more than there was a demon in your toilet."

Great. Curtis had come up with a "monster," like Sam had done. She wasn't about to give in, however. After everything that had happened since the aerator incident, she knew for certain it had not been an accident. She wondered if perhaps there *had* been a demon in her toilet that day (which seemed so long ago now, when they were eleven or twelve). Maybe there was no such thing as an accident after all.

"Did I tell you I paid my fine?" asked Curtis.

"Curtis, please, don't change the subject. I don't want any more explanations from anybody. The aeration tube was pulled under by something. I know what I saw, and I know I'm not crazy."

"I wouldn't worry. They don't ship people off to Evanston over things like this."

No, but what about the other things? There were probably loonies in the state hospital who had done lesser things than see dead bodies of their boyfriends that weren't really there. Jill could see the men in the white coats now, waiting in Curtis's driveway in a white, nondescript van— waiting to ambush her with butterfly nets. Before they dragged her away, she would write on the side of the truck with her finger, in the layer of dust: *Evanston or Bust*. Then she would laugh, because they would be doing her a favor getting her away from Sherman, the high school, the cops, the lake...

"I think Sam is dead," she said.

Curtis smirked crookedly and said nothing.

"Did you hear what I just said?"

"Calm down, Jill. I wouldn't worry about Sam. He's probably on his way back right now, wherever he went. I'm sure he's perfectly safe."

"No, you don't get it. You don't understand at all. This morning, when I was jogging, I found him dead. His body was mutilated, but I'm almost sure it was—"

"You're kidding, right?"

"No, I'm not, dammit. I panicked, and I couldn't tell if it was Sam, but I was pretty sure. His tape player was crushed on the ground next to him, and I found a tape in the mud—the same tape he was listening to when he left my place last night. It was Sam's body. Oh God, Curtis, what am I going to do?"

Jill started to cry, and Curtis set his drink aside and held her close. She put her head on his shoulder and squeezed him tightly. He placed his hand on her head and stroked her hair.

"Something killed him last night," she said into his ear, sobbing. "At Stink Lake. It was awful."

"That can't be. You know that can't be. How could Sam be dead? It just isn't possible."

Finally, they moved apart, and Jill looked at Curtis's face. It was strained; he looked confused.

"Mr. Prenez was killed last night."

"Yeah, I know. Everyone was talking about it upstairs."

"So was Sam. No one knows about it but me. And now you. Everything about it is really strange. After I came across the body, it started getting sucked up into the mud. Then I almost got sucked up myself, but somehow I managed to get free. I don't know. I was dazed. It's hard to remember everything that happened."

"You're slightly drunk."

"You've got to believe me, or I'm really stuck. I went into shock, and Maggie took me to the hospital. Then I reported the body. The police spent all day looking for it, and dug around the shoreline where I had spotted it, but they came up with nothing. Nothing at all. It was gone."

Curtis sighed heavily. "Are you trying to tell me there's an evil wizard at Stink Lake who knocked out the aeration tube, killed our French teacher, killed Sam, and then made off with his body?"

I wish I had a cigarette, Jill thought. I don't smoke, but I want to start right now. "Curtis, I'm sorry. I don't know what I'm saying. The police want Dr. Benson to run some psychiatric evaluations on me next week at school. Maggie thought it was a good idea. So did Celia. I don't. I don't think it's a good idea at all. Something is going on. Without you on my side, I'll be totally helpless."

"Shit. What do you expect me to do? Whittle off some wooden stakes so we can go vampire hunting?"

"Please don't make fun of me."

"I'm sorry. It's just that I bring you over here, and you tell me all these crazy things. If you were anyone else, even Sam, I would have told you to get the fuck out of my house. But you're not. You're Jill. You're still my best friend. I'm going to take you home."

"But—"

"You're in no condition to be partying tonight, and you could really use some rest. How much sleep did you get last night?"

"About four hours."

"See? And then whatever it is that happened to you today—I mean, you said you were in shock, right? I think if you just get a good night's sleep, all of this will be over. Sam will probably come back before you wake up, and then you'll see everything's okay."

"Don't you believe anything I've said?"

"No," Curtis said. He paused and took Jill's hand in his own. "No, Jill, I don't."

➤ TWELVE

"Are we trapped in here?" asked Jeff's voice in the blackness. It was the first time, Simon realized, that he had spoken all evening.

"No," said Simon. "Don't worry. There's a door in the boiler room that'll let us into the basement. There's another door at the end of one of the tunnels, and there's a couple of other hatches around. We can use any of them. Right now we're pretty close to the boiler room."

Troy flicked his lighter again. Its feeble light barely made visible a wide rectangular hole in one of the four walls. That, aside from the hatch in the ceiling, was the only exit.

"And from the basement we can get into the high school?" asked Jeff, looking anxious.

"Of course, you dildo," said Troy. "The basement is part of the high school."

"I want to get out of here, is all. It's too hot, and it's kind of ... uh ..."

"Dark?"

"No. I mean yeah, but ..."

"Spit it out, Jeff," said Troy. "Smelly?"

"No. Yeah. No, I mean ..."

"Illegal?"

"Creepy?" offered Kraig. "Weird? Scary? Spooky?"

"Yeah, that's it," said Jeff.

"Aw, cut it out," said Troy. "All you mean is you have to take a piss. Go do it in the corner."

Jeff turned around and faded into the darkness.

"It is pretty fucking hot in here," Troy declared.

"I told you, it's a steam tunnel," said Simon. "There's all these radiator pipes going down these little tunnels, like to all parts of the building."

"Nice."

The odor of mildew, mixed with the chalky cement dust they had kicked up, helped to make the stale air even less bearable. The smell of urine wafted over from the far corner. The hot dampness of the air made Simon's T-shirt cling to his chest, and was making his crotch itch. His jeans had been creeping up his crack all night and were pinching him in several places, but he couldn't adjust himself, not in front of these guys. They would all think he was a fairy.

"Ouch! Fuck!" said Troy, quickly letting go of his lighter. It clattered, in total darkness, to the gritty floor.

"Burn your thumb?" asked Kraig's now faceless voice. "I told ya, didn't I?"

"Yeah, I know. Shit! Now I can't find my lighter."

Blinded by the dark, Simon got down on his knees to help Troy look for it, scraping the floor with his fingers. His hands were rapidly coated with a layer of dust, but he failed to come up with the small plastic lighter. He wiped his hands on his jeans. His head suddenly struck someone else's, hard.

"Ow!" he and Troy shouted simultaneously.

"Sorry, Troy," added Simon, rubbing the bump on his forehead.

"Jeez, what a bitch," said Troy.

Simon hoped he meant either his own bump or the loss of his lighter. He quickly took advantage of the darkness by slipping a hand into his jeans to rearrange his dick and nuts, so they wouldn't keep getting pinched whenever he moved.

"Here," said Kraig's voice. His hand appeared all of a sudden, next to Troy's head, and was illuminated by a high flame rising above his clenched fist, coming from his own lighter.

"Fuck, man, why didn't you light that thing before I became a casualty? But Christ! Get it away from me— you're gonna burn my hair off!"

"Yeah, with all that grease in it, it'll go up real nice." Kraig was the only person in the world who could get away with speaking like that to Troy.

"Aha! There it is!" Troy spotted his blue lighter a couple of feet away and picked it up. Kraig turned his own off. Everything was dark once more. "Anyway, it's not grease, Kraigie, it's *gel*."

"Still goes up real nice."

"What are you—some kind of pyro?" Troy and Simon both got up.

"Just trying to be helpful."

"Why don't you 'help' Jeff over there? He'd look good as a skinhead." Troy flicked his lighter and they found Jeff's pimple-encrusted face had returned to the circle.

A terrified Jeff protested: "Uh . . . uh . . ."

Troy smiled and mussed Jeff's hair with his hand. "Jesus, kid, I'm not going to set your hair on fire!"

Jeff looked relieved. The lighter went back out.

Simon wondered just how he had forgotten to bring a flashlight. "C'mon, guys," he said. "This room's really dumb. There's other stuff I want to show you."

All day, he had thought about a story his brother had told him from work, back when Sam was sacking groceries at the Safeway. There was one day when one of the female cashiers had been on the toilet in the back, when she looked up to see a ceiling panel pulled back directly above her, and a man's face looking down at her. She screamed, ran from the toilet, and told the manager there was a man in the ceiling. At first he didn't believe her, but then he set up a stepladder in the middle of the store, near the frozen foods, and went up into the ceiling to take a look. A minute later, he brought the man down the ladder, in front of all the customers. The man smelled bad and was dressed shabbily; he said his wife had kicked him out of the house three weeks earlier and he admitted he had been living in the ceiling of the Safeway since then, sneaking down into the store at night to get his food, and hiding in the rafters by day. Simon couldn't remember what had happened afterwards to the guy, but it hardly mattered.

What mattered was that maybe Sam was doing the same thing, hiding out down there for a while, in the tunnels. If so, Simon was sure to find food, or clothes, or something, even if he and the Skunks had already scared Sam away with all their racket.

"All right. Lead the way," said Troy. "Here, Simon, you want my lighter? My thumb's still burnt; I can't use it."

"Naw, give it to Jeff. I'd know my way around here blindfolded."

Simon felt his way to the wall and found the passageway. "There's a little drop here, past this hole."

"Okay," said Troy. "You still aren't a real Skunk yet. Let's see you find your way through here in the dark. Kraig, take my lighter and don't let anyone use either of them. I'll grab onto Simon's shirt. Jeff, grab onto mine, and Kraig, grab Jeff's. And don't anyone let go. Those are the rules. Okay, Simon, let's go."

Simon felt Troy's hand fumble for the end of his T-shirt. Then, instead, it clutched a better hold onto the waist of his jeans and held it tightly in a fist, the knuckles pressing firmly right above his buttocks.

"All aboard," said Kraig.

"Hang on," said Simon. He crawled through the hole carefully, stretching one leg down to meet the lower floor on the other side. "Don't stand up once you're in here. You can walk—but you got to bend your knees and crouch down low." He turned to the left, feeling a slight tug on his jeans as the Skunks followed him into the narrow tunnel. Crumbled pieces of concrete, scraps of metal, and bits of broken glass crunched beneath their feet. Simon reached ahead, expecting to find a pipe crossing his path at head level. It was there, and he had to grab it to help himself crawl under it. "Watch your heads—there's a pipe right here."

"Got it," said Troy.

"Jeez, I'm roasting," said Kraig.

"We're going to the boiler room," said Simon.

"Watch your head, Jeff," said Troy.

"Okay."

"And watch where you step," Troy added. "Some sharp shit on the floor."

"There's a turn up ahead a little ways," said Simon. "Guide off the wall, on your right."

"Simon says," said Kraig, and laughed. There was a sudden *clang*. "Shit! Who put that pipe there?"

Simon was jerked slightly backwards, and fell over, as the train came to a halt.

"We told you to watch out," said Troy.

"Fuck you."

"Well c'mon, let's go."

Simon soon brought them around the turn. They were almost to the boiler room. Sweat dripped down his face in rivulets, and his breathing grew more rapid. The sound of hissing steam became stronger until suddenly they were upon it.

"Okay, guys, the boiler room."

"Kraig," said Troy. "Light one of the lighters."

There was no response.

"Kraig? Kraig! Where are you?"

"I'm right here," said his voice from behind them. "What did you think?"

"Well, c'mon, give us some light here."

"Hold onto yourself, why don'tcha?"

"Okay," said Troy, "I'm holding on. Tight." He made moaning noises. "Uhnn.... Uhnn.... Uhnnnn.... Ahhhhh!"

"Troy, don't be a pervert."

"Sorry, didn't mean to invade your turf."

"Fuck you!"

"No, thanks."

Kraig flicked the lighter a few times before it caught, illuminating his face. The flame didn't reach far. The four of them could see each other, barely, but couldn't see much else of the room around them. Kraig stood up, since the ceiling there was high enough. The others stood, too. Kraig started walking slowly into the blackness of the room, one arm stretched out in front of him and flickering with the feeble flame.

Slowly, the tall, round, cylindrical end of one of the boilers came into view. Pipes wormed around it, ran to it, and hung above it, along the ceiling.

Kraig shut off the lighter.

"Hey!" shouted Jeff.

"Hey nothing, man. It was about to burn my fucking thumb off. Simon, you should have brought a flashlight."

Shit! Simon wished no one would have mentioned that. "I forgot," he said. His shirt was drenched with sweat. The boiler room was like a sauna. There was no way Sam would be living down there.

"Kraig," said Troy. "Give me my lighter."

"OK."

Troy flicked on the lighter. Crumpled in his left hand was the T-shirt he had been wearing, and on his face was a malicious grin. He set fire to the shirt, held it in the air while it caught, then tossed it on the ground. He was barechested beneath his jean jacket, his flame-colored skin glistening wet.

The room came into full view in the dim, orange light from Troy's small fire. Three huge, iron boilers sat side by side down the length of the cement-walled chamber, their shadows shifting and wavering as the light grew stronger, then receded. At the other end of the room was a second tunnel, the same size as the one they had just come through. The firelight stopped at its black, square opening. On the nearest wall was a door, with several steps leading up to it, and a crack of bluish light shining at the base.

"That door takes us into the high school, right?" asked Troy, looking at Simon.

"Yeah, but we have to go this way." Simon pointed at the other tunnel on the far wall.

"What do you mean, we have to go that way?" asked Troy, grinning down at Simon like a wolf.

There was no way to explain. He felt like an idiot for even thinking Sam might be hiding out in the steam tunnels. There was no way he was going to tell the Skunks the real reason they were all down there. At the same time, now that he was there, Simon felt he had to complete his mission, and search through all the tunnels, until he was certain. He would have to further impress Troy, to keep him from wanting to leave the tunnels just yet.

"Do you know where that other tunnel goes?" said Simon. "The one over there? At the very end of it, there's a little iron door. It opens up into this huge tunnel beneath Seventh Street."

"The storm sewer," Troy muttered, as if turning the idea over in his mind, formulating a plan.

Simon had heard about this tunnel from Sam, but had never checked it out himself. He hoped Sam hadn't been kidding.

"Sewer?" Jeff whined. "I don't want to go near any sewer."

"It's not a real sewer," said Troy. "It's like a big drain where all the water goes when there's a rainstorm. The lake drains into it."

"Stink Lake? Oh, swell." Jeff looked longingly at the blue crack of light from underneath the door.

Troy's T-shirt didn't last any longer. The flames died until there were but a few glowing embers in the charred pile of cloth.

Simon felt a hand on his shoulder, and someone's hot breath on his ear. "Private Skunk conference," whispered Troy's voice. "Don't worry, Simon, we'll find your brother." Troy gave his back a brief pat.

"How did you know..." Simon whispered back.

"Not too hard to figure out. Now where was the last place he was at?"

"Jill Beaumont's."

"You called her, didn't you?"

"Umm, no." Simon hadn't even thought of it.

"Then what are we doing down here, anyway?"

"Just a hunch."

"All right. After we're through here, we'll go see her, see if she knows anything, OK?"

"Sure."

"End of conference." Troy moved away, and then his voice returned to its normal brassy volume. "Okay, Simon, let's go. Lead the way. We'll all grab on like we did before, but take one of the lighters this time so you can see where you're going when you have to."

"Sure thing." It was nice knowing Troy was on his side.

The going was tough through this tunnel.

Every few feet, they had to step over or slide under a radiator pipe crossing their path. Simon lit Troy's lighter periodically, checking for pipes. The ceiling was so low, it made getting past the pipes even more difficult.

"Wow," said Kraig. "It's kinda like in those TV shows, when they have to slide under a light beam or else a huge door will come slamming down on their head."

"You're so full of shit," said Troy.

"This tunnel's really long."

"I think it goes beneath the gym," said Simon. "At the end of that, it runs into the big tunnel."

"I want to see this storm sewer," said Troy. "I bet you could get anywhere in Sherman from there."

Simon came across another pipe. "You can step over this one, guys."

"Gotcha."

"Hey!" Simon shouted. He flicked the lighter and showed Troy what he had found: an empty bottle of strawberry schnapps. He handed it to Troy.

Troy unscrewed the top, sniffed it, and examined the bottle. "Still a swallow left," he said, and handed it to Jeff. "Go on."

Jeff looked reluctant, but grabbed the bottle and downed the last of it. "Gross."

"I know," said Troy. "I hate strawberry schnapps."

They kept a tally of the empty bottles they found: one of Black Velvet, one André Cold Duck, two Jack Daniel's, three Michelobs, and five Bud Lights. They found one used prophylactic.

"I can see Simon comes down here often," said Kraig.

"Jeez, are we going to have to come back this way, too?" asked Jeff.

"I think there's another hatch into the high school at the end of it," said Simon. "And here it is."

They had reached the end of the tunnel. Simon shone the lighter all around, so they could see. In the wall was set a small, iron door, hinged at the bottom, with a sturdy iron latch at the top—the door to the storm sewer. In the ceiling a similar hatch opened upwards—the door to the high school.

Simon turned off the lighter and unlatched the hatch in the ceiling. He poked his head up into the opening, without letting the door swing all the way open. "Hey, guys, it's the girls' locker room!"

"No kidding?" said Kraig anxiously.

Jeff said, "Really?"

Simon laughed. "No, not really. It's just a supply room."

"You jerk."

"Sorry."

"C'mon, Simon," said Troy. "Open up the other door. Let's see what's behind it."

Simon flicked on the lighter with one hand, and tugged at the rusty latch with the other. "Shit! It won't budge." He turned off the lighter and stuck it in his pocket, then used both hands to try to break open the latch. He pushed on the handle with all his strength, until it finally gave way. A brief gust of cool wind escaped from the opening, as the door swung inward and banged against the concrete.

"Whew!" Troy said. "That smell's really . . . putrid!"

"It's Stink Lake, like you said," said Simon.

"Jesus!" said Kraig. "It's like a million farts."

"At least," said Troy.

The hole was a foot and a half high and two long, and very dark. Simon took out the lighter, lit it, and leaned over the edge. He could see very little, but he could tell it was quite a drop to the floor below. "What the—" he began.

A shape shifted in the darkness. Simon's words echoed in whispers, as if being repeated by small voices.

"What is it?" asked Troy. He kept a firm grip on the seat of Simon's pants, to keep him from falling in.

"I don't know," said Simon. "I can't see anything."

Something moved in the shadows.

I don't know, I can't see anything.

"There's an echo in here," he said over his shoulder.

"Must be pretty big, then," said Troy. "Let me have a look."

"No, wait a second." Simon turned back toward the darkness, and tried squinting his eyes to see better, but it was no good. The stench was unbearable. A lump formed in his throat, and his heart beat faster. He whispered into the chamber: "Sam?"

Dead silence was all he heard.

He tried again, softly: "Sam? Are you in here?"

Behind him, Kraig had brought his lighter closer, adding more light.

Out of the darkness, two strong, slimy vines appeared, and coiled themselves around Simon's wrists like snakes.

"Holy fuck!" shouted Troy.

Simon screamed as the tentacles pulled him in. Troy's grip failed, and Simon was yanked from the tunnel and down, into the depths.

THIRTEEN

"Simon!"

Whatever the fuck it was, it had snatched Simon right out of Troy's hands, like a frog catching a fly with its tongue. Troy's fingers were raw where he had been holding on to the waist of Simon's jeans.

"Simon!" yelled Kraig, lighter still in hand. Simon's shrieks from the other chamber had stopped.

Troy stood back from the hole, his back flat against the tunnel wall. Kraig was nearer the hole, Jeff behind him. Troy had turned his head away, but his eyes stayed fixed upon the black opening. He expected six more green vines to spring from the opening and drag the three remaining Skunks into the sewer.

"Fuck it, Kraig!" he said. "Let's get the fuck out of here and get some help. C'mon!"

"Simon!" yelled Kraig. "Simon, can you hear me?"

"Shh!" said Troy.

They all listened carefully, and heard the gurgling of running water. No noise came from Simon. Kraig's lighter went out.

"Kraig, let's go!"

"Shit, man!"

"Kraig!"

"Shit! Holy fuckin' shit!"

"Kraig, Jesus!"

"But—Simon!"

In the darkness, Troy groped until he found Kraig's shoulder. He grabbed it firmly and shook him.

"We'll have to come back. Fuck it, Kraig. We can't go in there. What if that thing gets us?"

"We can't leave him!"

"Shut up!"

"But—"

"Shut the fuck up!" Troy shouted. He turned, found Jeff, and said, "Jeff, go! Through the supply room, up here!"

"Where?" Jeff cried, his voice breaking. "I can't see."

"Here!" Troy grabbed Jeff by the waist and dragged him beneath the ceiling hatch. "Right here! Go!" He shoved Jeff up. The iron door banged open, and blue light entered through the square hole. Jeff scampered up into the room; then Troy could hear him open a door and run off, into the gymnasium.

"C'mon, Kraig!"

"I'm shutting this door first."

"Leave it!"

With the light coming in, Troy could make out Kraig moving toward the hole.

"C'mon!" Troy pulled himself up through the ceiling hatch, into the moonlit supply room. He stuck his head down the hole, to see what the hell Kraig was doing down there. "Hurry up!"

"Almost got it! Simon must have busted this latch when he—Jesus Fuck!" Kraig disappeared, screaming, into the hole.

"Kraig! Kraig!"

Several shrieks followed, then nothing.

Leave him! he thought. He had to get the fuck out of there.

Troy glanced around the supply room for something heavy. A wooden desk was nearby. He slammed shut the iron door and threw the desk upon it, then grabbed some chairs and added them to it, then leaned a small bookcase against it. It was the best he could do. He sure as shit didn't want those vines coming after him.

He opened the door and ran out into the gymnasium,

heading as fast as he could toward the closest exit. On the wooden gym floor, his steps echoed loudly, making it sound as if there were ten other guys running after him. He looked over his shoulder, tripped, and fell headlong. Nothing was behind him. No green vines—nothing at all—slithered in his direction. He struggled to his feet, his right side bruised, and burst open the closest door, beneath a red "Exit" sign.

He was outside.

"There he is!" he heard. It was a deep, authoritative voice coming from his left, many yards away.

He glanced to one side, and saw a policeman chasing after him. *What the fuck?* he thought—until he saw another policeman standing near the high school entrance, with Jeff in his clutches, and Clint standing nearby, smiling.

Clint! That fucking rat!

"Hey, buster, hold it right there!"

No way, thought Troy. Without even looking for cars, he ran across Seventh Street, aiming toward Grant. A pair of headlights screeched, but missed him, the driver shouting obscenities at him. A long string of cars followed. Troy looked back. The cop had been cut off—now was his chance.

He ran down the length of Grant Street, the cold air biting against his bare skin beneath his open jean jacket.

The cop called after him: "I'm calling your probation officer, you little shit!"

Troy turned around and gave the cop the finger. "Suck me, pig!" he yelled.

He still had no clear idea what had just taken place, down in the tunnels. Something was *alive* down there. Simon and Kraig had been snatched by it. Jeff and Troy had escaped, but Jeff was in the hands of the police. Troy had to get help, but not the police—*not* the police! They would never believe any of it. He had to find some other way to get to Simon and Kraig.

Troy kept running, on the other side of the street from

the park, and decided to head for the Buckin' Bronc Motel, just up Grant, on the other side of Third from the trailer court. They had a pay phone there, and it would be less conspicuous than going to the shopping plaza. But who could he call?

Troy dashed across Third Street, swung open the door to the lobby of the motel and headed straight for the phone, much to the chagrin of the girl at the registration desk, he could see. He stood and stared at the phone and drew a blank. No one in his family would be of any help, and his dad was out working for the railroad the next couple of days anyway. Troy didn't know Simon's parents—they would simply think he was crazy. Kraig's mom might be OK...

Then he realized that whatever had gotten Simon and Kraig must have had something to do with Sam Taylor's disappearance as well, and the only person who seemed to know anything about that was Jill Beaumont. Troy dropped a quarter into the phone and listened to the dial tone. Thumbing his way through the Sherman directory, he landed upon the Bs, but failed to find anything reading *Beaumont, J.* But then, Jill lived with her aunt.

Screw it, he figured. They live right in the trailer park over here. Troy hung up the phone and ran out the door, leaving his quarter behind. He flipped up the collar of his jacket as he crossed Third Street again, in case there were any cops patrolling around. The Lucky Z Trailer Court was right here in this block. Jill's had the little white fence around it.

Troy went up the steps and pounded on the door. Jill's aunt appeared at the door with bags under her eyes.

"I need to see Jill," said Troy.

"She's not here," said Jill's aunt. "Sorry."

"This is urgent!"

"Well, Jill's out, and I don't know when she'll be back. Good night." She shut the door.

Troy decided to wait on the steps, but as he began to sit down, a flashy red Porsche drove up to the curb and let Jill out. Looking upset, she slammed the car door and stalked away, through the gate and up the path to her trailer. The Porsche peeled out.

"Jill!" Troy jumped down the steps and stood directly before her.

Jill raised her head up and tossed the hair from her face. "Troy? What do you want?" She looked preoccupied.

"Something's happened to Sam's brother—"

"Shit!"

"—and my friend Kraig."

"What is it? What's happened?" Jill's face had gone pale. She definitely knew something.

"I . . . I don't know. There were these vines . . . I don't know . . . They grabbed Simon and Kraig!"

"Was this at the lake?"

"No, we were at the high school, kind of . . . We were down in the steam tunnels, you know, that run under—"

"Yeah, I know, sure. That's right across the street, close enough." Jill looked over her shoulder. "Shit. Curtis's already gone."

"We've got to do something, go help Simon and Kraig. I don't think they're dead or anything. You were the only person I could think of. I saw the pigs talking to you today. Do you know what's going on? Is this what happened to Simon's brother?"

"I wish I knew. Listen, we've got to go see a friend of mine. I'll tell you everything I know on the way to his house. I was just up there, and told him what's been going on, but he didn't know what to think. If you tell him what you told me, maybe he'll believe me. We've got to get him to help us. This was in the steam tunnels?"

"Yeah, that's what I—"

"And you think they're still down there?"

"I don't know, but it's worth a look." Troy didn't know if he'd be ready to go back down there just yet.

"Well, come on, let's go! I don't have a car or anything. We'll have to run."

"OK, but let's watch out for the pigs. I think they're looking for me."

Jill grabbed Troy's jacket collar and tugged him along behind her until they started running down Grant Street. The cops were gone from the high school. The coast was clear. Troy had to run hard to keep up with Jill's pace.

This girl's crazy, Troy thought, but what the hell else have I got?

➤ FOURTEEN

The pizza Curtis had eaten for supper came up from his stomach, while Erik held his head.

Crouching on his knees before the toilet, there was nothing else he could do but stare at the disgusting mess his body was purging. Then, the last convulsion seemed to have gone. He sat, caught his breath, and wiped off his face.

"Finished?" asked Erik. Curtis nodded, and Erik flushed the toilet.

Curtis wished he could also flush the repulsive taste out of his mouth and the rank smell from the air. "Man, whoever invented vomit was a sick bastard."

"You said it."

The toilet bowl filled up with a marvelous blue; Curtis no longer had any reason to be staring at it. He got to his feet. "Thanks, Erik," he said—a dismissal. "I'm going to clean myself up a little here."

"Sure, buddy. I'll go tell everyone you're still alive," said Erik with a smile. "Talk to you later."

"OK."

Before, Curtis hadn't quite made it to the bathroom in time, and a stream of vomit had gone down the front of his Clash T-shirt. He removed the shirt now, threw it in one of the two bathroom sinks, and let it soak.

Splashing cold water on his face brought him to awareness, but failed to make him any prettier. He was repulsed by the goon he saw in the mirror. The glare of the fluorescent lights made his pale, unshaven face coarse and unattractive, while the sweat dripped from his brow.

Curtis stared deeply into his eyes, looking for something that was beyond his grasp. His face stared back at him devoid of expression. Squinting, he examined himself with more intensity, but it was no use. It was as if the piece of glass separating him from his own image were a great barrier, hiding some important, intangible secret.

What is wrong with me?

He felt like a heartless bastard, the way he had treated Jill. Sometimes he was too stubborn, but this time he had gone farther than ever before, to the point where he hadn't trusted Jill. That, he knew, was a mistake.

After testing the water, he stepped into the shower and let the hot stream engulf him. He washed the dried vomit from his chest.

Of course, Jill would have been the last person to pretend she had found a dead body, then actually report it to the police.

No matter that they didn't believe her—they seldom believed anybody.

And if Jill said it was Sam's body, there could be no doubt about it.

So, that was that.

Sam was dead.

That knowledge—not the slight bit of alcohol he had had that evening—was what had made him vomit.

He let the shower head spray a continuous stream into his face while he kept thinking, *Sam is dead, Sam is dead*.

He stayed in the shower for thirty minutes.

"And how's our widdle Curty-Wurtis?" asked Becky Roth, pouting. Her thickly applied mascara was running, and the rouge she had smeared on her cheeks was a bright, loud red, as if she had been snuggling up to a freshly painted fire hydrant. The huge mass of moussed, gelled, sprayed, and cremed hair on her head had transformed itself into a wild mess of stiffened tangles, but Becky was past the point of caring. Her heavy breasts, like water balloons, were an obstacle blocking Curtis's path. "Oh, you want by?" she asked, gazing crookedly. The way she slurred her words, it sounded as if she had said *you aren't bi?*—but she hadn't. Curtis ignored both her and her breasts and worked his way past the people in the hallway, to the living room.

An album by The Smiths was blasting over the stereo. Although he liked the band, he had to get to the turntable and put on something else, because their songs were all about loneliness, alienation, and pain, and were the last things he wanted to be listening to. He needed music into which he could escape—something fast-paced, something hardcore—but the stereo was on the other side of the room. Most of the people Curtis knew only casually, but they were welcome as long as they didn't destroy the place. The smell in the air was a bizarre mixture of Camel filters, clove cigarettes, marijuana, and perfume. Curtis found himself squinting; the thick smoke stung his eyes. He squeezed past several people, mumbling "Excuse me" repeatedly, like an automaton.

Curtis had never known the house to feel so close.

On the far end of the couch sat Frita Schmeckpeper, a nice girl he knew from Literary Criticism, sitting by herself and looking very bored. He waved tentatively at her, and she returned the gesture with a vague hand motion. Frita wore a short, asymmetrical haircut that framed her pale, freckled face and looked very modern. Her two layers of shirts were an original mix of bright, busy patterns pieced together from old clothing, hanging big and loose around her. She wore very little makeup: a subtle bit of lipstick and a touch of eyeliner. Erik wore as much. Frita was more real to Curtis than any of the other girls at Sherman High School. She was intelligent, reserved, and never played dumb. She motioned for Curtis to sit beside her.

He shook his head and said, "Fuck that, let's dance."

Removing the Smiths album from the turntable brought a few cries of "Hey!" from around the room, which Curtis ignored as he carelessly set it aside and put on a record by the Dead Kennedys. He was up for some slam-dancing. Frita got up from the couch to join him. Once the fast, furious strains of "Chemical Warfare" began to play, several people, including Erik, came out to the floor to take part.

Curtis wanted to forget, just for a little while.

Slam-dancing was the greatest thrill Curtis knew. Of course, here at his party it was only halfhearted, not entirely legitimate. But with Sam, Curtis had gone to a couple of punk shows down in Denver, where they had slammed until they were practically dead. It was an incredible rush, being at a terrific club with a hardcore punk band thrashing away on stage, while slamming on the floor below. Curtis and Sam would push their way through the outer crowd, heading for the floor close to the stage, where all the fun was going on. With the music drilling through the core of their beings, they would push each other, and suddenly Curtis was there, bouncing off bodies, shoving others away, ramming into a cluster of guys, tossing one of them out of the crowd, getting mashed against the stage for a second, charging back toward the center of the floor. At times, he would glimpse Sam's wildly excited face in the midst of the chaos. A skinhead would jump on stage with the band, and dive headfirst into a sea of Mohawks, spiked hair, and bare sweaty arms. Then would follow another punk on stage, another stage dive, another body swallowed up in the sea. People would slip on the slick floor and fall on top of each other, unhurt. Nobody ever seemed to get hurt, from what Curtis had seen. Sometimes Curtis wouldn't do anything at all; everyone else would keep him from falling over, and he would just get tossed around aimlessly for a while—until he got squeezed out of the crowd, and then he would get up on the stage and dive back in. The tempo of the music was like the rapid fire of machine guns, faster, harder, louder, more raw than anything in the world. It drove him on, and as long as the band played, as long as the punks in the crowd slammed into one another, Curtis was in a kind of sensual ecstasy. The amount of energy in a crowd like that was unbelievable, and that, coupled with the energy coming from the band, produced a greater high for him than any drug could ever give.

Here in his living room, however, there weren't enough bodies to make the slam-dancing very fierce. Besides that, even with Erik and Frita among the immodest crowd, there was something very important missing from the scene—or rather, someone.

The song ended, and the telephone rang.

"Hey!" Curtis shouted. "Don't anyone answer that. It's probably my parents. Let me get it." He smiled at Frita apologetically, then grabbed Erik's wrist and pulled him along as he headed down the hallway, down the stairs, to his bedroom, where he had a phone away from all the noise. Erik stumbled behind. After the seventh ring, Curtis reached the phone, sat on the floor, and picked up the receiver.

"Hello?"

"Curtis, hi," said his father on the other end, amid the crackling, fuzzy noise of long distance. "Just calling to let you know everything's going great down here. Your mother and I have had quite a day."

"Uh-huh," replied Curtis. He smiled at Erik and rolled his eyes upwards. Erik, sitting across from him, laughed. "So how's the dental conference?"

"Fantastic, so far." Curtis's father went on about the new techinques he was learning, and some marvelous talks he had heard from respected dentists. Once he started talking about work, he would never stop.

Curtis listened to the phone, occasionally offering an "Uh-huh" or two to let his dad know he was still there. He watched as Erik removed a small brown plastic prescription bottle from his pants pocket. With his free hand, Curtis grabbed a nearby hand mirror and set it down on the carpet between them.

"So, what are you up to this evening?" asked his father.

"Oh, not much. Erik's over. We're spinning some discs, hanging out, you know."

Erik tapped a small amount of white crystals onto the glass, withdrew a razor blade from his hip pocket and cut it into a fine powder, then created two short but adequate lines.

"You're supposed to be grounded. You're not allowed to have anyone over."

"Is it my fault I couldn't get him to leave? Anyway, you know Erik. He's an OK guy."

With a truncated straw, Erik snorted a line of cocaine up his nose.

"I guess. You guys aren't drinking, are you?"

"No, Dad. Here, talk to Erik a second." Curtis handed the receiver to Erik.

"Hey, Dr. Bowles. How's it hanging down there?"

Curtis took his turn, quickly snorting his share of the coke. Abruptly, he felt better, getting tingly all over.

"Is that right?" Erik was saying. "Well, did he have nice teeth?"

"Give me that," said Curtis, snatching the receiver.

"You fellas take it easy now," said his father. "I'd put your mother on, but I'm afraid she's already asleep. You know what a little wine does to her."

"Uh-huh."

"I'll see you Sunday evening, and then we'll talk."

"Right, Dad. See you." Curtis hung up.

Erik laughed out loud. He licked his fingers and pulled some strands of spiked blond hair down from his forehead, trying to create a cowlick. It wasn't working; his hair was too stiff from styling gel. This evening he wore a large, gold hoop earring in his right ear that, along with his bleached hair, created a nice effect against his deeply tanned skin. Erik was beautiful.

"I knew they'd call," said Curtis. "They don't trust me. I don't know why."

"Fuck. Your dad would be shitting bricks if he knew we were sitting here doing coke."

"Maybe. He might be doing it himself right now down in Denver. How should I know? Three dentists in Laramie were just busted for dealing the stuff."

"No shit? Well, that's it then. Your dad went down to that dental conference so he could make his connection, probably."

"I ought to become a narc. I'll turn in my dad, and give my evidence over to you."

"Sounds like a deal."

The drug was taking its effect. Curtis's senses were heightened. He kept rubbing his tongue along the roof of his mouth, amazed at all the fine ridges, valleys, and bumps he found there.

Sam is dead.

"Erik, talk about something," Curtis said, staring at the wall.

He felt about to burst forth with tears again, like he had done in the shower. Sam was dead, and had gone at the worst time imaginable. They had not even spoken to one another since the Rawlins track meet on Thursday, when Sam had blown up at him so suddenly. Curtis had stalked off without another word, and that had been it. The last time he had seen Sam's face, it had been grim, pained, uncertain, and red with anger. It was a wretched last memory to have of the best friend he had ever known. Their argument was now in limbo forever. Too many questions were left unanswered.

"Like what?"

"I don't know. Anything—just talk, all right?"

"Yeah, sure." Erik was still trying to form a cowlick, with little success. "Hey, you know that guy Becky brought over?"

"Billy Hedgecoe? Yeah, he's on the track team—" Curtis was going to say *with Sam,* but stopped short. Of course, Erik wouldn't have noticed the slip anyway, because he didn't know.

"Yeah, Billy. Well, I was upstairs sitting next to him on the couch. I guess you were in the shower. Anyway, he was getting all paranoid about the cops coming and busting up the party and carting everyone down to the courthouse. We were sitting there drinking beers, and Billy was pretty drunk. I tell him, 'All you can do is hope they don't come. Isn't much we can do about it if they show up, anyway, so don't worry about it.'

"So he says I'm right, but there's a way to make the cops leave you alone. He's grinning at me and everything, with a funny look in his eye.

"So I say, 'What are you talking about?'

"And he says he was at this party once, and the cops came to bust the place up, and so these two guys in the corner started making out. You know, kissing, tongues and everything, really getting into it. The cops checked everyone's IDs and all the underage people got in trouble. But they ignored those two guys. Just fucking left them alone.

"So then," said Erik, slyly raising one eyebrow, "I say, 'That's interesting.'

"And Billy says, 'So like, if the pigs show up, we could do that and they won't do shit to us.'"

Erik laughed self-consciously.

"No kidding," commented Curtis.

"Yeah, I think Becky's out of luck if she wants to get nailed by this guy."

"So, what did you do?" Curtis's laugh was uneasy. "With Billy, I mean."

"Nothing," Erik said with a slight smirk. "The cops didn't show up, did they?"

"Some guys get pretty weird when they're drunk," Curtis said.

Erik lay down on his side, propping his head up with his elbow. "Yeah," he said in a husky whisper. He placed his warm hand on Curtis's thigh and started stroking it lightly. "Some guys do."

"Erik—" Curtis began. This time, he couldn't allow Erik to seduce him. Things were different from the night before. Sam was dead. Curtis couldn't decide what to do. But the coke had made his skin more sensitive, and Erik's hand felt terrific there, moving slowly up his inner leg. "Erik, don't," he said, nervously turning his head away with his eyes closed.

"Why not?" Erik's hand crept up to Curtis's crotch and gave it a light squeeze.

Curtis was getting an erection. His stomach quivered; he drew a sharp breath. "Just don't, all right? I don't want to—"

Upstairs, someone screamed.

"What the hell?" said Erik, startled.

"Jesus!" yelled Curtis as he jumped to his feet.

The scream came again, high-pitched, female, and desperate.

Curtis and Erik looked at each other with alarm. Erik pocketed his prescription bottle and darted out of the bedroom and up the stairs, shouting, "C'mon, Curtis!"

Amidst the screams came a confused babble of voices.

Curtis grabbed his ivory-handled switchblade from where it was sticking out of the wooden door frame, snapped the blade shut, and shoved it in his pocket. He followed Erik up to the living room.

Becky Roth was struggling and kicking on the floor, waving her arms wildly and shrieking. Billy and Dean grabbed her wrists briefly, but she broke their grip. Gale held her shoulders down to the ground.

At first, Curtis thought it was a rape. Several other people were standing around perplexed, beers in hand, trying to figure out what was going on.

Gale was trying to talk to Becky. "Becky! Becky! What's wrong? What is it?"

Becky looked into Gale's face.

"Calm down, Becky," continued Gale. "Everything's all right."

Becky screamed again, as if horrified by her friend's face. She kicked and fought her way to her feet, hitting people who tried to grab her arms, kicking Gale's knee in the process. Shoving people aside, she went to the front door, wrenched it open, and ran out into the street.

Curtis rushed out after her.

"She's out of control," yelled Erik, following close on Curtis's heels.

Becky stopped in the middle of Green Hill Drive and began screaming at the top of her lungs.

At this point, Curtis couldn't think of anything but getting her back inside before she attracted the police to the party. She was obviously drunk off her ass, and had probably taken some drugs as well—not that Curtis was an expert.

Curtis and Erik caught up to her in the street. "Becky, shut up!" said Erik. But she wouldn't stop. Erik slapped her face, but it did no good. After that, she started crying, wailing at the top of her voice. "Let's get her inside." Curtis took her arms, Erik her legs, and they started forcibly carrying her up the hilly lawn of the Bowles home. Curtis kept losing his grip while she thrashed. It took every ounce of their energy to keep from dropping her, the way she was struggling. Gale came running up to help.

"What the fuck's the matter with her?" Curtis demanded.

"I don't know," said Gale, who didn't seem to be entirely there herself. "I guess it was all the NōDōz she took, and Jim Beam, beer, pot, and—dammit, Curtis, I don't know what all she's on." Now Gale was crying.

Curtis backed his way through the front door. "Christ, Gale, she might have to go to the hospital or something. How many NōDōz did she have?"

"I don't know. She eats them like candy."

"With all that alcohol—" Curtis speculated.

"Shit." Erik was having a hard time as they came through the door. Becky kicked with more vehemence. After they got through, Erik's grip faltered on one of her legs, and she kicked a hole the size of a fist in the drywall near the door.

"Oh, fuck!" shouted Curtis, exasperated. "Gale, can you deal with her? Billy, Robin, Dean? Somebody?"

Becky stopped struggling, but her crying and wailing

continued. Curtis and Erik set her out on the floor, telling people to back off and give her some air. Her hair was a mess, her makeup smeared worse than before. She lolled her head back and forth, moaning.

"Gale," Curtis said, "maybe you should take her to the Emergency Room, just to make sure she's all right. Erik could go with you."

"I think you're right," said Erik.

Just then Becky looked straight at Curtis. Her lips sputtered spittle, then she broke out laughing.

"Becky?"

"Oh, shit, Curtis!" said Becky. "I really got you this time! I got you!" She cackled hysterically.

"Are you OK?" he asked.

"I got you! You fell for it. God, what a sucker. You all fell for it, even you, Gale. Jeez, what a fucking riot. You should all see yourselves."

"You bitch," said Erik, standing up. "You fucking, bloody, rotten cunt."

"False scare," said Frita tonelessly, to no one in particular. "What a bore."

Curtis could do without stupid little pranks like this, especially from the likes of Becky Roth. He took the switchblade from his pocket and undid the catch, letting the blade spring forth. He sat on top of Becky's torso, pinning her to the ground.

"Curtis! Get off! Let me up. What are you doing?"

He held the cold blade close against her fat, fleshy neck. At that moment, he despised her. He had thought she was going to die, and he was the only one who had tried to make sure she would be safe, and here she was laughing at him.

"Curtis, no," Becky gasped.

Curtis leered at her and chuckled menacingly. He had drawn the switchblade as a joke at first, but now he was beginning to wonder about the possibilities. The blade was pressed against her flesh. He had just sharpened it a few days ago, and it could cut through anything.

The people standing around them were simply watching. They knew Curtis was only joking.

But Curtis realized it would only take one simple, brief slice, and Becky Roth's life would be over.

"Should I do it?" he asked the crowd.

Among them, in the smoky air, stood a shadowy figure Curtis couldn't quite make out.

"Yeah, go for it," said one of the drunken revelers. Other people echoed the sentiment, knowing it was only a game.

What did he have to lose? All his plans for the future were dashed with Sam's death. But he understood the enormous power he had in his hands at that moment: the power of life and death. One casual flick of his wrist, and Becky would die. If he withdrew his hand, she would live. It was an interesting dilemma.

He felt a compelling urge to act quickly, one way or the other.

Becky's face was petrified with terror.

"You really want me to do it?" Curtis asked, grinning. He looked up at all the smiling faces staring down at him saying *yes:* Billy, Dean, Robin, Gale, Frita, Erik . . .

. . . and Sam. Except Sam's face was saying *no!* and flickering madly, fading from stark white to dark shadow, and back again, one moment there, the next gone.

Curtis closed the blade without looking down and returned the switchblade to his pocket. He sprang to his feet as Sam's face disappeared from the crowd.

"Jesus! I thought the jerk was going to slit my throat!" said Becky as she got up off the floor. The crowd shied away from her.

Sam's figure appeared again bright and glimmering, and glided down the hallway before dimming into nothing. Curtis shoved his way past the circle of faces and followed. No one else had noticed, he could tell. Sam, now a visible dull gray, started down the circular staircase.

Maybe Jill and Sam had been pulling an elaborate hoax, just like Becky. Perhaps Sam was really alive after all. If that were true, he felt at that moment he could slit Jill's throat for real. If she had been fooling him all along...

Curtis ran down the staircase in pursuit of the shadow.

Opening the door to Curtis's bedroom, Sam turned his milky white head and gave Curtis a wide grin, eyes pitch-black and staring. He swept inside, closing the door behind him.

"Sam!" Curtis shouted, stumbling down the last steps and opening the door. Dr. McCoy was asleep on his perch; the fish were swimming back and forth in the aquariums; and in the terrarium, Dino sat wiggling his front legs and blowing bubbles in the slimy water.

A tall, man-shaped shadow shifted in the corner, then faded, and was gone.

"Sam?"

Curtis looked all around, but there was nobody there—nothing but an odor. He started to gag, and nearly tripped over the piles of clothing in getting to the small basement window. Then he slid the glass open, as far as it would go, trying to get rid of the wretched rotten-egg smell.

FIFTEEN

Jill and Troy were taking a shortcut through the Elk Mountain Golf Course when they heard the screams.

"C'mon, Troy, let's hurry."

It was against the law to be out on the golf course after dark, so they were taking a considerable risk. The nearly full moon bathed the greens in pale gray and cast long, dark shadows from the blue spruce trees. Jill's hair blew back past her shoulders in the strong, steady wind, and Troy, wearing no shirt beneath his jean jacket, had complained three times about the cold. The silhouetted trees were nudged rhythmically by the wind, making their shadows shift back and forth on the grass. Jogging their way across the course, Jill and Troy moved from one clump of trees to the next, wary that a policeman's searchlight would come shining out of nowhere to halt them dead in their tracks. The police were already after Troy, and by now Celia had probably phoned and asked them to find Jill and bring her home.

That was the last thing she needed.

But it was quite possible they could get caught, Jill realized. Curtis and Sam had discovered that a year earlier, when they had gone streaking nude across the golf course after dark; it was a regular part of the Sherman Police's nightly patrol. Trespassing was something they didn't take kindly to, whether the offender was naked or clothed.

To make matters worse, they were out past curfew.

Jill saw a suspicious pair of headlights coming down the road, though she couldn't tell whether or not it was a police car. Several of her friends could distinguish, from a single glance in a rearview mirror, between the headlights of a patrol car and those of a station wagon, but Jill could not. Besides, these headlights were too far away for such scrutiny. But they were rapidly coming nearer.

"Is that the cops?" asked Troy.

"I don't know. But whoever it is, we shouldn't let them see us."

Jill and Troy were out in the open. Jill made a mad dash for the closest tree, a squat spruce shifting in the gusty wind. After a moment's hesitation, Troy followed.

A third, brighter light lit up suddenly from the unseen body of the approaching car, its wide beam arcing quickly across the vast expanse of the golf course.

"Troy! Quick!" Jill ducked behind the cover of the thick tree, and pulled Troy in next to her by his denim sleeve.

The searching spotlight swept past without lighting upon them, and the police car drove on.

"I wish they would leave me alone," Jill muttered, kicking the ground with the toe of her Top-Siders.

By the time they reached the Bowles residence near the top of Green Hill, they were out of breath.

"Looks like a party," said Troy.

The house was large and angular, its natural redwood siding set in a diagonal fashion, its flat roof slanting downwards from south to north; most of its windows shot vertically up the southern face, which looked out over Green Hill Drive. Cars familiar to Jill's eyes lined either side of the street, and six had been crammed into the Bowles's driveway. An engine roared to life, headlights were turned on, and a carload of six inebriated high school students sped off down the hill with a screeching of tires, leaving in their wake the smell of burnt rubber. Many people were coming out of the house now, searching for their cars or a ride home. Their high, giddy laughter, drunken screams, and macho grunts pierced the chill autumn air. Car doors slammed shut and stereos were blasted to the hilt.

The party was apparently over, a little early by Jill's reckoning.

This time, she was determined not to let Curtis get the better of her. Ever since he had dropped her off back at the trailer, she had been brooding about it, trying to figure out how she could make him understand. Then she had run into Troy. On their way to Green Hill Estates, she had learned what had happened to the Skunks in the steam tunnels. With Sam and Curtis, she had explored those tunnels many times herself, including the vast storm sewer into which Simon and Kraig had been yanked. She doubted not a word of Troy's tale. Simon and Kraig were clearly in trouble, perhaps dead.

They needed Curtis's help. Jill would make him believe, if she had to hit him over the head with it. And if he wouldn't help after that, then he could go to hell.

Erik, looking very alert and happy, was showing people out the door. "All right," he was saying absently. "Go on home. Party's over."

Billy, Dean, Robin, Gale, and Becky left looking sullen, the last of a large throng of people.

Rick and Deb had just arrived in the Vega and were trying to get into the house. "Wherza beer?" Rick slurred drunkenly. Deb was whining unintelligibly at Rick and tugging on his fleshy, football-trained arm. "I said, wherza beer, faggot?"

"Yeah, faggot," echoed Deb. "Let us in."

Erik sneered at them both and gave Rick a strong shove. Rick stumbled backwards slightly, then lost his balance altogether. Clutching at Deb's arm for support, he fell clumsily off the cement porch, taking his shrieking girlfriend with him.

"Hey!" was all Rick could manage.

"Listen, shithead," yelled Erik. "The party is finished, understand? Everyone has left, and there's no more goddamned beer. So why don't you and your whore get back in your piss-mobile and find some other party." With that, he slammed the door.

"Come back here, you fucking flamer! I'm not finished."

The front door remained shut.

Dazed, Rick and Deb weaved their way back to the Vega, parked halfway on the sidewalk. Rick muttered, "Damn fucking bastard."

On their way past, Troy said, "Hi, sis!" and laughed.

Deb grimaced, but then asked him if he knew where any good parties were. Troy said he didn't, and that was that. Obviously, there was no love lost between these two.

Jill and Troy went up to the front door and pounded on it.

Erik answered it with a look of fury on his face, Curtis's switchblade drawn and gleaming in his fist. "Listen, asshole, I thought I told you—oh, Jill!" He grinned innocently and snapped the blade shut. "Sorry. Party's over."

"Erik, I don't care about the party."

"Becky pulled one of her stunts."

"We heard screams."

"Like I said."

"What about Curtis?"

"He's around. Wish you had been here." Erik's eyes fell upon Troy, and his face brightened into a wolfish grin. "Who's your friend?"

"We need to see him," said Jill as she pushed her way past.

"I'm Troy." Troy smiled coolly at Erik. "You're Erik Mürer."

"Yeah. How did you know?"

"Lucky guess."

The living room and kitchen were a complete disaster. Plastic cups and crushed beer cans seemed to be growing like mold on the carpeting, tables, couch, and chairs. The kitchen countertops were hidden beneath empty bottles, orange rinds, open pizza boxes, and depleted bags of tortilla chips. Melted vanilla ice cream oozed from a cardboard half-gallon left out beside the blender.

"Where is he?" asked Jill.

"I guess he's down in his room," said Erik.

"I'm right here." Curtis appeared from out of the hallway. His voice was nasal, his eyes red and bloated, as if he had been crying. "Jill, I need to talk to you."

"Same here. I brought Troy Zografi with me. He—"

"Alone, down in my room."

Jill followed him down the staircase, unwittingly kicking over a half-full beer can.

"All right. But this is urgent. We don't have any time," said Jill.

"I know."

Jill shut the bedroom door behind them, and no sooner had she done that than Curtis began crying like crazy. He put his hands to his face as if to hide it, and sobbed into his palms, his chest convulsing heavily. He was still standing, legs apart, hair mussed. Against the cluttered walls of his room, he struck Jill as someone utterly alone.

"Oh God," he said, but it was muffled by his hands.

Jill rushed to his side. "Here, sit down." She sat with him on the edge of the bed, her arm across his shoulders. Curtis nestled his head against her neck.

The room was cold, and Jill found the warmth of Curtis's body comforting.

"I'm sorry, Jill," he said. He sniffed. "I'm sorry. I didn't believe you."

"Here, have a Kleenex."

He chuckled softly, briefly. "Solves world problems."

"What?"

He blew his nose.

"Generation X," he said. "The band Billy Idol used to be in. They had a song called 'Kleenex.' They said it solved the world's problems. Thanks."

Jill squeezed him more tightly, and kissed his cheek.

"I know now you were right." He spoke in a quavering voice, so unlike his usual confident tone it was scary. "I mean, what you told me earlier, about Sam being dead."

Jill nodded, speechless.

"Yeah," Curtis continued. "After I dropped you off, I knew you were right. I threw up. I still can't bear it. Sam will never—"

"I know, I know. Let's not talk about it. I've been going through it myself all day."

"Jill?"

"Yeah."

"You know the other stuff you were saying, about how there was something weird going on at Stink Lake, like monsters, and evil wizards, and shit? I still think it's fucking bizarre, but I believe it. Every word."

She didn't know exactly what she thought about it herself, but she knew something was very wrong somewhere.

Curtis looked into her eyes. Tears still trickled down his cheeks, his dark eyes were glassy, and a heavy frown was pulling at his mouth. A sparse growth of beard was poking out from his pale skin.

"I saw Sam's ghost."

Jill's heart sank.

"Right here," Curtis added. "In my house, just a few minutes ago. Jesus, Jill, I'm scared."

They sat for a minute in silence, holding each other.

"Look, Curtis, we can't just sit here right now. I wish we could, but Simon Taylor and some other kid are in trouble."

She told him everything Troy had told her.

"OK," he said. "I guess we have to go check out the steam tunnels."

"That's what I thought, but we needed you first."

"If there's any way we can help him—"

"Well, c'mon, let's go. Troy's waiting upstairs."

"Jill, wait. We've got to find Simon and this other guy, but what the hell are we supposed to do if we meet up with that thing Troy saw, with the tentacles?"

Jill pulled him to his feet and handed him his leather jacket. "Don't ask me," she said. "You're the one who reads those Stephen King novels."

SIXTEEN

Simon's head was throbbing when he came to, and the first thing he noticed was that there was a song he couldn't stand stuck in his head, repeating itself over and over. It was the kind of song he could never get rid of once it planted itself there, the kind he suffered through on MTV while waiting for the veejay to show something good. Now that it was there, there was nothing he could do about it. He tried to think of a different song—one he liked—but it was no use. The stupid song kept returning.

Abruptly, Simon remembered where he was.

And he was afraid to open his eyes.

All around him, he heard hissing noises, like lighted matches being doused in water. The wretched smell of the place was inescapable, a rotten, musty odor that made him sick to his stomach; the cool drafts of air did little to alleviate it. The trickling sound of running water was persistent, but merely a background to the hissing, which was everywhere.

Simon lay, wet, in a pile of muck.

"Kraig?" Simon asked hesitantly. He had seen him getting pulled in shortly before going unconscious. "Kraig, are you in here?"

He tried to bring one of his hands up to rub the back of his head, but they were both held firmly at his sides by slimy cords of algae coiled about his wrists. He squirmed where he lay, and groaned as he felt sharp, seething pain from the cuts and bruises all over his body. One of his legs was bound by the same sinewy, rope-like things binding his arms, and he seemed to have a twisted ankle on the other leg, perhaps a sprain.

"Oh, man!"

Still the hissing sounds continued, and still Simon kept his eyes clamped shut.

A wave of extreme cold wafted down his body from head to toe. His heart skipped a beat, his teeth chattered, and then it was gone. He broke out in a sweat.

Little brother.

Something cold and clammy was on his neck.

He jolted his head upright and struggled violently, trying to shake it off, and unintentionally opened his eyes.

A clump of algae slid off, leaving a trail of slime along his skin.

Simon had expected to see absolute darkness around him, but instead found an erratic, dim, orange glow. All over the floor of the long, eerie tunnel, a teeming mass of salamanders was aimlessly crawling about; wherever the creatures stepped, jets of flame shot up from their feet, but were quickly extinguished by the half inch of water they were prowling in. Brief bursts of fire, like lighter flames, were everywhere, covering the blackened floor of the storm sewer, illuminating the stark cement walls and ceiling, and reflecting off the slick skins of hundreds of restless amphibians.

Simon.

This wasn't right. Salamanders weren't supposed to be able to do stuff like that... *nothing* was. And vines of algae weren't supposed to pull people from steam tunnels and hold them captive in storm sewers.

Near the ceiling, high on the wall, sat the small rectangular hole he had fallen through. It was too high for him to reach on his own without a ladder.

At the base of the wall, a charred human body lay smoldering in a denim Skunks jacket. Salamanders were all over it, crawling under the collar, emerging from the sleeves....

"Kraig!" Simon screamed. He shivered, and could feel

the hairs of his body standing on end. He felt about to gag, knowing part of the ghastly air he was breathing contained the smoke still rising from the body of his dead friend. Bile rose in his throat.

Simon, don't panic.

Sharply, as hard as he could, he pulled against the taut vines. He writhed on the slimy floor, trying to wrench himself free. The vines didn't resist him; they didn't seem to be alive. They were merely holding him securely in place. It was no use. Simon gave up and tried to catch his breath.

"All right, dammit, so you're real!" he shouted aloud.

It's real.

"Sam?"

Simon couldn't mistake the voice, but there was no sign of his brother anywhere to be seen, and it didn't seem to be a *voice*, either.

"Sam, where are you?"

I'm here.

"Where?" But as soon as he had asked the question, he suddenly felt his brother's presence, somehow, there inside him.

"Sam," whimpered Simon. "Sam, I'm scared."

Me, too.

The voice that wasn't really a voice seemed right on top of him. The hissing continued all around, the dull orange light flickering constantly.

"Help me."

I am.

Simon felt a hand on his shoulder. He could see nothing there, but he could feel it. Its presence was cold, but somehow calming, soothing, comfortable. He began to breathe more slowly. The unseen hand gently touched his cheek.

Sam's dead, he suddenly realized. This was Sam's ghost talking to him, a shadow, and very real. Simon swallowed hard. This was too much for him to take. First the vines, then the salamanders, then Kraig, then Sam. . . . He wished he could deny his brother was dead, but he could feel his presence, and hear his voice, and he definitely wasn't dreaming. "Sam, am I all right?"

You're alive.

The salamanders had killed Kraig—Simon was sure of that. They still remained busy over near Kraig's body, and hadn't yet wandered over to the far corner where Simon was, but he had a queasy inkling they would soon find him as well. He suddenly felt a sense of impatience coming from his brother. Sam wanted him to get the hell out of there.

"The salamanders?" Simon asked.

And worse.

"But what about these vine-things?" Simon realized they were only coiled around his limbs, and all he had to do was twirl his arms and let the vines unwrap, instead of pulling against them as he had been doing. Then he could untie his leg, and he would be free. Or was Sam telling him these things?

"I wish you weren't dead."

So do I.

Suddenly, Simon heard some people coming down the steam tunnels. A call, nothing more than a feeble echo: "Simon! Kraig!"

The salamanders' activity seemed to be quickening; the hissing sounds made by their fiery feet were becoming louder, more intense. The place was getting hotter.

"Simon! Kraig!" The call was louder, and Simon could make out the voice.

"It's Curtis!" Simon said.

No!

Sam didn't want Curtis coming down there.

"But how am I going to get out?"

Just do it! Hurry!

Sam's spirit was confident, but agitated. These salamanders were dangerous, and Simon had to find a way out fast.

If Curtis were to come down into the storm sewer, he might die, too. Like Kraig. Like Sam.

"Jesus, Sam!" Simon didn't even want to think about that. As he started working loose the vines, he noticed in disgust the same damned song was still stuck in his head, and started crying, just like a girl.

SEVENTEEN

Just don't think, she thought. *Just don't think. Keep your mind on the present, don't think about what's happened, and don't worry about anything. Stay cool. Don't fuck up.*

"Curtis," she said. "Park it in front of that house on the other side of the street, so no one will notice it."

Curtis chuckled. "Are we getting paranoid?"

"No, being smart." She sighed. "The student lot's deserted, and your car doesn't exactly blend in with the scenery. I don't want any policemen to come snooping around. It's Saturday night, you know. They're all over the place."

"Thanks, Mom."

While he parked, Jill finished her Cherry Coke, the second she'd had in the last ten minutes; she had to stay awake. Her mind was still alert, but her body was dragging, eyes dry and aching. Curtis had it easy. With that cocaine Erik had given him, he would be bouncing off the walls all night—not that Jill approved. He had told her on the way over how he and Erik had done cocaine together the last two nights, and enjoyed it, which upset her. On principle, Curtis had never been a big drug user. The most he, Jill, or Sam had done was marijuana or alcohol, and not very much of either. Curtis and Sam always talked about the "natural high" they had together, which made taking drugs redundant. They had told Jill that one time, attending a concert perfectly straight at Red Rocks Amphitheater outside of Denver, they had been so wild that more than one person had come up to them and asked them what they were on, and if they could have some. Now Curtis was doing cocaine, and liked it. Jill didn't understand, and hadn't yet decided if she ought to do anything about it. It was the last thing she wanted to deal with.

Don't think, she reminded herself.

"Troy," said Jill. "You got the bag?"

"Yep."

"Then let's go."

The wind grabbed Jill's door when she opened it, and she scrambled to catch it before it sprung. She loved Curtis's car as much as he did, and would have hated to see anything happen to it. He had let her borrow it a few times, but she never ceased to be amazed whenever she was allowed behind the wheel. If she had a car like this, she would be gone from Sherman in an instant, and never look back.

"Some wind!" said Curtis. "The lake is really smelling like shit."

"You said it, dude," said Troy, getting out of the car.

Jill had lived with Stink Lake all her life, and had never known it this bad—and it had certainly never worsened so much in the course of one day. On top of that, the wind was cold. Sherman would likely wake up the next morning with its first frost of the season. It was probably snowing already on top of Elk Mountain.

They scrambled across the street when there were no cars to spot them, and crept around the outside of the high school building until they had reached the iron door that led to the steam tunnels.

"Just as I figured," muttered Curtis. "The cops threw a lock on it. Troy, pass me the hammer."

Jill kept watch from a clump of trees, but couldn't see any police cars cruising around. Her hair blew in her face, and the cold stung her nose and ears. "Hurry," she said.

"Shows you how these cops think, Troy." Curtis hefted the hammer in his hand. "Hinges on the outside, and they figure they'll keep us out with a stupid lock." He tapped the rusty hinges noisily, then proceeded to pry the hinge pins out with the crook of the hammer.

Troy seemed impressed, but he didn't say anything. He had been strangely quiet, and Jill could tell he was still shaken up by whatever he had seen. He was fidgeting constantly, and looked scared.

Curtis slid the iron door to one side, giving them a diagonal opening a foot wide. The chain on the inside prevented it from budging any farther, but the hole was still big enough.

Curtis went down first, and had Troy toss the bag to him. Troy went next. With one last look around, Jill crossed her fingers and dropped down into the hole. The jolt of the landing was a shock; it had been a while since she had last been down there. But at least it was warm.

"Jill, have a torch," said Curtis. A bright beam shone in her face from a standard flashlight. She took it from him and aimed it randomly along the walls of the musty cement-walled room. Troy and Curtis grabbed flashlights for themselves out of Curtis's canvas book bag: a small plastic disposable for Troy, a bright lantern-sized one for Curtis. Curtis slung the bag over his shoulder.

"C'mon," said Jill, leading the way to the dark hole in the wall.

"Hey, Jill," said Troy. "Watch your step."

"Thanks." She looked down the length of the passageway, which stopped abruptly several feet ahead, where it turned toward the boiler room. It was grimy, filled with cement dust, scraps of iron, and broken glass. A few pipes traversed the tunnel near the low ceiling, but nothing out of the ordinary lay in their path. "OK, everything looks fine to me. Let's go."

She stepped down into the passage. With Curtis bringing up the rear, they squatted low and waddled down the tunnel. Jill scrutinized their path as they went, making sure nothing was slithering about. The heat was already making her sweat, and along with the stale air, it made her heart beat faster. She ducked under the pipes and came to the turn in the tunnel. She stopped.

With trepidation, she shone her stark beam around the corner and listened, but heard nothing except the scuffling of Troy and Curtis behind her. She looked down the tunnel at what she could see of the boiler room, but nothing strange could be seen. Relieved, she turned the corner. "Looks all right, guys."

In the boiler room, they found a pile of ashes, all that was left of Troy's shirt. Troy unbuttoned his jean jacket and wiped the perspiration from his chest with his hand. "Man, this heat's a bitch."

"And smelly," said Curtis.

Jill tied her jacket around her waist by its sleeves. "This is it, guys. Are you ready?"

"Yeah," they said.

"Curtis, what all is in that bag, anyway?"

He rummaged around, shining his light inside. "Well, there's the hammer, some nylon cord, a lead pipe, Mace, some darts, a fondue fork, a few bottle rockets, and some beef sticks."

Troy laughed. "Some arsenal. If you see this thing, all you can do is run. That stuff won't do us any good."

"I also brought this," Curtis said with a diabolical grin, unzipping his leather jacket to reveal a sweat-drenched T-shirt, and a large pistol shoved into the waist of his pants. "My dad's Colt .45 automatic."

"No shit," said Troy.

"Plus I've got my switch," Curtis added.

Great, thought Jill. *Curtis is high on cocaine, armed, and dangerous. We'd better not get caught, or we'll all be put away.*

"Well, c'mon, let's grab some weapons," said Jill. "Maybe they'll be some good. They won't if we leave them in the bag." For herself, she grabbed the lead pipe, which she held in her right hand with the flashlight in her left. She put the fondue fork in her back pocket, and a beef stick in her mouth, like a cigar, and began munching on it.

Curtis and Troy took the rest of the weapons, and then they all went around the boilers to the other side of the room, to the small, dark hole, the entrance to the long tunnel.

"I hate this tunnel," said Troy. "I hope to fuck that thing is gone."

"Simon!" called Curtis. "Kraig!"

Jill looked down the narrow passageway. It smelled like the lake. She could feel hot, damp air blowing from the other end of the tunnel, hotter than the air in the boiler room. With all the pipes in the way, she could not quite see the end of the tunnel. They would have to step over pipes every few feet or so, but some were so high they would have to crawl under.

"Simon! Kraig!" Curtis yelled once more.

"I don't see any tentacles yet, Troy," said Jill, finishing the last of her beef stick.

"Good," said Troy, hammer in one hand, Mace jutting from his jean jacket pocket. "I hope it's gone."

Stepping quickly and gracefully through the gauntlet of pipes was not a problem for Jill; she had been this way enough times. Troy seemed to be having some trouble, but Curtis was egging him on from behind. Some of the pipes were wrapped with asbestos; apparently the health of the maintenance men was not a top priority of the school's administrators. Jill hoped her many excursions into the tunnels wouldn't give her lung cancer someday. She could see the principal visiting her deathbed, wagging his finger slyly, saying, "Told you so, little lady. You're a black spot on the face of this school, Jill—"

Stop thinking, dammit! she thought. *Jesus!*

"Simon!" Jill called. "Are you down there?"

Simon's voice echoed down the passage: "Jill! Down here, in the storm sewer."

"Simon!" Curtis was exalted. "Hey, buddy, we're coming, just hang on. Are you all right?"

"Yeah, I'm OK."

"Kraig, are you there?" yelled Troy, and was met with silence. "Simon, where's Kraig?"

"Troy, is that you?"

"Yeah, it's me. What about Kraig?"

Simon was sobbing. "He's dead."

"No." Troy came to a halt. "Oh man, no."

Jill clutched Troy's wrist and pulled him along behind her. "C'mon. Deal with it later. We've got to hurry. You can't stop now. We've got to get Simon." She sniffed the air. "Do you guys smell smoke?"

"Yeah," said Curtis. "And it's hotter than hell."

Simon said, "You guys have got to go back!"

"But we're coming to get you," shouted Curtis.

"No, don't! You've got to go away."

They were getting closer. Jill could see the hole at the end of the tunnel, from which was coming a dim orange light. She had to get down on her stomach and slide beneath a set of thick, hissing pipes. Then she realized the hissing was coming from the storm sewer.

"Simon," said Curtis. "We're coming whether you like it or not, so just stay put."

"But you can't!" Simon yelled. "There's all these things down here, waiting to get you."

"What things?" asked Jill, stepping over a pipe.

"Slimy things! There's a whole freakin' army of salamanders down here, and they're trying to set fires everywhere. They got Kraig. They burned him up."

"Hey, I saw what got him and Kraig," said Troy. "I'll believe anything, now."

"It's true, you guys!" Simon's voice was high-pitched, frantic. "These salamanders will kill you, if you come down here."

"Why haven't they gotten you?" asked Jill.

Simon didn't answer.

"It's OK, we're coming to get you."

"No! You can't! You've got to get away fast. I'm getting out of here, going down the sewer. I'll find a way out.

Somewhere away from the lake and salamanders and stuff."

Jill stopped. She looked at the pale faces of Curtis and Troy, and said, "I guess we should go back."

Curtis didn't seem certain. "Simon, are you sure you're OK?"

"Yeah, I'm fine. I hit my head, and I've got a twisted ankle, but I can walk. I'm ready to get out of here."

Troy looked anxious, motioning back the way they had come with his flashlight. "Let's go," he urged.

Jill couldn't think.

"The salamanders!" Simon shouted. "Christ!"

"Simon, I'm coming!" called Curtis. He stumbled past Jill, clambering over pipes, heading for the opening.

"Don't, Curtis! They're climbing up the walls, they're coming after you! Get out!"

"I'm going to pull you up, Simon." He reached the hole.

"Curtis, no!" yelled Jill, going after him.

"Get over here, Simon!" Curtis looked over the edge and gasped. "Holy shit!"

Jill grabbed him by the arm and pulled him back. "Don't be an idiot."

Salamanders started scrambling over the top, crawling into the tunnel, setting it aflame.

"Simon, get out of there!" Jill yelled, dragging Curtis back down the tunnel with her.

"I'm going!" called Simon.

"Wait! The hatch," Curtis said. "This way." He tried to open the small hatch in the ceiling, but it wouldn't budge. "What the hell—"

A salamander was heading for Curtis's tennis shoe.

"Fuck it, Curtis," said Troy. "I blocked it on the other side. C'mon, hurry!"

Jill pulled Curtis's arm. Troy was already fifteen feet ahead of them, going as fast as he could over and under the pipes. Curtis pushed Jill ahead of him. She couldn't go very fast. Crouched this low, it was nearly impossible to shuffle along quickly enough. Her head bumped into the hard concrete ceiling, and she cried out. She dropped the lead pipe, leaving her right hand free to help her get over the pipes in her way. Her grip on the flashlight was tight; she wasn't about to lose it. The walls of the passage began to glow with an eerie, orange light, and the heat behind her made her feel as if she were crawling through an oven.

Quickly, she glanced behind her. Curtis was right on her tail, behind him a wall of flame creeping along at a faster pace than the approaching mass of salamanders.

"Move, Jill!" yelled Curtis.

The salamanders were coming through the fire unscathed.

She looked ahead again and hit her head on a pipe. She got on her belly and slid under it, then grabbed Curtis's hands and yanked him through. They dashed down a short distance with no pipes, getting ahead of the flames. Troy was still ahead of them.

Jill came to another pipe and had to slide under. She turned around to help Curtis.

Curtis screamed, and clutched fast onto the pipe. A long, slimy algae tentacle had snapped out of the flames like a whip and wrapped itself around his leg. It was trying to pull him back, into the fire. "Jill! Get my switchblade! Cut it off me!"

She slid back under the pipe, took the ivory handle from his back pocket, and pressed the catch, releasing the blade. "Hang on."

"Get it off! Christ, Jill! Cut it!"

Jill began sawing at the tight vine. The hair on her arm was singed by the heat, and the salamanders were coming. But the flames were too bright; she couldn't look. She pressed her arm down hard, cutting back and forth. Curtis's leg was up in the air. The vine was pulling strongly, trying to get Curtis before Jill cut through.

Curtis shrieked, letting go of the pipe. He fell to the floor, the tentacle snapping in two and flying back down the tunnel. Jill had almost managed to cut through; the vine itself had done the rest.

"Thanks," he gasped. "C'mon!"

Flames began to roll along the top of the ceiling. The roaring noise became louder.

Jill and Curtis dove under the pipe. The tentacle lashed out again, barely missing Jill's foot. It wrapped itself around the pipe, yanking it out of the wall, and releasing a hot, continuous purge of steam.

Jill and Curtis scurried as fast as they could down the tunnel, pulling each other along every bit of the way. The smoke was getting thick, but they were ahead of the flames and the hissing army of amphibians. Curtis dropped his bag. They saw along their way the hammer and can of Mace Troy had been carrying, as well as the beer cans and empty bottles of alcohol they and others had left behind in times past.

Finally, they emerged from the smoking tunnel into the boiler room, hacking and coughing. Troy was there already.

"Through that door, Troy!" shouted Curtis. He shone his wide beam on the wooden door perched atop several cement steps. "Hurry!"

Troy ran up the steps, swung open the door, and darted out into the hallway. Jill and Curtis shambled up after him, her arm around his shoulder. Once in the corridor, they shut the door behind them. It locked automatically.

They were outside the band room, Jill realized. She and Curtis stood and coughed for a moment, trying to clear their lungs. Curtis was dark with soot, and Jill's arms were filthy. At the end of the hallway were the doors to the outside, a green, glowing exit sign hanging above.

"We've got to get out of here," said Jill. "The place is on fire."

Troy caressed the red fire alarm set against the wall, and smiled wide with anticipation, like a child opening a present at Christmas. "I've always wanted to do this," he said, and pulled the white lever down.

EIGHTEEN

The hot water streamed over Troy's naked body, washing the grit and soot away in a grimy current that went spiraling down the drain. As he reached for the soap, the spray suddenly went cold and shot out at half the pressure. He gasped convulsively. Fucking Curtis must have started the washing machine already. Troy shivered, then braced himself against the frigid water and began soaping his limbs, cursing under his breath. First, he had been "granted" the third and last shower, and now this. He yawned; a trickle of deodorant soap slipped into his mouth. If he weren't so goddamned tired, he'd let Curtis know just how he felt about his hospitality. Just because he was younger didn't mean he was any less human.

Kraig was just killed, you fucker. You could at least let me have a hot shower.

Hey, shitheap, he told himself, *hold on. Curtis and Jill just went through the same thing with Simon's brother. Don't act as if you're so fucking special.*

He had little right to complain. He had had four shots of Cutty Sark, courtesy of Dr. Bowles's top dresser drawer, while waiting for his turn at the shower to come around. He still couldn't picture his buddy Kraig as a corpse; the whiskey would help him defer that till later. He planned to drink until he passed out, and to continue drinking whenever he woke up.

Troy dried himself; the towel had been hanging above the furnace vent, and was warm and soft. He threw on the change of clothes Curtis had loaned him: bikini briefs, athletic socks, sweatpants, and a Billy Idol T-shirt. He appraised himself in the mirror and decided he looked OK. His arms and shoulders were big and solid; he had done twenty pull-ups the other day in P.E.—a new school record. In the eyes of the ninth-graders he was an asshole; the seventh-graders thought him a god; yet to Kraig he had been neither. *What the fuck am I going to do now?* he asked his reflection, and saw Billy Idol's face sneering back at him in answer. That was it, of course. He would have to play it cool, as always.

In the party-trashed living room, Jill was seated on the couch in Curtis's bathrobe and house slippers, leaning sleepily against Curtis, who had changed into another pair of jeans and a red sweatshirt. Jill's eyes were half closed, puffy, encircled by purple; she looked exhausted. Curtis nodded a greeting to Troy. Troy grabbed the half-empty bottle of Cutty Sark from the cluttered coffee table and sat in the plush recliner, sloppily gulping a swig as he did so. It tasted *fine*.

"We all need some sleep," said Curtis, whose eyes were wide and staring. He seemed far from tired, but of course he was all coked up, Troy remembered, and he had poured half a bottle of eye drops into his eyes. Of course, so had Jill, but the eye drops didn't seem to be keeping her awake at all. Nothing could have done that. Her arm was draped across Curtis's chest, hanging onto his shoulder. Curtis's arm was leaning on the back of the couch, his hand hanging loosely in Jill's silky hair. Troy wondered offhandedly if Curtis and Jill had ever humped. In fact, Jill looked a little like the first chick Troy had nailed, at his cousin Minnie's birthday party in Cheyenne last April. Troy's eyes fluttered, trying to close. Jill was already asleep. They were all too worn out to be scared, and Jill almost looked content. Her long hair rested, fluffy and billowy, against the back of the couch, part of it bunched up against Curtis's rigid cheek.

"S'Erik still 'sleep?" Troy mumbled. None of them had told Erik anything about their tunnel mission before going, and Erik had stayed behind to start cleaning up from the party. When they had returned, they found him sound asleep in Curtis's bed, snoring. It was a lucky break, considering the fire at the high school had already been talked about on the radio. It would have been uncool for Erik to have seen them all straggling into Curtis's house covered with black soot, coughing and hacking, while Sherman High was going up in cinders.

Curtis said, "Out like a log."

"S'good."

Troy smiled crookedly and took another sip of whiskey. In a few seconds, his eyelids felt like lead weights; they closed; he slept.

A knocking, as from a slow and heavy fist, jolted Troy awake. Some whiskey sloshed out of the bottle still clutched in his hand; he set it on the coffee table and absently rubbed the wet liquor stain. Jill, alone and deep in sleep, was stretched out on the couch. The chime clock on the mantel rang once to announce 3:30 a.m. Curtis was nowhere in the room.

The knocking came again—three solid raps—followed by the gruff, loud bark of a large dog.

Shit, thought Troy, it's the cops, come to arrest us for arson . . . or murder. Or drugs—the dog had probably been brought along to sniff out Erik's cocaine. He ran to the door, looked through the peephole, and was relieved to find the filthy, battered face of Simon Taylor, illuminated by the porch light and grotesquely distorted by the fish-eye curve of the tiny lens. No pigs were in sight. Troy unlocked the bolt, unhooked the chain, and opened the door.

"Simon!" Troy couldn't believe it. Simon must have walked all the way across town. "You OK, kid?"

Simon didn't speak. With his tattered clothing, cuts, and bruises, he looked as if he had just run a gauntlet. He seemed barely able to stand. His eyes were glassy, and nothing so much as a look of recognition was on his face.

Nuzzling his leg was a black Labrador retriever, glistening in the light of the doorway.

"Shit, man, you look half dead."

Troy put his arm around Simon's shoulders and helped him inside, the dog following at their heels. Even with Troy's support, Simon was limping.

"Jill, get up!" Troy yelled. "I'm putting Simon on this couch."

Jill awoke with half her senses, but still understood enough to scramble off the couch when she saw Simon. Troy laid Simon out on the cushions and propped up his head with a pillow.

She was cold, and her first thought was: *Where's Curtis?*

"Jesus," she said, looking at the clock, then back at Simon, then at the dog, who was licking Simon's wrist. It was Claude. Simon looked like hell. Jill rushed to his side and brushed the hair away from his grimy forehead. Small cuts marked his face, and there were more on his legs and arms; she wondered what terrible things he had seen in the storm sewer, what had happened to him, how he had managed to escape. She held his head and looked into his glassy eyes. "Simon, you made it out of there! You're all right! Say something—please!"

Simon stared silently at her.

Jill hugged him. "Everything's going to be fine. You're alive!"

"Ask him," said Troy, "about this fucking dog."

"Must have followed him."

"Huh?"

"Never mind. Go find Curtis. I'll clean Simon up a bit."

Grumbling, Troy left the room.

Jill went to the bathroom and prepared a hot, damp washcloth, then went back to Simon and began wiping the dirt and slime away from his cuts. He didn't even flinch. Thinking he might be in shock, Jill took some blankets from the master bedroom and draped them over his body.

Simon mumbled something quietly. Jill moved closer to hear better. *"Attrapé!"* he said. *"Attrapé!"*

Jill didn't know what it meant. Whatever it was, it was French, and she couldn't keep her hands from trembling— Simon didn't know a word of French, and it wasn't his voice, either.

Suddenly, she remembered the strange dream she had had after Sam had left the trailer Friday night, the dream in which Mr. Prenez had come to visit her, wanting her to take care of his dog. Her heart fell to her stomach when she realized it hadn't been a dream at all.

Troy scowled. He didn't like this girl bossing him around all the time. But he said "OK" and went off to look for Curtis. Curtis wasn't in the kitchen or any of the upstairs rooms, so Troy went down to his bedroom. The door was closed and there was no light coming from underneath it, so he decided to knock.

Groans came from the other side, and then Curtis said, "Hey, hang on a minute." Troy stood waiting longer than that before Curtis opened the door, naked except for a towel wrapped around his waist. He looked as if he still hadn't had any sleep. "Yeah, Troy, what is it?"

"Simon," Troy said. "He looks like shit. Walked all the way here, hasn't said anything. There's some dog with him."

A voice came from the darkness of the bedroom, wondering what was going on.

"Nothing, Erik. Troy, I'll be up in a second. Tell Jill I'm coming up."

"Better hurry."

When Curtis, barefoot and clad only in a pair of jeans, joined them in the living room, Jill told them the dog was named Claude, and had belonged to Mr. Prenez.

"The dead teacher?" Troy asked.

"Simon's ankle is swollen," Jill said. "I can't believe he made it this far on his feet."

"Well," said Curtis, "let's get him to the hospital."

"I don't think we should—" Jill began.

Simon stirred, letting out a low moan.

"Simon, do you know where you are?" asked Jill, lightly stroking his forehead.

The voice that came from Simon's lips was deep and croaky, not his own, and it said: "Jill, I asked you to take care of Claude."

Jill gasped and backed away from Simon's body.

Troy asked, "What the fuck was that?"

Jill knew what it was, but Curtis was the first to answer. He spoke in a shaky voice: "Jesus—Prenez—" He met Jill's gaze, his mouth hanging open. "Prenez. That was his voice!"

Claude, looking up at Simon's face, wagged his tail and whined.

Curtis put his arm around Jill's shoulders, but she still felt cold in the bathrobe. "He's staring at me," she said, and hid her face against Curtis's neck.

"Claude," said the voice coming from Simon's mouth, "go to Jill. She's your master now."

Claude whined, shifting his weight back and forth on his legs.

"Go! Don't beg. Jill will look after you."

Claude backed away from Simon and sat before Jill, eyes downcast. Jill looked down, and her quivering hand reached out to stroke his head. "It—it's OK," she stammered, but she didn't know whether she was speaking to Curtis and Troy, or to Claude, or to herself. She looked up at Simon's face. "I'll take care of him"—Jill swallowed hard—"Mr. Prenez, I—I promise."

A look of relief momentarily passed Simon's face, then was gone. Once more, he was catatonic.

Claude barked.

Jill was worried. "We can't take him to the hospital like this."

"But his ankle—" said Curtis.

Jill glared at him. "Curtis, you can see he isn't Simon right now. What do you think a doctor would say about this?"

"She's right," said Troy. "Can't let a doctor see him, not with this ghost or . . . or whatever in—" His voice trailed off to nowhere. He was clearly drunk; he collapsed in the recliner. Dammit, he wasn't going to be any help at all.

"All right, all right." Curtis had come to his senses.

Simon smiled and said, "You got an A, Jill."

"I know. You told me—"

"You got an A."

Curtis pulled Jill closer to him, his face long and drawn. Jill glanced at Troy; he had already fallen asleep.

"Curtis?" said Simon. "Jill?" Mr. Prenez's voice was gone, and the one replacing it was closer to Simon's own, but not quite, since Simon's voice was still high and prone to cracking. This voice was deeper, but still young.

"It's Sam," said Jill in a strained whisper. For a second, Simon looked like Sam, before Jill shook the image from her mind.

"Yeah," said Curtis. He addressed Simon: "Sam? Is that you?"

"Curtis, put it back!" said Sam's voice.

"What does he want?" asked Jill. Curtis's grip on her shoulders was firm, painful. He didn't answer her.

"You've got to put it back! The lake—a curse—"

"Curse?"

"—unleashed. Jill—help—"

"How? What can I—"

"Horrible—it hurts!" Tears came from Simon's eyes and rolled down his cheeks onto the pillow. "We're trapped. Jill—help us—"

Attrapé.

"Dammit, Sam! How? I can't do anything!"

"Curse," he said, or was it "Curtis"? Jill couldn't tell, the voice was so strained. He sounded in pain. "Curtis—Curtis—"

"Yes?" asked Curtis.

"Your fault," said Sam's voice. "All your fault."

"The sugar bowl," Jill mumbled, then looked askance at Curtis. "The sugar bowl, remember? You took it out!"

"It's not my fault!" snapped Curtis.

"Put it back," urged Sam's voice once more, before Simon's body collapsed against the pillow. Curtis rushed to Simon's side, checked his pulse, felt his forehead, and said that for all he could tell, Simon was going to be all right.

Jill backed up and leaned against a wall for support. Stink Lake was under a curse, because Curtis had removed the sugar bowl from it. That was why Sam was dead?

Jill stared at Curtis in horror.

"Don't look at me like that," he said. "Maggie's the one who wanted the sugar bowl, not me, so stop looking at me like that!"

NINETEEN

A vicious wind came in the night, feeding the flames at the high school and providing every possible hindrance for Sherman's firefighters, so that by morning the two-story brick edifice was nothing more than a blackened, crumbling, hollowed-out bier with one collapsed wall, housing pile after pile of charred, useless rubble. Although the fire was burnt out by midmorning, the wind was still raging, stealing people's laundry, trying to lift the Sunday dresses of Sherman's women, and ready to rend and tear any brave kite that might go up.

Jill stood, leaning against the weathered white fence in front of her trailer, gazing at the remains of Sherman High and all the hunched-over people standing behind the police line pointing, and wondered what she should have been feeling, instead of this intense satisfaction. But she realized it didn't make any difference. The bitter cold stung her face, and she noticed that to the west, gigantic, darkening thunderheads were approaching the town. She rolled a butterscotch candy around in her mouth, and remembered when she was ten years old and had nearly choked to death on one of these things while watching *Star Trek* after school; Celia had somehow managed to dislodge it just in time. Morbidly, Jill wondered what would have happened if Celia hadn't been home. She supposed she would have first turned blue, then passed out, then . . . she shuddered at the thought, and spat the undissolved disk from her mouth. She decided she should take up something a little less dangerous, like smoking.

It was ten-thirty; Curtis wouldn't arrive for another half hour, and then, while Maggie was out shopping, they would check her trailer together for the sugar bowl.

As Jill went back inside her own trailer, she took a deep breath, and could smell the coming rain.

She let poor Claude out of her bedroom, and crumbled up some leftover meat loaf into a bowl for him. Jill had no idea what Celia would say about him, but she didn't care, either. She fixed herself a glass of Ovaltine, and looked out the window at Maggie's trailer. Maggie's kitchen light was still on; she hadn't left yet.

Routinely at eleven on Sunday mornings, Maggie walked the five blocks to the Safeway to get her weekly bag of groceries, since most other shoppers were at church and there were therefore no crowds. Once she left, she would be gone for at least forty-five minutes—plenty of time for Jill, Curtis, and Troy to go in, find the sugar bowl, and throw it back in the lake before Maggie could find out.

Curtis was wrong, of course. Maggie couldn't have know anything about the curse, and she certainly wasn't a witch. All she knew was it had belonged to her old fiancé from forty years ago, and she only wanted it as a memento. She had told Jill so herself. She must not have known everything about her fiancé, but that was understanable. Maggie could never harm a soul; she didn't even eat red meat. Jill couldn't bear the thought of having to explain it all to her, about Mr. Prenez, and Sam, and Kraig, and the salamanders. But then, there was probably no point in telling her anyway, once everything in Sherman was back to normal.

Which would be soon.

Jill sat down at the kitchen table to finish her glass of Ovaltine. By her feet, Claude was finishing the last of the bowl of meat loaf. He was probably still hungry, having gone an entire day without food. Jill would have to go buy him some dog food. She scratched his head, but as he was still eating, he ignored her. Jill made a failed attempt at a smile.

A knock at the door made Jill jump.

Jill was expecting Curtis and Troy. "Come in."

"It's me, hon," said Maggie's voice. "My hands are full."

"Maggie!" Jill got up and opened the door. Maggie was standing there in the wind, smiling, with a steaming pan of freshly baked cobbler clutched between two oven mitts. Her hair was hidden beneath a pale green silk scarf, and reeked of hair spray. As she looked distractedly over her shoulder at the approaching clouds, her orange lipstick and blue eye shadow caught the dull sunlight in an odd way. Jill wondered why older women were color-blind when it came to putting on makeup, while Maggie stepped inside and set the pan down on the kitchen counter.

"Just thought I'd come see how you were doing. Celia called me last night, said she was worried sick about you, running off in such a state."

"Really?" Jill was suddenly, unexpectedly, on the defensive. "I don't know what came over me."

"We all go a little crazy sometimes."

"I know." *What was that supposed to mean?*

"When did you get in?"

"This morning."

"I know how much you like peach cobbler, so I thought I'd simply have to make some and bring it over. You are feeling better today, aren't you?"

Jill nodded, forced a smile. "Oh yeah, much better," she lied.

"Good. There was an article in the paper this morning about Sam. Apparently, his brother is missing, too. Did you know that?"

"No."

Maggie grinned. "Well, I'm sure it'll all be straightened out soon enough. Terrible thing about the high school. They'll probably have to move you all over to the junior high for the rest of the year. How in the world are they going to manage?"

"I don't know."

Maggie didn't seem to notice Claude, who was sniffing in the kitchen right around their feet, or if she did, she didn't say anything.

"I'm going to Safeway before the storm hits," said Maggie, removing her oven mitts and setting them by the cobbler. "Care to join me?" Maggie was heading for the door.

"Oh, I'm sorry, Maggie, I can't. I'm doing fine, really, and I've got some things to do. Thanks anyhow."

"Some other time?"

"Yeah, sure. Thanks a million for the cobbler. It looks fantastic."

Maggie's smile drooped. "Oh, it was nothing. I'm just being neighborly."

They said good-bye, and Maggie left. Jill shut the door and looked out a window, and watched Maggie walk down Grant Street until she turned the corner at the Buckin' Bronc Motel. Now there were only about forty minutes before she would be back.

Jill tried to reach Curtis by phone, but there was no answer. Perhaps he and Troy were on their way, but Curtis had said he would call before coming over, and all the same, Erik should have answered, since he was supposed to be taking care of Simon, according to Curtis's plan.

She would have to do it herself. Curtis and Troy weren't supposed to show up for another fifteen or twenty minutes, but she couldn't afford to wait any longer.

 # TWENTY

Getting into Maggie's trailer was no problem, since Jill had long ago been entrusted with an extra key. She slipped it in the lock, opened the door, and entered the musty-smelling place. Maggie hadn't vacuumed in a while. Warm sunlight filtered in between the half-parted, yellow curtains. Jill shut the door behind her and flicked on the funny living room light fixture, the sorry attempt at a miniature chandelier, with light bulbs trying hard to be candle flames, and gold spray-painted filigree. The air seemed cloudy, either from dust or from the cobbler Maggie had made. Peach smell lingered still, along with the must. Jill couldn't help the feeling that came over her, and she smiled. It was as if nothing had happened, as if she would go to the high school tomorrow and Sam would be there with a kiss for her, and Mr. Prenez would hand back the tests he had graded, and Curtis and Sam would be friends again, and ... there was something about this room, something calming. Here, she felt comfortable.

Jill knew Maggie's household upside down and backwards, and since the sugar bowl wasn't on the shelves of knickknacks lining the wall, there was only one logical place to look: the old rolltop desk against the far wall. That was where Maggie kept her private things, everything that had made up her life. If she kept the photo of her dead fiancé there in one of the drawers, it only made sense that was where she had put the sugar bowl that had once been his.

Jill looked at her watch; there was still plenty of time.

She went over to the desk. She didn't know what type of wood it was made of. It was either a naturally dark wood, like mahogany, or a lighter wood that had been stained, but the thick coating of old, sticky varnish made it hard to tell. The top squeaked as she rolled it up. Inside, there were many small drawers on either side, and a shallow desktop intended for letter-writing. Ballpoint pens were scattered about the desk, and a jewelry box sat in one corner.

Directly in front of her lay an overstuffed, unaddressed, plain white envelope that was also unsealed, its back flap merely tucked inside snugly. Jill reached for it to look inside, then hesitated, feeling guilty. This was Maggie's private business. The sugar bowl wouldn't be inside the envelope. She knew she should have left it where it lay, but now that she had picked it up, she decided it couldn't hurt anything to take a peek. What she found was a thick pile of stiff hundred-dollar bills, and a withdrawal slip from Maggie's bank dated Saturday morning.

Maggie had closed out her account, and her entire life savings was now grasped between Jill's thumb and forefinger.

Jill hurriedly slipped the bills back in the envelope and set it on the desktop exactly where it had been before, so Maggie wouldn't know. Now why had Maggie done that? she wondered. She was sorry she had even looked. She didn't want to know Maggie's secrets, she decided, and began to have second thoughts about stealing the sugar bowl and throwing it in the lake.

Because it would be stealing, after all.

Oh bullshit, she thought. If returning the sugar bowl to Stink Lake would keep any more people from being killed, she couldn't give a flying fuck if she broke the law. But she did care about hurting Maggie's feelings, and breaking the trust she and Maggie shared.

Too late now, I've committed myself. Maggie will agree it was the right thing to do, once I tell her, once she knows what happened to Sam.

She opened the topmost of the large drawers beneath the desktop. Inside were assorted crochet hooks, knitting needles, embroidery hoops, a pin cushion covered with pins of all sizes, sewing needles, patches, bits of cloth, a few needlepoint patterns, and nothing else. Jill shut it and went to the next one down. In this one Maggie's paints were piled —tubes of acrylics and oils, jars of tempera, plastic cases of watercolors—along with a bundle of old, used brushes bound together with a rubber band, and a few brand-new brushes still in their cellophane wrappers, but that was all. Jill sighed, closed the drawer, and went to the next. It was locked. She shook it violently, but it held firm and wouldn't open, despite its age. It was tempting to try picking the lock, but Jill had never had any luck with that in the past, and knew she wouldn't be successful going that route, not without damaging Maggie's desk in her frustration. So she tried to think of where Maggie would keep the key to the drawer. Surely not on the key chain she carried with her. Jill checked all the tiny drawers beneath the rolltop, searching through all the small items they contained, but came up with nothing. Then she checked the jewelry box, and after digging through all the ornaments, amulets, brooches, and earrings, came upon a set of three tiny brass keys on a ring. They looked exactly right. She tried each key until she found the right one and the lock gave, then she opened the drawer. It smelled of mold, and everything inside was covered with a layer of dust. A small cloud of dust particles flew up from the opening, making Jill cough. She blew the dust from the objects inside—a dozen small jars, similar to the tempera paint ones, only they contained many diverse things, and were labeled: *Hedda's hair 2 Nov 46, Mr. Conroy—fingernail clippings 21 Feb 47, Mayor Thompson—saliva w/tobacco 3 Mar 47. . . .*

Jill shut the drawer fast. She didn't want to know. She nearly forgot to lock it back up before she tried the next drawer down. She had to unlock that one, as well.

She was relieved to find it was merely filled to the top with letters. Acidic dust emanated from the yellowed papers—the same sort of dust Jill encountered whenever she tried to read an old, used paperback book. She felt around the drawer, thinking the sugar bowl might be hidden underneath, but it wasn't. Everything in the drawer was what it appeared to be, except there was something strange about the letters. None of them was addressed to Maggie, and there wasn't a single date more recent than August, 1948. Jill thumbed through to check, but they were all letters, their ink fading, to someone named Emily: *Dear Emily, My Darling Emily, Dearest Emmy, Dear Emmy Margaret*....

Margaret? *Maggie?* But that couldn't be! The dates on the letters went backwards from 1947, to 1936, 1922, 1911, 1902, *1896, 1881, 1877*....

No, that was a stupid thought. Maggie had to have been keeping her mother's letters—or her grandmother's—but they certainly were *not* her own.

Jill frantically put the letters back in the drawer and locked it. Beads of sweat trickled down her forehead, and her clammy palms were sticky with dust from the aging paper she had been handling.

One drawer remained, deeper than the rest, also locked. Jill merely had to open it halfway before she saw the shiny silver of the sugar bowl, sitting atop an old, worn, leather notebook. Maggie must have cleaned it up, for surely it had been tarnished or covered with mud and silt, but here it was, at last. Its lid had been welded shut, Jill noticed. She picked it up and could tell from its weight and the way it shifted when she tipped it that there was something within.

"You found it, I see," said Maggie's voice behind her.

Jill jumped, and dropped the sugar bowl back into the drawer. "Oh, hi, Maggie," she said turning around, her voice quavering. Maggie was smiling pleasantly, which put Jill more at ease. "I'm sorry. I didn't mean to pry, I just—"

"You just had to see it."

"Yeah. I didn't expect you back for another half hour or so. I figured I could come take a look, out of curiosity... you know... because of your fiancé and everything, and you wouldn't have to know." Jill swallowed hard. If Maggie were the sane, normal person Jill knew she was, there would be no trouble, and everything would be all right. "How did you know I was here?"

Maggie came closer, shutting the front door behind her. "Honestly, I had no idea, Jill. It started raining on my way to the store. I came back for my umbrella, and there you were."

Jill nodded, not knowing anything to say.

"If you'd wanted to see the sugar bowl, you had only to ask. I would have shown it to you."

Jill stood up and moved away from the desk, trying to remove herself from what she had done. She had invaded Maggie's privacy, had broken their trust, and in so doing, had made a big mistake. "I'm sorry."

Maggie chuckled as she came up to Jill, and leaned against the desktop. "There's something else very interesting in that particular drawer, Jill. Would you like to see it?"

"What is it, that book?" Jill asked. "I know what it is. It's a book of witchcraft, isn't it?"

Maggie said nothing.

This time, Jill's voice came out in a mumble, because she was scared. "Isn't it?" she repeated.

"Yes," said Maggie resignedly. "But that wasn't what I wanted to show you." She bent over and rummaged around the half-open drawer, knocking objects about.

Maggie's face was grim as she stood, wielding a shiny, well-kept, black revolver.

Jill froze; she was looking down its barrel.

TWENTY-ONE

Curtis woke up with his face against the pillow and Erik's arm draped across his bare back. A light spattering of rain was striking his window in a low, steady rhythm, and the sky beyond the window well was gray. He couldn't tell from looking at the sky what time it was, but he knew one thing: he hadn't been woken up by his alarm clock, as he should have been. He rolled out from under Erik's arm slowly, not wanting to wake up, and searched for the clock. He found it on the floor beneath a dirty T-shirt. It read: 11:32 A.M.

Shit. He must have accidentally turned it off and gone back to sleep without knowing it, or maybe he had simply forgotten to set it. He was supposed to have woken up an hour earlier and taken Troy with him over to Jill's, so they could get into Maggie's trailer and look for the sugar bowl. Now it was too late. He hoped Jill had simply gone ahead and done it herself.

Getting out of bed, Curtis felt a twinge of sorrow, since he had hoped to be the one to return the sugar bowl to the lake. It seemed his responsibility, or perhaps his duty. Sam's ghost had told *him* to put it back, not Troy, not Jill. He yawned, stretched, slipped on a pair of flannel gym shorts, and made a nasty face at himself in one of the mirrors on the wall.

He wondered why Jill hadn't called when she saw he wasn't coming. The phone was still on the carpet next to the mirror he and Erik had used to cut their cocaine. Curtis picked up the receiver, thinking he'd better give Jill a call himself, and noticed the ringer had been turned off. Erik must have done that; it was probably a habit of his at his own home. No wonder Curtis hadn't gotten any calls. He turned the ringer back on, and punched out Jill's number.

"Hello?" said Celia's voice on the other end.

"Hi, Celia, this is Curtis. Is Jill there?"

"No, she's not."

"Did she say where she was going?"

"Nope. I woke up about ten minutes ago, but she was already gone, and she didn't leave a note."

"Oh."

"That girl, she's never here. Do you know how late she came in last night?"

"Yeah, I brought her home."

"Well, thanks for that, at least. But now she's off again, who knows where. She's not at church, I can tell you that much."

"Neither are you."

"Of course not, and neither are you, Curtis."

"Bad for my image."

"Look, if you see Jill, have her call me, all right?"

"Sure, Celia. Thanks. I've got to go."

"Bye."

Curtis hung up.

If she wasn't at her trailer, she must be over at Maggie's; or maybe she was at the lake, throwing the sugar bowl back in. Curtis decided to try Maggie's number. He had to look it up in the slim Sherman telephone directory: *Aldrich, M.* He punched the numbers and let it ring, but no one answered. Either Jill wasn't there, or she didn't think it would be right to answer the phone. He put the receiver back in its cradle.

Immediately, the phone rang. He picked it back up and said, "Hello?"

"Hi, Curtis." It was a young, female voice.

"Jill?"

"No... this is Frita Schmeckpeper."

"Oh, hi."

"How's it going? Are you still cleaning up?"

Cleaning up, cleaning up...oh yeah, from the party. "Uh, no, I haven't even started."

"Oh." Frita sounded disappointed. "I thought I'd call and see if you wanted to have lunch, at Holy Frijoles, or wherever."

"Frita, I wish I could, but—"

"I know, you still have to get the place straightened up before your parents get back."

"Yeah. Thanks for the call, though. I mean, I'd like to do that sometime, but today's just no good."

"Sure, I understand. Hey, um, I'll talk to you later, then?"

"Yeah, definitely. See you. Bye."

"Bye."

Curtis didn't know what to do about her. Frita was really nice, and he wanted her as a friend, but she seemed to be developing a crush on him, and he knew that wouldn't work out. He simply wasn't interested in girls—none at all, not even Frita Schmeckpeper.

Erik's body was shifting beneath the bed covers; he was awake. "Morning. Who was that?"

"Frita."

"Oh, of course. I think she likes you."

"No kidding."

"I like you, too." Erik smiled.

"I know that." Curtis smiled back, stretching his torso.

"Why don't you get back in bed?"

"Because I've got things to do, and I need a shower."

Erik put his hands behind his head, displaying his tanned arms and chest. "I'm going to lie here a while. I'll be up in a few and help you clean up."

"Thanks."

"Sure you don't need any help soaping up?"

"Uh-huh. I think I can manage." With that, Curtis left the room and went upstairs.

The living room didn't look as messy as he had remembered from the night before. Then he saw why: Troy was going around the room, picking plastic cups and other garbage up off the floor. Troy's clothes, now clean, lay in a bundle on the seat of the recliner, but he was still wearing the ones Curtis had loaned him.

Simon was still asleep on the couch. Troy had slept here in the living room so he could keep an eye on him, and would have awakened Curtis if anything had happened. Since he hadn't, nothing must have come up.

"Hi," said Troy, pitching some orange rinds into a green garbage sack. The sweatpants hung low on his hips, and molded themselves around the curve of his buttocks as he bent over to grab a beer can.

"Hey, you don't have to do that. You weren't even at the party. Just leave it. I'll get to it later." Curtis liked the shape of Troy's muscular arms, and the way his pectorals bulged through the flimsy fabric of the T-shirt, putting a strange cleft in Billy Idol's forehead. For an eighth-grader, Troy was really something.

"Weren't we supposed to go over to Jill's at eleven?"

"Yeah, we were. My alarm didn't go off, though. No big deal. I'm sure Jill can take care of it." Curtis examined Simon's face. Simon was breathing soundly, but looked as if he could still use nine more hours of sleep. "How's Simon doing?"

"Fine, I guess." Troy rubbed the back of his neck, cringing. He looked stiff. "He kept waking up every hour or so and talking gibberish, about a mile a minute. Whatever it was, it was freaky. He sounded real scared, and then he would drop off to sleep again. After a while, I didn't pay any attention. I could see he was OK and everything."

Curtis crossed his fingers.

Troy was wiping off the coffee table with a wet paper towel. The .45 automatic belonging to Curtis's dad was sitting on one corner; Troy picked it up and tossed it on the pile of clothes in the recliner.

"Hey, be careful!" Curtis snapped.

"It didn't go off, man."

"It could have."

"Shh! Curtis, you're going to wake up Simon."

"Listen," Curtis said in a quieter tone. "Stop cleaning up my place. It's not your job. Just hang tight, relax. I'm grabbing a shower and then we'll motor over to Jill's, and see what's up. We'll leave Erik here to look after Simon."

Curtis went into the bathroom and slipped off his shorts. Why can't they all just leave me alone? he wondered. He didn't want Simon, or Troy, or Frita, or Erik. He didn't even want Jill, not anymore. The only person he had ever wanted, the only one he had ever loved in the whole world, had been Sam.

And he had almost had him. *Almost*. If only there had been more *time*! If only...

It had only been a month and a half ago, when they were returning from a P.I.L. concert in Denver, that Curtis had told Sam he was gay.

"It's not like I think I should have been a woman, or anything like that. I mean, I'm real glad I'm a guy! That's the whole point. I like being a guy, but girls don't turn me on, you know? Other guys turn me on, girls don't. I don't know why. That's just how it is. I don't ever want to be prevented from loving another human being just because of its sex."

They were sitting at a booth in the Ever-Open Cafe in Fort Collins, Colorado, at three in the morning, eating hamburgers and onion rings. A waitress was mopping the floor, and there were only three other customers in the place, who looked like truckers. Curtis and Sam were talking quietly.

"So, what if you meet a really great girl someday?" Sam asked.

"I don't want to rule out girls completely. But so far, I've only been interested in guys. Sam, I've known I was gay since I was about twelve, but it was only a year or two ago that I admitted it to myself, understand?"

"Really? You've known since you were twelve?"

"Sort of. I used to sneak in front of the TV late at night and watch *Looking for Mr. Goodbar* on cable, because there was this great scene where Richard Gere was dancing around the room in a jockstrap—well, I guess you'd have to be there. That's the only reason I ever watched it, and Christ, that was a long time ago."

Sam munched on an onion ring, and was silent for a while. "So, what does this mean for our friendship?"

"I don't know. I've been terrified of telling you, but now that I have I feel fantastic. You're my best friend. I feel real comfortable talking about this with you." Curtis laughed. "It was a lot easier than I thought it was going to be. We've been spending so much time together this summer, I knew I'd have to tell you sometime. I was real worried you might freak out and our friendship would be over. But then I decided, I ought to be honest with you. If you didn't mind that I was gay, great, I figured it wouldn't really damage anything. And if you did mind, you wouldn't have been the sort of person I'd want to hang around with, anyway. I didn't have anything to lose."

Sam smiled. "You seem really happy."

"I am! You don't know what a great load this is I'm getting off my chest. You're the first person I've ever told."

"You haven't talked to your parents?"

"No."

"Not even Jill?"

"No. I don't know. She's my oldest friend, but I don't think I would be as comfortable telling her as I am with you. I don't think this is going to change anything between us, do you?"

"No. Jesus, Curtis, why would it? I'm straight, you know, but that doesn't mean I'm going to stop being your best friend."

"You mean it?"

"Of course, man. Just knowing you trust me enough to tell me you're gay makes me feel good. You're still the best friend I've ever had, too. I'm not going to toss you aside just because you happen to be gay."

"Good." Half of Curtis's burger had been sitting on his

plate for a long time, and was now cold. "I don't want you to take this the wrong way, Sam, but—I love you. Like a brother, I mean. I really love you."

Sam whispered, "I do too, man. I love you, like a brother, no more." He looked nervously about the cafe. "Shit, I've never said that to a guy before!"

"Me either," said Curtis. "Remember that time we said we'd never allow ourselves to be drafted if there was a war?"

"Yeah, what about it?"

"You said you didn't want to go to war, because you couldn't ever kill anyone. It didn't matter if he was the enemy, or even if he was pointing a gun right at you, but you wouldn't be able to pull the trigger and shoot him. And I thought so, too, remember?"

"Uh-huh. I could never kill anybody."

"I was thinking about that the other day, and I sort of changed my mind."

"What do you mean, sort of?"

"I was thinking how much you meant to me, how much I valued our friendship, and I realized I *could* kill someone else, if he was about to kill you. I'd have no problem with that. I'd shoot him on the spot, or throw myself in front of you to keep you from being killed."

"Wow." Sam's eyebrows sprang up. "Really?"

"Yeah. I would kill for you, man. I mean that. I'd die for you, too, if I had to—"

"Curtis, don't talk about that. Don't ever die for me."

"Okay, maybe I couldn't die for you, I don't know. But I would definitely kill, if it would save your life."

Sam's face had a melancholy grin, and his eyes were watery. He looked as if he were about to cry. "I guess I would, too," he said. "I would kill for you. You mean a lot to me. As a friend, I mean."

They didn't talk again for a long time, not until Curtis had finally finished his burger and the waitress had given them their check.

Then Curtis said, "We should become blood brothers."

It was something he had been thinking about for a long time.

"Blood brothers?"

"Like Tom Sawyer and Huckleberry Finn, you know."

"Yeah, I know what you mean."

"I've got my switch. We could do it right now."

Sam looked at the ceiling for a second, and said, "I don't know, mixing blood like that."

"Fuck, man, I don't have AIDS."

"I hope you don't, but how do you know?"

"Because I've still never had sex with anybody—male, female, or whatever. Unlike certain studs I know."

Sam smiled, vainly. "Okay, I'm sorry. Sure."

Curtis asked him to hold out his thumb, and then made a small slice with the sharp edge of his switchblade. He had Sam make a similar cut on his own thumb, and then they held their wounds together for a moment.

"Is that it?" asked Sam.

"I guess so. I don't know if we're supposed to say anything, or what. It's kind of gone out of fashion."

"I think we've said plenty already." Sam sucked the trickle of blood off his thumb. Curtis dabbed his with a napkin, then they paid their bill and left a small tip on the table. It was two and a half hours driving back to Sherman, and Sam slept the entire way, looking absolutely uncomfortable, slumped as he was in the Porsche's low bucket seat. Curtis kept the volume low on the stereo, so it wouldn't wake Sam, even though he was nearly falling asleep at the wheel himself. . . .

Curtis toweled his face dry, looked at himself in the mirror, and sneered. If you hadn't taken that sugar bowl out of the lake, none of this would have happened, he said to his reflection. Sam, your blood brother, wouldn't be dead, and maybe, just *maybe*, you could have worked something out.

But it wasn't my fault. It was Jill's friend, that old bitch, Maggie. She killed Sam.

Someone knocked on the bathroom door.

"Hold on a minute, will you?" said Curtis. He was still dripping wet.

"Roger—holding on. It's me, Erik. I just heard about the high school on the radio. You know it burned down?"

"Yeah, I know."

"I thought so, man. Your leather jacket is covered with soot."

"Shit."

"Don't worry, I won't tell anybody." On the other side of the door, Erik was laughing. "You really got balls, you know that?"

"Yeah, I know."

"Nice, big, juicy ones."

"Erik, shut up!"

TWENTY-TWO

Slanting, wind-whipped streaks of gray dashed across an ashen sky. Jill was looking out a small, vertical space of window not enclosed by the yellow curtains, and that was all she could see: *gray*. The steady drone of rain filled her ears.

"Groceries will have to wait," Maggie muttered as she pulled the last knot tight.

Curtis was right, Jill thought. Maggie is a witch.

She was utterly helpless, bound with nylon cord to one of Maggie's kitchen chairs that had been moved to the living room. Her ankles were secured to the back legs of the chair near the seat so her feet were suspended a foot off the floor. Behind her back were two cords tied to her feet that went up around her throat, tied in slipknots. Her wrists had been pulled down between her knees and tied to the chair's front legs. Even if she threw her weight and tipped the chair over, her struggling would surely close the loops around her throat and cut off her air. Besides which, Maggie was still in the room, with a loaded gun in her hand.

A gust of wind rattled the trailer. Jill swallowed hard and could feel the tight cords trying to keep her Adam's apple from going back down. The position Maggie had tied her in was more uncomfortable than she could have imagined possible.

"Will you let me talk?" Jill asked. She could feel tingles in her feet, as the circulation started leaving her toes.

"Certainly, child, go ahead."

The smell of charred nylon wafted into the air as Maggie took a lighter and burned the frayed ends she had cut, which crumpled into blackened blobs of molten plastic for an instant, then hardened into brown ones, but continued to stink. The odor made Jill wince, and she worried for a moment that some of that molten plastic might drip onto her hands. But it didn't, and before she knew it Maggie was finished.

"Are you going to let me go?" Sweat trickled from Jill's brow, running down her temple, along her cheek.

"Frankly, no. I'm sorry."

"Then you're going to kill me?"

"Foolish girl!" Maggie snapped, the blood rising to her face. "Why did you have to go through my things!"

She couldn't answer. Maggie *was* going to kill her.

"Jill, dear, it's not as if I wanted to."

Jill tried to keep the sob from rising; it was expanding in her throat, causing the ropes to constrict farther. She managed to hold it back, gritted her teeth, and said, "I don't understand."

"You will." Maggie straightened with some difficulty, her hand at the small of her back, and went into the kitchen. She pulled a chair from the table, turned it around and sat facing Jill, many feet away. The revolver remained in her hand; she rested it on her thigh, pointing it vaguely in Jill's direction. "You will, which is why I haven't done it already." She shut her eyes and rubbed the bridge of her nose, as if thinking very deeply.

Maggie was serious. Her grim countenance seemed strained, and her stiff hair looked as if it hadn't been combed. The grip she kept on the gun, however, was steady, and all her movements seemed deliberate. She appeared quite sane, which frightened Jill even more.

"Maggie, you don't have to kill me," Jill pleaded. "I won't tell anybody anything, I promise."

"Oh, bull!" Maggie shouted. "You won't tell them how I tied you up? Or that I'm a witch? Or about the curse?"

"They wouldn't believe me, anyway. They—they never believe me."

"Despite everything, Jill, I'm still your friend. I'm performing a kindness by killing you now, rather than letting you die at the hands of the lake, or the salamanders. You should be glad."

Glad! Jill couldn't hold back the sob any longer, and her eyes started to water. "Why don't you just stop everything, right now, before it gets any worse?"

"I could never do that. It's taken me forty years to find that damned sugar bowl. It's eluded me all this time, and now I've got it. Do you honestly think I'm about to go and throw it back in, just because you asked me to?"

"Why not, Maggie? Then you wouldn't have to—to kill me. Oh God, why are you doing this? You aren't a cruel person."

"Oh, I never used to be. Not when I came out here to Sherman, at least. I went bad much later."

"Went bad?" For a moment, Jill almost felt like laughing, but it turned back into a sob, because of the ropes, and because she was so confused, and because she didn't know why Maggie was doing any of this. "Maggie, get serious."

"I am, Jill." Maggie sighed heavily. "You really think you know me, don't you?"

Jill didn't answer.

"How old would you say I am?"

"I don't know."

"You saw my letters when you pillaged my desk, you noticed the dates. Go on, take a guess. How old?"

Those letters couldn't have been hers. "You can't be any more than seventy. I know that."

"I can't, can I? What if I told you I was one hundred and thirty-six years old?"

"I'd say that's bullshit."

"Oh, really?"

"You're not a hundred and thirty-six years old, Maggie!"

"Am I so young and beautiful?"

A crack of thunder shook the trailer, making Maggie's piles of junk jingle on their shelves.

"Could I have some water?" Jill asked. She was dying of thirst, and eager to change the subject.

"I don't see why not." Maggie thought a moment, then got up and went to the kitchen. While she filled a tall glass with water, she looked out the kitchen window. She stared out into the rain. "It used to be a dump, you know."

"What did?"

"Stink Lake. Up till the end of the war it was the city dump. Before that, it was cattle grazing. And before that, who knows—buffalo hunts?" Maggie shut off the water and came into the living room almost smiling. She allowed Jill a few large gulps before setting the glass down on the end table beside the couch. For a moment, she seemed like the same old Maggie. Then she returned to her chair in the kitchen.

"The only time Sherman ever grew a whole lot was after the war," Maggie explained. "All those GIs came home and everyone started building, all on the north side of town. Pretty soon the residential area reached the dump, and the city council decided it might be a good idea to move it. I would have had no quarrel with them, mind you, except they also decided to turn the site into a park, and put a lake there. They owned the land, you see, so they could do whatever they wanted with it."

"I still don't get it."

"When I came out here, Sherman was just outgrowing tents, starting to become a permanent railroad town. I told everyone I was a widow—not true, naturally—and was looking for privacy and seclusion. I had a small house built a couple miles north of town, just a little north of where we are now, on a tiny bit of property. But it was enough. It's gone now, of course. I lived there for a long time, off and on, since the 1870s, changing my name every generation or so, and claiming to have inherited it from the previous owner. A rancher owned the grassland between myself and the city, but I intended to buy a hunk of it someday. Initially, I was unable to do so, which didn't really matter at the time. But it was that small hunk of land that had drawn me out to Wyoming in the first place, from back East, do you understand? There was a great concentration of power—earth forces, if you like—in that land, and I intended to use them."

"For your witchcraft, you mean?"

"Yes."

"But I can't believe you're a witch. You've always been such a good person—"

"Haven't you ever heard of a good witch? Well, that's what I was when I came out West, like I said before, and for a long time after that. I'm from a long line of witches, and as far as I know, none of my ancestors have ever harmed a soul, except in defense, of course. I can't say the same for myself. But in the beginning, I was very 'good.' I didn't hex anybody or cause any damage. I was only interested in experimentation. If I could tap the power in that land, I could learn more than any witch had before me. But I didn't have to own the land to be able to use it. I would go out at night, into the pasture, and try my spells, see what worked and what didn't, and no one was the wiser. I did this for many years, and then, around the turn of the century, the ranch got tied up in a legal matter with the city. To make a long story short, the land ended up in the hands of the town, and that was where they put the municipal dump. But I didn't stop my midnight rituals just because the place was filled with garbage. The smell was annoying, but I endured it. With all that power at my command, there was little I couldn't do. I was able to keep myself young, and attractive in my own way. I was even able to change my appearance. Now, a normal witch, born with power, would be drained of all her energy long before she could do that. If every witch could stay young, we would be far more visible in the world today, believe me!"

"But you could."

"Not because I was better than any other witch, but because I learned to use a great source of power. For seventy years of my life, I didn't age a single day." Maggie's eyes were glazed. She was staring beyond Jill, into the past. "It was wonderful."

Jill examined Maggie's wrinkled face, and wondered if she could possibly be as old as she claimed. Jill couldn't even picture Maggie as a young woman. It was impossible to tear away the aged flesh and old, brittle hair, and expose the smooth-complexioned, smiling face of youth. Jill had the same problem with all old women. None of them could ever have been seventeen. The difference between the girls she knew at school and the old women in nursing homes was too drastic. She wondered how different she would look when she reached eighty. If she ever got the chance.

"I tried to stop them from building a lake at Burroughs Park. This was just after the war. Wolf and I went to all the meetings, and opposed their ideas with all sorts of concrete, logistical baloney. We told them it would be far too costly. When that didn't work, I tried casting spells on the council members. That did work, of course, and they did change their minds. Unfortunately, the idea had already been aired, and with a referendum, the townspeople decided in favor of it. There was nothing I could do—*nothing*—against all those people. The lake would have been built anyway. I had no choice but to engineer a curse. If I had sat back, instead, and let all that water sit there for long, it would have neutralized all the power that lay beneath. I had to delve into black magic, for the first time in my life. It was scary, but also necessary."

"Why couldn't you just let it go?"

"That's what Wolf said, too, way back then."

"Wolf?"

"My fiancé, Wolf Lesch. He wanted me to forget about it. He didn't want to see all those people get hurt, but I was to the point where I didn't really care. I was mad with rage. If all that power were taken from me, I would start growing old again. I'd been young all my life, and I couldn't let all those stupid people steal it out from under me. I just couldn't bear the thought of that!"

"But you did grow old." Jill's voice was getting

scratchy. She wasn't getting much oxygen, but when she tried taking deeper breaths, the cords simply tightened more.

Maggie got up and gave Jill another drink of water.

"That's because Wolf turned against me," Maggie said. "He pried into my notebooks and found how to counteract the curse. He prepared the sugar bowl and threw it in, just when everything was getting under way."

"And then you killed him."

Maggie started. "How did you—"

"It was spontaneous combustion, they said."

"Which, of course, doesn't really exist."

"Curtis told me about it." *If only he would come, and wrestle the gun from Maggie's hand* ...

"It wasn't spontaneous combustion. I had the salamanders get him, just before the sugar bowl plunged through the surface of the lake. He certainly didn't expect it. But it was for his own good, believe me."

"But that was forty years ago! Why bring back the curse now? It doesn't make any sense."

"I had to, for Wolf."

"But you said he was against it."

Maggie scowled. "Why did I think you would understand? I should have known I could never explain it to you."

"I'm trying."

"Perhaps I should just get it over with."

Jill started to cry. "Oh, Maggie! . . . You're my friend . . . you've always been . . . so kind to me . . . like yesterday."

"But I killed Sam."

"I know, but—"

"But nothing. I killed Mr. Prenez. I burned down the high school. Why hon, I've only just started."

"But . . . but that's not you . . . that's the curse!"

"There's no difference."

"Yes there is!" Tears were rolling down Jill's face. Her

words were being choked off. "The curse... the curse is evil, but you—"

"The curse is evil, I'm evil, there's no difference."

"But you're not! You're... you're good and kind—"

"No, I'm not. I'm rotten."

"Please, don't!"

"Did you eat any of the peach cobbler I made?"

"Y-yes... it was delicious."

"You're lying."

"No, I'm not! I... I had a whole piece, and—"

"I know you're lying, Jill. If you had eaten any of that cobbler, you wouldn't be here right now. It was poisoned."

Jill stared at Maggie, and the image was blurred because of her watery eyes, but even that didn't make the gun go away. It was still there, clear as anything.

"Poisoned. Now do you still think I'm so kind?"

"I don't believe you."

"Don't be foolish. I didn't want the curse to get you, so I poisoned the peach cobbler. You didn't eat any of it, so I'm going to have to shoot you. That's all there is to it. Why should I lie?"

The cobbler was poisoned. "Celia!" Jill shouted. "Oh God, she'll eat it!"

"Good. I hope she does. It will be much better for her. You're really very lucky, you know. Once the curse was unleashed Friday afternoon, it should have simply gone out and killed everybody. The town should have been entirely destroyed by Saturday. It's actually quite powerful. Everything that makes up the lake is entirely at the disposal of the curse. The curse can spin algae together into very effective whip-like things..."

"Yes, we... I've met up with those."

"And it can turn harmless salamanders into the most vicious little creatures, shooting off fire everywhere; they can cause an amazing amount of destruction. The lake water can be whipped up into a huge storm, nearly hurricane strength. The mud can be made to shift and slide. What the curse can perform with all the materials it has at hand is probably beyond your comprehension. But I suppose after forty years of waiting, it's having a hard time getting started. Once it really gets going, nothing will be able to stop it. The sugar bowl will only work if someone can get close enough to throw it in."

"What about you?"

"I cast the curse in the first place. It can't do anything to me. As a matter of fact, that was one of the last things my power ever accomplished for me. When Wolf suppressed my curse, I lost all my power. I had been so dependent on the forces from that land, I hadn't had to rely on my own for years. Then, suddenly, it was all gone, even the power I had been born with. I started to age once more, the same rate as everyone else. There was nothing I could do about it. If I had had a little power left over, I could have found the sugar bowl instantly. Instead, it took all this time, as you can see, and even that was mere chance. It's all I've been able to think about, for forty years. I used to go out at night in a canoe, trying to dredge for it, but I kept getting arrested. I still can't believe Curtis managed to find it. At last!" She smiled, gazing up at the ceiling. "After taking the sugar bowl from the lake, I thought of trying to get you out of town, but what was I supposed to tell you? You wouldn't have gone. I couldn't have found a proper excuse for sending you out of town. And then, once Sherman was gone, you would have known who was responsible. So I realized I could let no one escape, not even you. But I am glad it's taken so long to get going, so I could kill you before it does."

"But I don't want to die—"

"Why not? You're always telling me how horrible everything is at school, how you have no future, and you're stuck in Sherman, and you'll never get to college, never find the right man, never be married, never do anything worthwhile. Well, perhaps you're right."

Perhaps.

"You might have ended up like me, a bitter old maid."

"Maggie, don't say that!"

"Don't patronize me, Jill. You have no idea how sick I am of people always treating me like a child. 'Oh, Maggie, don't say such awful things! Oh, Maggie, why don't you make another one of those lovely afghans for the senior craft fair? Here, let me carry those big, heavy bags for you. My, don't you think it's past your bedtime?' I get it from you, from the girls in my bridge club, even perfect strangers. I can't take any more of that crap. You don't know the first thing about me. You've only seen what you've wanted to see, ever since you were a child. You have this ideal, the 'perfect grandmother,' or maybe the 'perfect mother,' neither of which you've ever really had, and you believe I'm it. But I'm not. I've played along with your game, but now it's all over."

That sobered Jill up fast, and now she was trembling.

"Every generation thinks they're the first to discover sex. And do you think I've never been drunk? Do you think that in 1900 there were never any wild parties? No opium addicts? Do you think there were no whores, no rapes, no abortions? Do you know how many people died of venereal disease before they came up with penicillin? Things are no different today from what they were back then, despite all our technology. Or perhaps because of it. New generations never learn anything at all, and life keeps getting worse and worse." Maggie stared down at the floor.

This was Jill's chance. She had to talk Maggie out of it.

"You haven't learned anything, either," said Jill.

Maggie looked up. "Pardon?"

"You say you've lived all this time, and you've watched everybody, and no generation is any different from the last. But here you are, about to shoot me."

"And you think I've learned nothing?"

Jill was feeling an adrenaline rush, like she had when talking with the police. It was now or never—victory or death. "You would kill a whole town just to be young again, over something that happened forty years ago. And even then, no one in Sherman knew they were hurting you."

"Jill, what I've learned is that once something is done, it's done. Back in 1948, I put a curse on this lake, and I killed my lover. I had to, though I know you'll never understand. Once Wolf threw the sugar bowl in the lake, he would no longer be Wolf. He had to sacrifice his soul to do what he did; it left his body the instant the sugar bowl left his hands. If I hadn't killed him, he would have walked the earth as a mindless zombie for all his remaining years, having no consciousness, no soul. I can't ever take back the curse, any more than I can bring Wolf back to life. Both were unfinished business, in a way. I couldn't let the curse stay suppressed forever, and now I've set it free. I've set Wolf free."

"You simply don't care about human life, do you? You don't understand what it means."

Maggie laughed.

Jill's throat was parched once more. Rain was beating against the window. The sky was getting darker, even though it was only noon.

"That's something I do know," Maggie said.

Maggie stood up, cocked her revolver, and thrust it in Jill's face.

"It really doesn't mean a thing." And she was grinning.

Jill whimpered. Out the corner of her eye, she saw a dark shape with spiked hair appear in the window, and gasped. It was Curtis, in the rain; he could see everything. His hand appeared against the window screen, his fingers forming a V, for victory.

Maggie followed Jill's glance. "What was that?" she asked.

"I—I don't know." Jill looked again, and there was nothing, but she could hear footsteps outside.

Maggie heard them too, took the gun out of Jill's face and hurried to the front door.

Curtis burst inside, drenched from head to toe, holding his dad's automatic pistol up against his chest. Troy was behind him.

Lightning lit up the doorway. The wind blew inside the

trailer, blowing junk mail off the kitchen table.

Hurriedly, Maggie brought up her gun.

"Maggie, no!" Jill shouted. "No!"

Curtis ducked in surprise just as Maggie fired. The bullet went right past his ear, shattering a Hummel figurine on the shelf behind him.

Troy said, "Son of a bitch!"

Curtis thrust out his gun with both hands, his dripping face contorted into a look of disgust and terror, and fired twice.

A stream of blood gushed from a wide hole in Maggie's forehead, and her body collapsed onto the floor, knocking over one of the kitchen chairs. Her gun skidded across the linoleum and banged against the refrigerator.

"No! Maggie!" Jill cried desperately. She wanted to run over and help her, to call an ambulance, to do *something*. But she was still bound to this damned chair. She couldn't believe what she had seen. The shots reverberated around the trailer, and kept echoing in her head, over and over, throbbing, pulsing...

Thunder boomed.

Curtis was still standing there, frozen. Troy gaped at the body as it lay there twitching, before it finally stopped moving entirely.

Then, in a flash, the quickly spreading pool of blood dried into a flaky coat of rust on the floor. Maggie's corpse caved in upon itself and the skin and muscle flaked away, down to a skeleton.

Jill screamed.

The bones stayed intact for a brief instant, before collapsing into dust themselves, covered by the rumpled, empty clothing. The wind was blowing the bone dust around the room, pushing it into small piles like snowdrifts against the baseboard.

Maggie was all gone.

Jill kept screaming. There was nothing else to do.

☛ TWENTY-THREE

That was stupid, Curtis thought. *I should never have let her take the Porsche. With the state she was in, she could have an accident, especially in this storm. And I would be responsible. Me.*

"Hey, man," said Troy, his hand on Curtis's shoulder. "Sit down, take a breather. I'll find it."

"A sugar bowl, like from a tea set, made of silver," Curtis reminded him. He sat on the gray speckled couch and glanced at the vinyl-and-chrome chair to which Jill had been tied. The white cords dangled around its legs, severed by Curtis's switchblade.

"Yeah, I know already. Jesus, you've told me enough times."

Curtis stared at the pair of pants and the blouse lying on the kitchen floor, and couldn't believe the linoleum was so clean. There had been so much blood. Now there was nothing; Troy had swept up the dust and dumped it in the kitchen trash.

"Curtis, do you think the cops are going to come?"

"No." No one would have noticed the gunshots, not with all that thunder crashing all over the place.

He couldn't stop thinking of what his mother had always told him: *If you don't put on some muscle, you're going to dry up and blow away.*

But that wasn't what had happened to Maggie. She had been some sort of witch, just as he'd thought. "You were right," Jill had said, when Curtis, without thinking twice, had handed over his keys. She had snatched the key ring from his outstretched hand as if it had belonged to her. "You were right, damn you!" Then she was gone.

Curtis had stared after her in a daze, unable to do anything as he watched his car's single functioning taillight vanish in the distance behind a gray veil of rain.

So Maggie had put the curse on Stink Lake, as he'd figured. She had killed Sam. She had ruined everything.

Curtis felt no remorse, and paid no attention to the loud whine of fire engines outside.

Wednesday evening at ten, Curtis had received a call from Sam. Sam's parents had gone to an Elks Club dinner, one of the few times they had gone out in months. Sam said there were some buddies of his over from the track team, and they were all sitting around drinking beer, and he wanted Curtis to come over. He sounded as if he had already had a few. Curtis went up to the master bedroom where his mom and dad were propped up in bed watching the news, and told them he was going out, that he would be back later, he didn't know when. His dad nodded and he left.

Sam had two guys over, Billy Hedgecoe and Ray Pautz. Ray was really a good guy, and Billy seemed all right too, although Curtis didn't know either of them very well. Curtis had let himself in, and everyone was sitting around the TV room in the basement, watching MTV on the 25-inch Trinitron. On both the coffee table and the floor, empty beer cans were scattered, four for each drunken guy.

"Hey, guy," said Sam, getting up from the sofa as Curtis came down the stairs. He smiled warmly, his toothy grin brightening up the darkly paneled room. "Let me get you a beer. You know Billy and Ray?"

"Yeah, kind of." Curtis smiled at them.

"Don't just stand around. Go on, sit down." Sam disappeared up the stairs.

Curtis sat on the floor, where he had a side view of the TV. He wasn't really interested in watching MTV, but he wanted that beer. "You guys have a track meet tomorrow."

"Yeah," said Ray taking a gulp. "No big deal. I can handle it."

"What's a little beer?" said Billy. "Anyway, we don't have to go to class tomorrow, 'cause we're leaving at nine for Rawlins. Meet won't get going for awhile. I don't give a shit. I'm getting shitfaced and staying out all night. Maybe go over to Becky's."

Ray laughed knowingly. "Shit, man, she's a cow."

"But she fucks like a horse."

"How would you know?" Ray punched Billy's shoulder. "Ow! Hey!"

Sam returned with several beers, which he passed around. He sat on the floor beside Curtis.

They sat around drinking, talking about the idiots on the TV, and about girls. Curtis felt distanced. Yet he drank one beer after another, and they tasted real good. He didn't like most of the videos being shown, and he didn't give a flying fuck what kind of an expert Becky Roth was at giving blowjobs.

"What about Jill?" Billy asked Sam. "Have you scored?"

Sam said nothing. He had locked up, as he frequently did, was hiding his emotions. Curtis could read him easily.

Billy kept pressing. "She give good head? C'mon, does she ride you hard, or what?"

Still Sam kept quiet, and sprayed his chin as he opened another beer. If he didn't say something, Curtis would have to. After all, Jill's reputation was at stake, and nothing mattered more to a girl than her reputation, although Jill would be the first to deny that she gave a shit.

"Oh," said Billy. "Are you through with her then? Is that it?"

"Shut up, man!" There it was, the Explosion. "I'm not 'through with her.' Christ, man, don't ever talk about Jill that way, at least not around me. She's not like Becky. I mean, she's not a cunt. She's a great girl, and it's really none of your goddamned business, all right?" He poured barley and hops down his gullet. "So just shut up," he mumbled.

"Hey, I'm sorry. I didn't mean nothing, honest."

Ray said to Billy, "You should have known better, you dumb fuck," and thwacked him on the head.

Curtis got up to go to the bathroom. His bladder felt stretched to the breaking point. While he was relieving himself in the toilet, Sam came stumbling in; Curtis saw his reflection in the mirror.

"What's up?" Curtis asked, zipping himself.

"Nothing," Sam slurred. "Grab some more beer. I've got a ton. Mom and Dad won't be home till late. Simon's in bed. You having fun?"

"Yeah," said Curtis thoughtfully. Sam was blocking the doorway. Curtis felt silly, standing there and talking with Sam in the bathroom. He wanted to get back to the TV room. "Billy and Ray are nice. I'd ignore the stuff about Jill. They don't know her at all. They're nice guys. They're just drunk."

"You're a nice guy." Sam's eyelids were droopy. He had had a lot of beer. He placed his hand on Curtis's shoulder and looked drunkenly into his eyes. "I don't care if you're gay, or bi, or anything."

Sam's hand lightly brushed Curtis's crotch. Curtis smiled, astonished.

"You're my best friend," Sam added, looking suddenly sad.

Curtis didn't know what to say. He didn't know what Sam was doing. Sam was drunk, that was all. Friends always acted funny when they were drunk. It didn't mean anything. Besides, Sam was a physical kind of guy, and had always been real chummy. Just because he had touched Curtis's crotch didn't mean he wanted to jump in the sack with him.

"C'mon, Sam," Curtis said, leading him out the doorway, back to the TV room. "I need another beer."

Billy and Ray hung out for another hour, and then took off in Ray's Gremlin, heading for Becky's.

Sam and Curtis sat around on the sofa drinking, and changed the channel to Marilyn Monroe in *The Seven Year Itch*. It beat the hell out of Madonna. They talked about nothing much, how Tom Ewell was such a goof, and the movie was corny but funny as hell, and school was so much bullshit.

Then out of the blue, Sam repeated what he'd said before—exactly the same words, in exactly the same drunken mumble, as if he had practiced it for hours beforehand. "I don't care if you're gay, or bi, or anything."

Curtis was drunk, but still in control. All he could say was, "Good. I'm glad." He didn't dare hope for anything else, even though he would have given his left nut to be sitting right up against Sam, flank against flank, their arms around each other, Curtis's head nestled in the crook of Sam's neck. Instead, they sat on either end of the sofa, the way it would always be.

"You kill me," said Sam, laughing. "You really kill me!" He didn't go on from there. Curtis didn't know what he was getting at.

"I'd better go," Curtis said. "It's real late, and there is school tomorrow."

"Aren't you coming to my meet?"

"If you want me to, sure. I can swing it."

"Good."

"But I really ought to get going."

Sam followed him upstairs, to the front door. Curtis opened it, and the cool midnight breeze gave him a shiver. The sky was clear, the street quiet.

"Drive carefully," Sam said, pointing an unsteady finger at him.

"Yeah, sure. See you tomorrow."

"See you."

Curtis had turned and gone down the first step when Sam spoke again.

"Curtis?"

Curtis looked over his shoulder. Sam was standing in the dim light of the doorway, leaning against the edge of the half-open door. "What is it?" asked Curtis.

"C'mere."

Curtis went back to the threshold and stood facing Sam. Sam wouldn't look him in the eye; he was staring down at the doorjamb.

"After the track meet tomorrow," Sam whispered, "I want you." Then he started closing the door.

Curtis couldn't believe what he had heard. He pushed against the door, opening it back up. Sam staggered slightly backward but didn't speak. Curtis went inside. "Are you serious?" he asked. His heart was racing.

"Of course I'm serious," Sam mumbled, finally raising his head and looking into Curtis's eyes. He smiled sheepishly.

"You—you're really not kidding?"

Sam came forward. His face filled Curtis's vision, or so it seemed, because his eyes were so intense. Curtis had been amazed since their first meeting how similar their eyes were: a rich, dark brown no one else in the world seemed to share. Comparing only their eyes, anyone would have said they were brothers. Sam hugged Curtis tightly, resting his head on one shoulder. Curtis felt Sam's hot, damp breath on his neck, the fingers clutching the flesh on his back, the pelvis pressing hard against his own. Sam's body was warm. Curtis's hands roamed up and down Sam's wide back, exploring the taut muscles. Their two bodies together felt like one, only exaggerated: the two deep chests, narrowing down to two trim waists, rounding out to two sets of muscular buttocks, standing on two pair of legs slightly spread, four feet firmly planted. It made Curtis feel superhuman, like Hercules.

"Tomorrow," Sam whispered into Curtis's ear, "I'm going to run just for you."

Curtis held him tighter, savoring the way Sam's muscles rippled beneath his fingers.

Sam's head shifted. His stubbly cheek rubbed Curtis's. Curtis shut his eyes. Their faces lost contact for a moment before Sam's lips brushed against Curtis's, pulled back and hesitated, then pressed down, warm and wet. Sam's tongue pried apart Curtis's lips and thrust inside, while his hands traveled down and grasped Curtis's ass. Their tongues played with each other, rolling, poking, and sliding around. Sam licked the ridge above Curtis's teeth and reached far into his mouth. He sucked Curtis's tongue down his throat, and Curtis did the same, until their lips were sore and felt ten times their normal size. They were out of breath. Sam's hand was holding Curtis's crotch. Beneath Curtis's jeans was the hardest, fullest erection he had ever had, and it was being rhythmically squeezed and stroked by Sam's fingers.

"Oh man, I love you," Sam said.

Curtis took Sam's head between his hands, so he could get Sam to look him right in the eye. Sam's eyes were nearly closed; he looked as if he were about to fall asleep on his feet. "I love you, too, more than anything. Don't you ever forget that." Curtis had got the line from some movie, knew it was sappy, but meant it all the same.

"I won't."

"Not ever."

"Nope."

Spontaneously they kissed again, and it seemed to go on forever. Curtis's mind kept playing Sam's words over and over; Sam *wanted* him, he *loved* him—more than a friend or a brother, and he was going to run just for him. Curtis was already looking forward to the track meet, while they were still kissing and making funny noises and fumbling around with their hands. Curtis felt Sam's crotch, and found he had an erection, too, and a nice one at that.

Then, inexplicably, Curtis sensed a presence behind them, in the doorway.

"Curtis!" shrieked a voice. "Sam!"

They split apart like pepper running away from soap, looking away from each other, trying to pretend they hadn't just been making out and feeling one another up.

It was Sam's mother. His father, at least, was still parking the car, or Curtis might have had the shit kicked out of him. Sam's dad already thought he was a "fag-assed bastard."

Curtis made a hurried exit, waving at Sam while Sam's mother slammed the door in his face. On his way home in the Porsche he got picked up for DWI. The cop wouldn't even have pulled him over if the car hadn't had a busted taillight.

But he didn't care. While he sat in the back of the police cruiser, he was thinking of Sam. All he had ever wanted had now been given him, and not even Sam's mother could take it away.

Or so he had thought.

At the track meet, Sam pretended he couldn't remember anything he had done the night before, claiming he had been too drunk. Curtis could tell Sam was trying to brush him off, for some reason.

"Don't you want to know what you did?" Curtis asked.

"No." Sam wasn't smiling.

"Are you sure? I mean, I think I ought to be honest with you. I feel—I don't know—obligated to tell you what you did."

At that point, Sam scowled, and said through clenched teeth, "You mean the kiss?"

"Yeah." Curtis knew Sam hadn't forgotten. "I've never been kissed like that before. You said you wanted me, and I just—"

"Shut up!"

Curtis did.

"Do you think I'd ever do anything like that again?"

After a moment's thought, Curtis replied, "Yeah, I do."

Sam's jaw squared itself. He seemed to be grinding his teeth. "I'm sorry. I was drunk."

"So was I, but—"

"Curtis, I'm not gay. And now my mom—" He lowered his voice. "My mom saw us kissing! Jesus!"

"So?" Curtis was getting desperate. Everything was going wrong.

"Now my mom thinks I'm a fag."

"Well, fuck your mom!" This was the wrong thing to say. Curtis knew that if he weren't Sam's best friend, his jaw would have received a mighty blow.

As it was, Sam merely looked at Curtis in disgust, and said, "No, Curtis. Fuck you." Then he turned and walked away.

Tears streamed down Curtis's face as he thought, *Anytime, man, anywhere.*

"I found it!" said Troy.

Curtis leapt to his feet. "Let me have it."

Troy handed over the sugar bowl.

Curtis clutched it tight against his chest and headed out the door, saying, "C'mon!"

The wind grabbed Maggie's screen and slammed it against the side of the trailer. By the time they got to the gate, they were already drenched and smelling like the lake. Lightning flared just beyond the shopping plaza through a dull orange mist; flames were climbing into the sky from the north end of the long structure. The rest of the sky was dark. A fire truck was parked in front of the Buckin' Bronc Motel, and the crew was scrambling around, hooking up hoses. The rain didn't seem to make any difference; the fires were already raging.

Fighting the wind, Curtis and Troy dashed across Grant Street. Curtis raised his forearm to shield his eyes against the rain, his other hand still clutching the sugar bowl. The muddy grass made running difficult, and the air was so thick with the smell of algae, Curtis felt he could hardly breathe. Troy fell flat on his face. Curtis stopped and yanked Troy by his slippery arm, helping him back on his feet. Slime and mud covered Troy from head to toe, and Curtis felt more than a little slimy himself. It seemed to be coming down along with the rain, which itself seemed to be coming from the lake. A bolt of lightning struck on the opposite shore, brightening the sky. Two houses over there were already on fire. A dark, shifting mass was climbing up the shoreline on all sides: salamanders. Most were on the southern and western sides, where all the fires had been started. But now they were crawling out of the water in all directions. The whole storm, it seemed, was emanating from the accursed lake.

"We'd better hurry!" Curtis had to shout above the wind. He was chilled to the bone, and wet all the way down to his socks. Now he was watching the ground for salamanders, but none had reached him yet. He couldn't let any touch him, or it would be all over. He had to get the sugar bowl back in the lake before it was too late.

"Look at that!" yelled Troy, pointing.

Gray-green waves were breaking in the middle of Stink Lake and crashing against the banks. The water was swirling around sluggishly in a spiral, like a galaxy, and there was a green mist rising up from the lake into the storm clouds above.

Curtis slipped and tried to catch himself, but ended up landing on his side. He hadn't let go of the sugar bowl, at least. Planting an arm in the mud, trying to rise, Curtis looked up and saw the salamanders coming fast. He struggled to his feet. He was still a short distance from the shore, but he had to throw the sugar bowl now. Where he was there were few salamanders, but several feet away stood an army. Before he got rid of the sugar bowl, they might attack; he also might need a clear retreat, in case something went wrong.

With all the strength he could muster, Curtis hurled the sugar bowl far afield. Now the storm would go away, the salamanders would return to normal, Simon would be all right, Sam's spirit would be free.... He saw the silvery object break the pale green mist and plunge through the surface of the lake.

The salamanders charged; it hadn't worked.

A ring of flame flew up all around the banks, following on the tails of the amphibians and being fed by the furious wind. It was rolling rapidly toward Curtis, who turned and ran as fast as he could, dodging the occasional salamander in his path and blindly heading back to Maggie's trailer. Suddenly, with great anxiety, he looked around as he ran, searching the rain, the grass, the lake, the trailer court, the flames—everywhere—but it was no use.

He had lost Troy.

TWENTY-FOUR

Jill could hardly see. The windshield wipers couldn't cut their swaths fast enough to keep up with the rain. It was as though the windshield were made of the sort of textured, opaque glass found in shower doors and bathroom windows. She had the defroster on full blast to keep the insides from fogging up. Outside, it was dark gray all around, the sky blending in with the road blending in with the sagebrush. She couldn't believe it was only one in the afternoon.

A semi truck began passing her, plastering the Porsche with a thick coat of rainwater. It took so long for the truck to glide by that Jill had to guide off its taillights; that was all she could see until the truck returned to her lane and climbed off into the distance. "Asshole!" she shouted, but since she had a headache, the sound of her own voice sent a sharp pain into her ears, and she winced. Then, finally, she could see the road again, in between the quick swipes of the wipers, but only for a small distance in front of her. All else was gray and misty.

But at least the crying was over.

It was all over, now. Sherman was behind her forever. Before getting out of Maggie's trailer, she had grabbed the envelope filled with cash, and stuffed it in the inside pocket of her jacket. Jill had enough money to set herself up, somewhere. She could go to Chicago. She could go to New York. She could go to Florida. She was on I-80, heading east, and she would just keep on driving, until she . . . stopped. Curtis could fly out to wherever she ended up and take his damned car back. Jill hadn't told him where she was going, but she didn't care. This was the first chance she had ever had to break out of Sherman, and she wasn't about to give it up. But right now, all she wanted to do was get past this stupid storm.

She tried turning the headlights up to bright, but that just made everything worse, so she flicked them back down.

Suddenly, there was a deer frozen in its tracks directly in her path, looking straight into the headlight beams.

Jill slammed on the brakes, and at the same instant remembered that was the wrong thing to do. The car slowed, the tires screeched, and then the brakes locked and she was hydroplaning. She tried to steer out of the lane, onto the shoulder, and the car started skidding to one side. It veered off enough to the right that it missed the deer and kept on going, until Jill had spun around 180 degrees with only one tire still on the pavement. She was off the road, at least, and safe. A red light was glowing on the dashboard; the engine had died. She saw the deer scamper off the road in the direction from which it had come, and disappear into the rain.

That was a close one, she thought. Tough enough.

Her heart was racing, and the windows were fogged, despite the defroster, from her rapid breathing. A car flew by on her right; she was facing traffic, tilted up at a steep slant, but it wouldn't take much to get the car turned around once more.

After she caught her breath.

That was the third time in the last few hours that she had nearly died. Maggie had tried to kill her with the poisoned cobbler, and later with the gun; now Jill had almost slammed into a deer at sixty miles per hour. She seemed almost to have a death wish.

And now she didn't have any friends left.

Sam was dead, and Maggie had been killed by Curtis. Curtis had to be crazy, if he could burst into the trailer and shoot Maggie like that. Maggie had been everything to Jill.

She had been there at every crucial point in Jill's life, helping wherever she could, as a friend, a confidant, a mother figure. No matter what Maggie had thought of herself at the end, she had been a truly good person. Jill knew she could have talked Maggie out of shooting her, if only she had had more time. But Curtis had come along and spoiled everything. Now Jill would never know, and Maggie would be lost to her forever. So would Curtis. The three strongest friendships in her life were over for good, and now she had to start back at the beginning, all alone.

Jill turned the key in the ignition, and the engine quickly came to life. The rain hadn't let up. Let it come down, she thought bitterly, as she turned the car back in the proper direction—toward Laramie—and gunned the engine. Soon enough, she was back up to highway speed, and watching the road for more deer.

Her headlights picked up a green sign coming up on her left that read: *Laramie—28*. She was far away from Sherman, now.

It was strange that there had been a deer on the road. Unlike many of the rural highways in Wyoming, the interstates were bordered with barbed-wire fences. It was common to see road kills every several miles along one of the little highways, but not on the interstate. Every now and again, however, it happened. Deer had to go to great lengths to get through the fences in the first place, and many of them got hung up in the barbed wire in the attempt. Every so often, one got through. Jill wondered why a deer would go to all the trouble, and then stand in the middle of the road, change its mind, and go back the way it had come. She was glad she hadn't killed it, not to mention herself.

She passed a green sign reading: *Battle Road Exit—2*.

She realized suddenly that she was very much alive. She had made it.

Curtis would take care of the curse. He knew what to do. Jill only wished she had shown him where the sugar bowl had been before taking off like that and leaving him in the lurch. But it wouldn't be too hard for Curtis and Troy to find it. The drawer to the desk was open, with the sugar bowl and Maggie's black leather notebook inside.

Half an hour before, just when she was leaving Sherman city limits, Jill had decided she really didn't care what happened to the town. There had been, for too long, so many things conspiring against her, holding her back, denying her the hope of a fulfilling life, that she was glad, in a way, to see Sherman meeting its end. It was the same feeling of satisfaction she had had when looking at the burned-out shell of the high school building earlier that morning. She could see why Maggie had lusted for revenge. A corner of Jill's soul craved it, too. And now that she no longer had any friends, it was easy to block out all those other people, the nameless, faceless idiots that made up most of Sherman. Their lives would never amount to anything. They would graduate from Sherman High, go to college, and return to Sherman to teach in the same high school. If the curse were to hold complete sway and destroy the entire town, Jill had wondered if it would even matter.

But now that she was halfway to Laramie, she had come to her senses. She hoped Curtis could stop the curse before it killed anyone else. Just because Jill didn't know them very well was no reason for her to dismiss them like that. Just because she didn't understand them didn't mean it was all right for them to die. Most people in Sherman Jill would never be able to understand, any more than she could understand the deer. Yet she had risked her own life to protect that of the deer, even though a few minutes later it could have easily gone farther on up the road and been killed by another driver. Jill didn't have the right to judge people she hardly knew. And even though Sam was gone, Maggie was gone, and Curtis had gone nuts, there was still Simon, Erik, Frita, Celia...

The cobbler!

Jill had forgotten to tell Celia. For all she knew, her aunt might already be dead.

She turned off at the Battle Road Exit, having made out the dim green light of a gas station. Her heart was pounding in her ears as she pulled up to the stop sign at the end of the exit ramp. She had to get to a phone. If she didn't reach Celia in time...

Beneath the bright, glowing plastic sign for Ernie's Sinclair Service was a phone booth. Jill pulled up sharply and came to a jolting stop, left the engine running, and darted through the rain to the lighted booth.

Using the only quarter she had, she dialed, with shaky fingers, her home. It rang, and rang, and continued to ring, until the connection was abruptly broken. "Hello?" said Jill. "Hello! Hello!" But there was no one there; the line was dead. She hung up and was about to dial Wells Memorial Hospital, to see if Celia was on duty, when the pay phone failed to return her quarter. All she had left in her pocket were a few pennies. "Damn!" she shouted, yanking on her damp hair. She struck the phone with her fist.

The rain soaked through to her skin as she ran to Ernie's Sinclair Service to get change. The old man behind the counter said he couldn't make change for the hundred-dollar bill she handed him. Jill thumbed through Maggie's envelope and discovered a few small bills at the back, handed him a one, and he made change for her, eyeing her suspiciously. "Thanks," she said.

The call she made to the hospital was fruitless; Celia's supervisor told her Celia had not come in to work, but she wasn't scheduled until much later, anyhow. Jill tried her home number once again, but a recording came on telling her the line had been disconnected or was no longer in service, and if she stayed on the line, an operator would come on to assist her with...

Jill hung up, got back in the car, drove to the other side of the overpass, and turned onto the interstate, heading back to Sherman.

➤ TWENTY-FIVE

Curtis was sweating as he tore the brittle, yellowed sheet of paper out of the notebook. He knew now what he had to do.

All the answers had been right there, in the book he had found, in the same drawer where Troy had found the sugar bowl. The old sugar bowl had already been used once, so it had been useless. It had had no more power than any of the rest of the junk on the walls of Maggie's trailer. If Curtis wanted to put an end to the curse, he would have to prepare a fresh sugar bowl to be thrown in the lake, and even then, he didn't know if he would be able to make it work. Maggie's scrawled notes made it sound simple, yet Curtis didn't know if he had the courage to go through with it.

He had still seen no sign of Troy, but Curtis hoped he had gotten away. He couldn't imagine what it would be like, to be touched by one of those salamanders, and engulfed by those scorching flames...

Curtis folded the torn page into fourths and shoved it in the back pocket of his jeans.

Several pages in the notebook had been devoted to the curse. He knew it was going to destroy the entire town, and not only would it kill everybody, it would trap every "soul" it could get its hands on, to "enhance the power of the earth in Sherman." Prenez's soul, and Sam's, had already been trapped, but the curse must have been weak enough the night before that they had been able to get their messages through, however eerily. Curtis wondered if Simon were truly safe, if he still had his soul.

He didn't have time to consider the implications. All he knew was that he had the power to end the curse, release those souls, and prevent any more from being taken.

He could get all the necessary materials, but they were at his house in Green Hill Estates, and Jill had his car. She had been gone over an hour, and Curtis was beginning to get the feeling she was never coming back.

He stared at the pulsing orange glow in the windows and realized he might not get the chance to set things straight with Sam. At least, not in this world.

On the way back to Sherman, Jill realized Curtis had, in fact, saved her life. Maggie *had* intended to kill her, and the poisoned cobbler was proof, if indeed it had been poisoned. Jill had only Maggie's word on that count, and if Maggie had been telling the truth, Celia might already be dead.

The radio reported there were several fires burning out of control, in spite of the rain, in the neighborhood of Burroughs Park. There was also a Tornado Watch and a Severe Thunderstorm Warning in effect until nine p.m. for the entire county. Jill had seen an ambulance on the other side of the interstate with its siren on and lights flashing, and wondered if someone else had struck the deer.

She turned off for Sherman at the Second Street Exit, which was the one closest to her side of town and the fires, which were coloring the sky a deep salmon.

Second Street was blocked off just past the Buckin' Bronc Motel, where two fire trucks were trying to fight the enormous blaze engulfing the shopping plaza. Jill couldn't get home that way; she would have to make a U-turn and go around the block from the other side.

Just as she was turning, a figure darted into view, caked with dark, oozing mud and slime. The figure was waving frantically at her.

Jill braked to a halt in the middle of her U-turn, when she saw the disgusting figure was actually Troy.

Troy opened the passenger door and climbed in. "Jill!"

he said, out of breath and gasping for air. He smelled as if he had been swimming in the lake. "It didn't work! Curtis . . . Curtis threw the thing . . . back in . . . in the lake, but . . . didn't work."

"Where's Curtis?" Jill asked, alarmed. She gunned the engine and they turned the corner, heading for the trailer court.

"Better stop here," Troy said, "and walk . . . Fires everywhere, and salamanders." He tried to wipe some of the grime from his face. "Curtis? I don't know. I . . . I chickened out. I saw him throw it in, and then the fire shot up everywhere, and the salamanders were after him. I got the fuck out of there, don't know what happened to him."

Jill parked the car, and they got out and ran to the trailer court. The wind was so strong that every raindrop stung her face, and the rain was still pouring. Troy was right; flames were shooting from the windows of several trailers, people were running from their homes, and salamanders were crawling on the ground. Encircling Stink Lake was a wall of fire. A blackened corpse was smoldering on the sidewalk at the corner of Third and Grant. Jill gasped. Troy told her to watch the ground for salamanders, or she'd end up like that, but she knew that already.

Her trailer was intact, although it would only be a matter of minutes before the flames spread from one of the neighboring trailers. No light shone from the windows. Jill unlocked the door and rushed in. The peach cobbler was still untouched, and on the kitchen table lay a note from Celia.

Jill—

They needed some extra bodies at work, so I got called in. What are you doing with Norbert's dog? He wanted to go to the bathroom, so I let him out. But I'm in a rush. See you later.

Celia

Celia hadn't eaten the cobbler, and was probably safe. Jill sighed in relief, but wondered what had become of Claude. Before leaving, she ground the peach cobbler down the garbage disposal. Then she grabbed Troy's arm and they hurried over to Maggie's trailer.

Curtis was inside, sitting on the couch and brooding.

"Curtis!" she said.

"Jill!" Curtis jumped up and embraced her. His arms were very strong; Jill could hardly breathe. "I didn't think you'd come back."

"I wasn't going to. Thanks for saving my life. I forgot to tell you that before."

"No prob." Curtis let go of Jill when he saw Troy. "Troy! You're alive! I thought they'd got you."

"Naw, I'm all right."

"Good. C'mon, we've got to go up to my house. The sugar bowl wasn't any good anymore. I've got to make a new one." He explained that he had found Maggie's notebook, and it had provided a formula for suppressing the curse, which he had torn out and put in his pocket.

"Let me see," said Jill.

"No," said Curtis. "I can't. I have to do this myself."

Jill glared at him. He was withholding something from her.

"My mom has a silver tea service," said Curtis. "I also need a salamander—one that isn't going to kill me first."

"You mean your pet, Dino?"

"Yeah. Let's go," he said impatiently. "We don't have any time." They left, and Curtis turned off the lights.

On their way to the Porsche, Jill came upon Claude, barking at salamanders. She picked him up, so he wouldn't touch any of the deadly creatures, and carried him back to the car with them. She hoped nothing had happened to Celia on her way to work.

* * *

When they got to Curtis's house, it was still a mess.

Erik was in the recliner, watching an auto race on TV. He looked over his shoulder and waved at them as they came through the door. "Hey, Curtis, Jill, Troy. Holy shit! What happened to you guys?"

"Nothing," said Curtis. In the car, he had told Jill not to tell Erik anything. It was too late—too much had happened, and Erik would never believe any of it. He would only get in the way. "How's Simon?"

Simon was still stretched out on the couch, covered with a blanket from chin to toe.

"He woke up a little while ago," said Erik. "But he just lies there and stares at the ceiling. I got him out of those dirty clothes and fed him some ice cream. He'll be OK, don't worry. All those cuts are really minor—they're healing up—and his ankle isn't sprained. At best, he might have a bruised bone, but that's all."

"How would you know?" asked Troy.

"Hey, my mom's a doctor. You sort of learn these things."

Curtis opened up one of the doors of his mother's Dutch china cabinet, which had miraculously survived the party, and grabbed the sugar bowl from the tea service on the middle shelf.

Jill went over to the couch and stood over Simon, looking down into his eyes. He didn't seem to notice her. She asked if he could see or hear her, but he said nothing.

Curtis ran down the stairs.

"Troy," said Jill. "We're going to take Simon with us."

"What do you want me to do about it?"

Jill sighed. Naturally, Troy would have to be difficult now. "Get him some clothes and help me get him to the car."

A cry came from the basement, and then Curtis yelled, "Christ!"

"I'm going to see what's the matter," Jill said. "Erik, you and Troy get Simon out to the car, all right?"

"Sure," said Erik.

The doorbell rang, but Jill didn't stick around to see who it was. She hoped it wasn't Curtis's parents, but then they wouldn't be ringing the doorbell, anyway. As she ran down the stairs, she smelled smoke, and then saw it coming from the open door to Curtis's bedroom. Curtis came running out of the bathroom with a soaking-wet towel, and handed it to Jill. "Here," he said. "See what you can do." He started back up the stairs.

"Where are you going?"

"The garage, to get the fire extinguisher," he shouted as he disappeared from view.

Jill ventured into the bedroom. Parts of the carpet were on fire, and the smell of melted rayon was thick. Curtis's parrot, Dr. McCoy, was now a pile of ash. The screen that covered Dino's terrarium was torn open from the inside, and Dino was nowhere to be seen. Jill swatted the fires with the heavy, wet towel, coughing and hiding her face from the smoke. She watched her step, being sure not to back up into Dino. He was in this room, somewhere.

Curtis appeared with the fire extinguisher. "Get back," he commanded. Jill stepped aside and he started spraying the flames. "You didn't see Dino anywhere, did you?"

"No. Who was that upstairs?"

"Rick and Deb, come to pick a fight with Erik."

"Oh, swell."

In a few minutes, the flames on the carpet and the water bed were out, but the water bed had a slow, gurgling leak, which they ignored. They crept around the room stealthily, searching every corner for Dino. Curtis flung open his tiny window to let out the smoke, and rain started coming in.

Then they looked behind them, and saw the bedroom door was now on fire, as well as the carpet at the entrance.

"Shit," said Curtis. He handed Jill the fire extinguisher. "Get those, will you? I'm going to find that son of a bitch." Curtis drew his switchblade; the blade sprang forth.

He went out the door, and Jill sprayed the flames. It wasn't too long before they were out. She searched the basement for Curtis, and to see if more fires had sprung up. Curtis was looking in his father's study, but he hadn't found Dino, and there was nothing on fire there.

"Damn," he said, running his fingers through his scalp. "Where is he? He can't have gone far."

As they searched the rest of the basement, Curtis told her he had to kill Dino, slice him up his ventral side, and stuff him in the sugar bowl. Then he had to add some drops of his own blood, and weld the lid shut.

"That's it?" asked Jill.

"Well, basically."

He was holding something back. Jill wished she could see what was written on that scrap of paper, but he wouldn't let her. She wondered if it had been a good idea, coming back.

Upstairs, people were shouting: Erik and Rick, Jill supposed. Accusations flew, from "Cocksucking flamer," to "Neo-Nazi macho shithead." A loud thud shook the ceiling. Something or someone had been knocked over.

"I don't think Dino's down here," said Jill.

Curtis nodded.

They ran to the stairs, and found the top steps on fire. Curtis took the fire extinguisher, while Jill scuttled past, dodging flames, to look for Dino.

Deb, standing near the front door and wearing her "Wyoming Shit Kickers" cap, shrieked, but Jill couldn't see any fires in the living room. Rick and Erik had knocked over the coffee table and were wrestling on the floor. Erik had got a hold of Rick's hair; he slammed his head against the carpet. Rick threw Erik off him and landed a punch in Erik's ribs. Deb cheered him on.

Simon was still on the couch, oblivious. Erik and Troy hadn't gotten very far with him.

Curtis joined Jill in the living room, having finished with the stairs. "Where is he?" he asked, blade drawn.

"I don't know. C'mon!"

Deb yelped, and said, "Watch out, Ricky—Curtis's got a knife!"

Curtis ignored both her and the fray on the carpet. He

looked under the couch. Jill took the other side of the room, searching behind and underneath the stereo. She tried to stay clear of Erik and Rick, but found no sign of Dino. "Not over here!" she yelled.

"Not here, either," said Curtis.

Troy joined the fight, pulling Rick off of Erik and receiving a good box on the ear.

Jill smelled fresh smoke. "Curtis! Over there—the china cabinet!" It was catching fire.

Curtis sprayed it with the fire extinguisher.

Deb said, "What are you guys doing?"

Jill paid her no attention. She looked under the china cabinet, but Dino wasn't there. "Damn!" She was beginning to wonder if Dino were invisible.

From the TV came the sound of a loud explosion, as a car burst into flames.

Troy and Erik now had Rick pinned to the floor, and Erik was pummeling him.

"Stop it, Troy!" shouted Deb, melodramatically. "You fucking queers! You'll kill him!"

Then, from behind the fallen coffee table crept Dino. He was heading for Rick's hair, and was only inches away.

Curtis dove over the couch, switchblade in hand. He landed across Simon's legs, one arm outstretched and hitting the carpet, his other hand coming down swift and hard. "Die, sucker!" he shouted.

Deb screamed as the blade came down, but shut up a moment later, when she saw that Curtis hadn't split open her boyfriend's skull. Then she looked baffled.

Curtis had stabbed Dino right in the middle; in a few seconds, the thing was dead. The knife was coated with salamander blood.

"What the fuck?" queried Rick, confused.

"Nothing, asshole, I just saved your life. Now get the fuck out of my house." Curtis got up off the floor, holding the bleeding body of Dino in his hands. "And stay away from Stink Lake."

Jill wondered how Curtis felt, having to kill Dino like

that. Sam had given Dino to him the previous year, and Curtis had always taken perfect care of him. Now Dino was just a slimy, lifeless mess, and Curtis was momentarily frozen as he stared down at it. But Jill couldn't tell what he was thinking.

Troy and Erik got off of Rick, and let him get to his feet.

Curtis and Jill went into the kitchen.

"I'm going to the garage. My dad keeps a blowtorch out there. I hope it still works."

Jill gave him a kiss on the lips. Curtis seemed taken aback. "Good luck," she said.

"Thanks." He was sweating, and then he was gone, down the hallway. Dino's blood dripped from his fingers.

The air was hazy from all the smoke, but at least the fires were out. The living room was a disaster area. Rick and Deb were going out the door, although Rick was limping.

"You wimp!" Deb shouted at Rick, emotionally. "Beaten up by my little brother and a fag!"

"C'mon, bitch," said Rick. And then they were gone. Jill heard the Vega fire, reluctantly, to life.

"Jesus!" said Troy, breathing hard. "That was fun."

"Erik, are you OK?" asked Jill.

"Oh yeah," he said. "I can take it."

"Go ahead and rest a few minutes," said Jill. "Troy, find those clothes Curtis loaned you last night, for Simon. Then we have to take him to the car."

Over the TV, the announcer was saying, "Let's take one more look at that spectacular crash...."

Jill wondered what was keeping Curtis.

Suddenly, she had a vision of Curtis lying on the floor of the garage in an old pool of transmission fluid, his fist clenched around the switchblade that was plunged deep into his stomach. Blood was gurgling from the wound the way the water had bubbled forth from Curtis's damaged water bed. She shook her head violently, and made the image disappear.

Although she had told herself she wasn't going to disturb Curtis, she was getting worried.

"I'm going to get Curtis," she said getting up. "Why don't you guys take Simon out to the car. Just lay him out in the backseat, and try to keep Claude off of him."

Troy said, "Sure." Erik looked bewildered as he sat there rubbing a bruise on his arm, but then, Jill realized, he didn't know who Claude was.

Jill ran down the hallway and thrust open the door to the garage.

The blowtorch, which looked just like the fire extinguisher except for the blue flame leaping from its nozzle, was standing up at Curtis's feet, hissing. The sugar bowl lay on the ground, its lid black from being welded shut; the job looked finished. Curtis was sitting on a stool with his back to Jill, his chest convulsing, his face buried in the oily canvas gloves on his hands.

"Curtis?"

He straightened up, stood, and turned around. His face was beet-red and grease-smudged. "I'm OK," he said, then repeated it. He seemed trying to convince himself, however, rather than Jill.

Jill stood there in the doorway. She found that she was afraid of him. It seemed she ought to hug him or something, but she couldn't bring herself to do anything except stare, and wait.

"Are you ready to go?" she asked.

Curtis threw his gloves on the ground and shut off the gas on the blowtorch. "Yeah," he said. "Definitely." He grabbed the sugar bowl, looked up at Jill, and smiled self-consciously.

Jill tried to smile back, but she knew it ended up a grimace. That wasn't what she had wanted. As they left the garage, she took Curtis's hand, which was trembling fitfully, and squeezed it tight. She couldn't think of anything to say.

When they got back to the living room, Jill grabbed the fire extinguisher from where it lay on the floor beside the china cabinet; it might be of some use when they got around all those salamanders at Burroughs Park. Erik and Troy were outside in the rain, and the door was ajar.

Curtis and Jill were going out the door when they nearly ran right into Curtis's parents on their way in, huddled together beneath a single dripping umbrella.

"Oh!" said Curtis's mother in surprise. She hadn't gone inside yet; she hadn't seen the "tornado" that had struck her living room.

"We're back," announced his father.

"Hi," Curtis muttered as he squirmed past them. "Bye."

Jill followed right behind him, offering the Bowleses her grimace, and swallowed a croaky, "Hello."

Curtis and Jill ran toward the Porsche, getting soaked. Erik and Troy were standing beside it. Simon was inside.

"Curtis!" shouted his father. "What the hell is this?"

"You get back here this instant!" ordered his mother. "I mean it!"

Curtis ignored them. "Erik," he said in a serious tone. "Listen to me. Can you get your mom's car?"

"Yeah, sure—"

"Great—you guys go over to your house and get it, all right? I want you and Troy to go to Laramie. Go see a movie. Do anything. But get out of Sherman."

"Why?" asked Erik.

Looking down Green Hill Drive, over the crest of the hill and past the golf course, they could all see the rest of Sherman laid out before them. The entire neighborhood around Stink Lake appeared to be on fire. Other isolated spots of orange could be seen elsewhere in the town, through a misty screen of rain. The rain that was coming down, even in Green Hill Estates, smelled like the lake, and felt slimy to the touch.

"Troy will tell you everything once you're both out of Sherman."

"Hey, man," said Troy. "I really think I ought to come

with you guys. I mean, I could give you a hand, and you guys could use it, you know?"

"There's only one thing left to do, and I can do it by myself. Besides, there's no room for you in my car. I want you guys out of here, fast, just in case it doesn't work."

Erik still looked befuddled.

"OK," said Troy. "Hey, if Simon makes it, give him this, and tell him I'll be seeing him." He took off his Skunks jacket and handed it to them.

Jill took it and threw it in the car, thinking sarcastically, *After all that's happened, I'm sure Simon will be thrilled.* She said good-bye to Troy and Erik, got in the passenger side, and shut the door, setting the fire extinguisher at her feet. Simon was stretched in the backseat, and Claude was asleep in his lap.

Curtis came around the other side, sugar bowl in hand, and got in the driver's side. He started up the engine.

Curtis's father was coming after him, running down the lawn, and cursing at the top of his lungs.

Erik rapped on Jill's window. She rolled it down and he stuck his face in.

"I still don't get it," Erik said, and laughed nervously. "What's the deal? *What is going on?*"

"Everything," she said.

Curtis peeled away from the curb.

➤ TWENTY-SIX

As they were speeding past the golf course, Curtis reached over and shoved his Sex Pistols tape into the cassette deck. It was in the middle of "Bodies" as it came blaring over the speakers.

"Curtis," Jill complained. She was staring out her window, trying to see whatever she could of what was happening to Sherman. "I really don't want to listen to this right now!"

Curtis let out an exasperated sigh. "Hey, c'mon, I just want to hear it one l—" He didn't finish.

Her head snapped around; she looked at him hard. *Had he been about to say "one last time"?* she wondered. She let it go. *Let him listen to his music.* But she wasn't going to let him die. He was the last one left. Her last friend.

The wipers slapped water back and forth across the windshield. Curtis turned down Seventh Street. It was a through street without any stop signs, so he wouldn't have to watch any intersections. On either side of the street, houses started flying past at forty miles an hour. Some of them were on fire already, even way out here. The traffic coming from the opposite direction was thick: people fleeing their homes, flashing their brights, honking their horns. Curtis's car was the only one driving toward the conflagration.

Jill heard someone scream, and wondered whether it had come from outside or from Curtis's tape.

Claude was whining. Jill looked back over her shoulder

and scratched him behind the ears. Simon was like a stone statue.

Curtis ejected the tape. "Why are some of these houses on fire? They're nowhere near the park."

The answer suddenly popped into Jill's head. "The storm sewers," she said.

"Yeah, you're right!"

"The rainwater will carry the salamanders all over town," she said, and realized what that meant. "Every house could be on fire in a matter of hours."

"Or," said Curtis, rubbing the stubble on his chin, "it could all go up like that." He snapped his fingers. "Right now, in a second."

Farther down the street, Jill saw, everything was a bright orange. Trees, houses, cars were all on fire.

Jill had to talk to him. There were things she had to say, things she had to know. Once they got to the park, Curtis wouldn't waste any time; he would get out of the car, try to get to the lake, and throw the sugar bowl in, or whatever it was he had to do.

The only sound in the car was the rain beating against the windows. From outside came the roaring and crackling of the great fires.

"Curtis, you aren't going to die, are you?" She had found the right way to phrase it; all he had to do now was say *no*.

"I don't know," he said. His face held a pained expression. It looked as though he had borrowed it from Sam. "Maybe we'll all die, for all I know."

That wasn't the answer Jill had wanted. Whether or not he was going to die, he seemed to believe it was certain. Curtis reached over and downshifted, and Jill grabbed his wrist and gave it a gentle squeeze.

"You can't die," she said, looking straight at him. But he was still looking out over the hood of the car as he drove. "I won't let you."

"That's very nice of you."

She wanted to tell him to stop being a jerk, but that was

entirely out of place here, now. "Curtis, my other friends are dead. If you die, I won't have anything left."

"If you're trying to lay a guilt trip on me so I won't go out there, don't."

Jill wondered if that were what she was doing, without realizing it herself. She wanted to see the end of the curse, but at the same time she didn't want anything to happen to Curtis.

"You think you have nothing left," continued Curtis. "What about me? I've killed somebody! Shot her dead, with a gun. But I'll never be convicted, because the body dried up and blew away, for Chrissakes!"

"Stop it—"

"And I wasn't even sorry. I know she was your friend, but I don't care. Sam died because of her. This is all her fault. I'm glad I killed her!"

"Curtis, stop, you're scaring me."

"You think I'm not scared? Not caring that you've killed somebody, that's terrifying. I feel like a monster."

"Curtis, watch out!" she shouted, pointing in front of them. In the middle of the road lay a black, smoking corpse. Curtis swerved successfully around it, and slowed down. Salamanders lay in the road ahead. Stink Lake was coming up.

"I have nothing left," said Curtis. "Even less than you. Dammit, Jill, Sam was my life. I've been dead inside ever since last night, when you told me what happened to him. Now everything's gone. I don't have a future. All I ever wanted was Sam. I don't want anything anymore, or anybody, not Erik, not you. Nothing."

This was a slap in the face. Jill had been so wrapped up in her own problems, she had hardly realized what Curtis was going through. She still didn't understand, but she felt she was beginning to. It all fit: the time Curtis and Sam had spent together, the way they had seemed to pass secrets back and forth through their eyes, the work they had put into their friendship. Jill knew they were blood brothers, but now she realized something more. Curtis had been in love with Sam; the earring jiggling from his right ear probably did mean he was gay, after all. She wondered why he had never told her.

"You were in love with him, weren't you?" she asked, but it was a statement, not a question.

"Yeah. I loved him. More than you can know."

"He loved you, too, didn't he?" This time it was a question.

"Yeah."

Curtis parked the car one block down the street from the burned-out husk of the high school. Most of the houses were burning down. Some were already gone. Another one abruptly exploded into flames on the other side of the street. Curtis turned off the engine. The heat was tremendous, even with the rain falling down.

"Were you guys more than friends?" That was the most polite way she could put it.

"Yeah. Sort of..."

Finally, now that they were stopped, he was no longer watching the road. Flames danced in his dark irises, as their eyes met.

"Did he ever love me?"

Curtis paused, and said, "Of course."

He would have said that anyway, whether or not it was true, she thought. Jill knew Sam had loved her, as a friend, but she didn't know if there had ever been anything more. He had never actually told her one way or the other, nor had she told him. Even now, she didn't know if she had loved him as anything more than a friend, even though they had slept together a few times. She didn't think she would ever know, not as strongly as Curtis seemed to.

"I'm going to go do it," Curtis said, grabbing the sugar bowl.

Jill picked up the fire extinguisher. "Here, take this, just in case."

"No. I won't need it."

Jill wanted to do it herself, just to make sure Curtis would be safe. She wanted to sacrifice whatever she could for him. But he would never let her, and if she asked, he would probably get angry, and she didn't want him to leave like that. He was determined to go through with it, and no matter what she might try, she could never stop him.

Curtis leaned over and planted a chaste kiss on her cheek. She closed her eyes. He placed something in her hand.

"Good-bye," she said. "I love you."

"Me, too. You'll always be my best friend," was what he whispered in her ear.

She kept her eyes closed until she heard the door slam shut. Then she looked at what he had slipped into her fingers. It was the page he had torn out of Maggie's notebook, folded in fourths, stained blue and sweat-drenched from being in his pocket.

Quickly, she opened it up and tried to read it. The old ink, now brown, was smudged, and the handwriting itself was a hurried scrawl, making it difficult to decipher. She held it up to the bright firelight shining through the windows, which made it easier. It gave the formula for suppressing the curse, with alternate suggestions for extenuating circumstances, some with question marks beside them. Toward the bottom of the page, she found what she was looking for.

"For a mortal man to make it work," it read, "he must forfeit his very soul, to watch over the lake, and keep the curse at bay..."

Jill let the page fall from her grasp; it drifted down onto the empty driver's seat.

Jill suddenly recalled something Maggie had said toward the end, before Curtis had come in and shot her. She'd said that if she hadn't killed Wolf after he'd thrown in the sugar bowl, he would have become a mindless zombie, walking the earth forever without a soul. Jill understood now; it had been a mercy killing—if there had even been anything left to kill. Wolf had given up his soul trying to save Sherman.

Jill froze. She couldn't let Curtis attempt it.

She grabbed the fire extinguisher and got out of the car. A hot wind blew against her, smoky and wet, coming from Burroughs Park. She tossed her hair back, slammed the door, and started running. In the street, there were fewer salamanders than elsewhere, so they were easy to avoid. She turned the corner, and there was the park.

Curtis was running just ahead of her. She hadn't lost much time.

The lawn of Burroughs Park was a patchwork quilt of Kentucky bluegrass and flames, and the portions not aflame writhed with tiny, dark, glistening amphibians. Stink Lake could not be seen at all; a wall of fire surrounded it, shooting many stories high, and swirling counterclockwise, like a whirlpool. It seemed to be slowly spreading outwards, as it spat balls of flame into the ground and crept even higher into the sky.

Curtis was heading directly toward it.

"Curtis!" Jill screamed. "Come back! Don't do it!"

He was running right through the swarm of salamanders, but he hadn't caught fire. His dark figure stood out, stark and alone, against the brightness. The wind was slowing him down. Where he was it seemed nearly hurricane force, and he was no longer running. He had one arm up in front of his face, the other clutched tightly against his stomach.

Jill ran after him, crossing Fremont Street. She had to save him, and she didn't care if she died trying.

"Curtis!"

The salamanders were waiting for her. Their eyes shone, black and dim, reflecting the flickering light all around them. Tiny flames shot up from their feet. They crawled all over each other, sneaking like assassins, but kept their eyes on Jill. Hissing noises sprang up wherever they stepped; even this close to the firestorm a light rain was falling.

Jill turned the fire extinguisher upside down and sprayed the creatures in a wide swath before her. They skittered away, hissing. *It worked*. She stepped ahead, into the path she had cleared. Behind her, the salamanders closed it back up. She sprayed again, and kept it coming as she continued forward, trying as much as she could to pick up her pace. Curtis was still far ahead of her. As she went farther, the wind became a greater hindrance, preventing her from going any faster. As she got closer to the lake, the salamanders thinned out little by little, until the great mass of them was behind her. Then the fire extinguisher sputtered out.

"Come on, come *on*," she pleaded. "Dammit!" She threw it aside; it was all used up.

She could avoid the salamanders from here on out. At least she had made it this far, even though her exit had been cut off.

The hot wind was excruciating, and growing ever stronger. She had to lean into it to keep on her feet, and kept her hand in front of her face to protect her eyes. She only looked down, to watch for salamanders, except when she had to glance up to find Curtis's figure.

"Curtis!" she screamed once more. But it was useless—she could barely hear her own voice above the roar of the firestorm; there was no way in hell that he could.

She had wondered how he could have made it as far as he had without a fire extinguisher, but when she saw him disappear behind the wall of flame without being touched, she realized he was being protected as long as he held the sugar bowl. Which meant Jill was in trouble. Now that Curtis had gone into the firestorm, she could never go in and get him. She couldn't go forward, or she would go up like a match. She couldn't go back, or the salamanders would have her.

Her throat was parched, and her skin felt as if she had been out in the sun all day. This close to the flames, no rain fell. The roaring and crackling and hissing were driving her crazy. It sounded like Niagara Falls.

She should have stayed in the car. She had left Simon unprotected. The Porsche might be on fire, and he would be trapped inside. She wanted to kick herself.

She looked down at her feet just in time to see a salamander gingerly stepping forward, trying to take her by surprise. It reached out to touch one of her Top-Siders. Jill jumped away, shrieking, and wished she had some way to defend herself in case more than one decided to come after her.

Then she saw something squirming on the ground out of the wall of fire. It was a skinny vine, like the one she had cut from Curtis's leg. It slithered forth like a giant bull snake, and Jill almost thought she saw a forked tongue fluttering out of its tip. It was sizing her up, ready to strike.

Jill tried to maneuver away, but it was difficult. She had to keep her eye on the tentacle, while watching the ground for salamanders and fires. But the tentacle was following her. She knew it would get her; she didn't know when, or what it would do to her. She had seen some of these algae vines wrapped around Sam when she had found him lying in the mud. This one might do the same to her.

"Go away!" she shouted. "Go away!"

It serpentined through the wilted grass, coming at her in an S-shaped path. Then it shot out and coiled itself around her leg, and yanked.

Jill fell flat on her back, screaming. She thrashed about on the grass, reaching desperately for something to grab onto, but there was nothing. It was dragging her forward, into the firestorm.

"Let go!"

Her back burned from being dragged. A second tentacle lashed itself around her arm, and a third came down hard across her thigh, slicing through to her skin. She cried out in pain.

The wall of fire came closer and closer.

She was about to die...

And then everything stopped.

The firestorm was gone. The tentacles lay limp on the ground, and their grip on her limbs had loosened. Jill lay motionless, twenty feet from the lake's bank. It was still raining, and she saw many houses still on fire. But she knew it was over.

She turned her head in the other direction and saw a salamander not two inches from her face. It stared at her suspiciously, and stepped on her muddy hair. But nothing happened. The salamander tried his other foot, but that didn't work, either. His Adam's apple, or whatever it was, contracted, and he skulked away.

Jill laughed, as the rain poured over her from the gray sky above. It smelled clean, fresh.

Curtis had done it; the curse was over.

But where was he?

Jill shook the slimy vines off her arm and legs, and stood. Her thigh hurt where she had been whipped, and her pants were cut, but she wasn't bleeding. And better yet, she wasn't dead.

Curtis's body lay, face down, at the edge of the lake. He was motionless, but he wasn't one of those charred corpses, at least. He might still be alive.

Jill walked, slowly, toward him. If he were dead, she didn't want to know. If he was alive, she had to.

Curtis stirred.

"Curtis!" Jill said, and went closer.

He got up on one knee, looking out over the lake, and then very stiffly rose to his feet.

Jill ran up and embraced him, holding him tightly against her, resting her head on his shoulder and closing her eyes.

"Curtis, you've alive! You made it! I don't believe it. Oh my God, I thought I was a goner. I came out after you. I thought you were going to die. I was going to get you, bring you back. I didn't care about the town, all I wanted was you. Oh, you feel so good..."

His arms wrapped themselves around her torso and squeezed her strongly, his fingers gripping into her flesh.

"Don't ever let me go," Jill said, hiding herself in Curtis's embrace. "I don't ever want to lose you. Promise you'll never leave me. Promise."

Curtis said nothing.

"Promise me," she repeated. Then she tried to look into his eyes, but his hold on her was too tight. She could feel his heart thumping against her breast. She pushed gently against his chest so she could see him.

His hair had been blanched white, and his skin was gray. A strand of algae clung to his face alongside his nose, and was dangling in his mouth, which was hanging open. His eyes had lost their coffee-brown tone; in fact, they were colorless, with no sparkle at all. A low, gurgling moan emanated from his mouth, and wouldn't stop. It grew louder and louder. He wouldn't let her go.

"Curtis!" she shrieked, struggling against his vise-like clutch. "What's the matter with you? Let me go!"

Then she knew. The spell had worked all too well; his soul was gone.

The more she squirmed and fought against him, the tighter he held her, until finally she pushed herself out from under his arms and threw herself free, falling upon the grass.

The thing that had been Curtis stumbled toward her with its arms outstretched. Its moaning droned in her ears.

As she got to her feet and started running for the car, she was screaming.

Curtis's body was still alive.

But he himself was dead, inside.

← TWENTY-SEVEN

By dusk, the sky had cleared.

To the west, cottony clouds flared up pink and orange above the jagged silhouette of the Rockies. The sun had disappeared behind the towering bulk of Elk Mountain, but daylight still reigned. The slowly darkening eastern sky was a midnight blue that allowed a few bright stars to gleam through, but the moon had not yet risen.

Jill could see Venus, earth's sister planet, shining, steady and bold. She wondered if she had a sister there.

Most of the water on the interstate had dried up, but there were still many puddles along the shoulder. Claude was sitting in one, panting. He patiently watched the cars drive past, and closed his eyes briefly to the short burst of wind each one left in its wake. Jill held her thumb out whenever another group of cars came toward the curve; she had stationed herself so the coming traffic could easily see her long before they reached the bend. So far, however, she hadn't had any luck.

Where she was standing, a small hill blocked her view of Sherman, but she knew a few fires were raging still.

Her muscles ached, and her mind was exhausted. She wanted to sit down on a comfortable car seat as soon as possible. She wished she could make herself look older. People were paranoid enough about picking up hitchhikers; Jill figured the last thing they wanted was someone they thought was a teenage runaway—which, in a sense, she was.

A bee came and hovered around Claude's nose. His ears

pricked up, his jowls twitched, and then he snapped at it. It buzzed away in a jagged course toward the pine trees on the hill. The breeze was cool, and carried the sharp scent of wet sagebrush mingled with car exhaust. Jill shifted her weight and sighed. She hated waiting.

When she had returned to the Porsche, Simon was there waiting for her, standing beside the car.

"Jill!"

She ran up and hugged him, and neither one could hold back the tears. Jill closed her eyes, and pushed from her mind everything that had just occurred at the lake, while Simon's small arms squeezed her tight.

"Simon, are you all right?"

"I think so." He considered a moment. "Yeah, I'm OK now."

Jill looked over her shoulder at the park, but the thing that had been Curtis was no longer following her. It was nowhere to be seen. She told Simon she was going to take him home. Simon got in through the open driver's side and climbed over the gearshift to the passenger's seat. Jill got in, but saw there were no keys in the ignition.

"Oh God," she said. "Simon, do you have the keys?"

"Uh-uh," he said, shaking his head. "Are they gone?"

Jill searched the floor, the seat, the glove box, but could not find them. Curtis must have taken them when he had left to throw the sugar bowl. He must have thought he was going to make it after all—or perhaps he had simply done it out of habit.

"Shit!" said Jill. She had been hoping to drive the Porsche out of Sherman, but she was damned if she was going to go back and wrestle the keys from *it*. The very thought made her flesh creep. "Shit!" She punched the steering wheel, accidentally honking the horn.

"What's this?" asked Simon. He had picked up Troy's Skunks jacket from the floor by his feet. "They didn't get Troy, did they?"

"No, he's fine. He and Erik got out of town. Troy said he wanted you to have that."

"You're kidding!" To Jill's surprise, Simon actually was thrilled. He put it on. It was too large for him, but he would grow into it.

They went back to her trailer, which was still, incredibly, untouched by flames. They sat on the floor in the living room and talked. Jill told him what Curtis had done, how the curse had been brought to an end. Toward the end of the story, she grasped his hand and held it tightly; otherwise, she would never have been able to finish. Then she asked him what exactly had happened to him.

Simon told her how Sam's ghost had gotten inside him down in the storm sewer to alert him about the salamanders. "Then," he said, "when you guys came down and the salamanders started going after you, I was able to get away. This other ghost got in me, this Prenez guy, see, and they helped me find a way out of the sewer. I went down a few blocks and got out through a grate in the street, and then I started making my way up to Curtis's house, but then I kinda blacked out, and they took over. It was freaky, 'cause I could still see what was going on, but I couldn't do anything. It was some trance or something. It kept going deeper and deeper. Later on—this morning, I think—Sam and the other guy left. They couldn't hang on anymore. The lake pulled them back, but I was still in this trance. I could feel the lake pulling at me. It wanted me to come, too, and the pull kept getting stronger and stronger. It was sorta like a dream, though, or when you're all spaced out in the hospital. Next thing I knew, I was in Curtis's car, and I saw you running. It's all gone now—I mean, the trance. I feel OK, really."

She told him she had decided to leave Sherman that night. He wanted to come with her. But she told him his parents needed him, especially now that they had lost Sam.

"He really is dead," Simon said.

"Yes. He's dead." Her fingers were at the nape of his neck, winding themselves in his hair. He was going to have to explain it to his parents. "I'll walk you back to your house, if you're up to it. First, I have to make a phone call."

She went to the phone and dialed the number and extension of Celia's supervisor at the hospital.

"This is Annette, may I help you?"

"Could I speak to Celia Parker?"

"One moment, I'll get her."

Jill was put on hold. Muzak played in the background. A minute later, the line was picked up.

"This is Celia."

Jill hesitated, then chickened out and hung up. Celia was alive, and that was all she needed to know before she left Sherman for good. She couldn't speak to Celia now. After she was gone and had set herself up somewhere, she would write her a letter, to let her know she was alive.

Jill and Simon walked the ten blocks to his house, which had also survived without a scratch. They hardly spoke the entire way. They both limped slightly, their arms around one another. They said good-bye on the walk in front of the house. Simon asked Jill to come inside, but she didn't feel like answering any questions; she remained at the curb as Simon went up the steps to his house. She watched Simon embrace his mother, and his mother watching her. From the purple bags under her eyes, it was obvious the poor woman hadn't slept since Sam had disappeared. As Simon stood there hugging her about the waist, she stared over his shoulder, through the screen door, at Jill, while tears rolled down her cheeks. After several minutes, they withdrew to the privacy of their home. Jill stood there, unable to shake the image of Mrs. Taylor's face, and her expression of both gratitude and derision.

Jill's jacket was barely enough cover against the rapidly dropping temperature. If she had to spend the whole night in the open, she would freeze.

A Ford Taurus drove past. Its three brake lights shone brightly—points of a triangle—as it slowed down, veered onto the shoulder, and came to a stop. Jill ran toward it waving. Claude followed at her heels, then bounded ahead, wagging his tail. The car backed up slightly to meet them.

Just my rotten luck, Jill thought. *A yuppie!*

The passenger door was pushed open for her, and Jill poked her head inside. The driver was a black woman of about thirty, with a short but conservative haircut. She wore glasses, a yellow polo shirt, khaki slacks, and a smile.

"Where are you headed?" she asked, one eyebrow cocked. Her voice carried a slight Southern twang.

"Chicago?" she said.

"You don't sound so sure!"

"Oh, Chicago, I'm sure." She was eager to get in and sit down.

"Doesn't matter, anyhow. I'm only going as far as Omaha."

"Omaha's fine. I've got a dog."

"I saw that, I saw that. Nice one, too. Lab, is he? Don't worry. Just put him in the back, long as he's no trouble."

"He's all right." Jill opened the back door and ushered Claude inside. He leapt onto the seat and curled up.

"Doesn't he look bushed!" said the woman, and chuckled. "He's a cutie. What's his name?"

Jill got in and closed her door. She noticed the driver was wearing her seat belt; she reached over and put hers on. "Claude," she said.

The woman checked her mirrors, looked over her shoulder, and started pulling away from the shoulder. "Claude, huh? That's nice. What's yours?"

"Sue." It was true enough. Susan was her middle name, had been her mother's name.

"That's nice, too. Debbie," she stated, offering her hand to shake, which Jill did. "Hope you don't mind if I smoke, 'cause I'm going to, anyway." She tapped a cigarette package until one sprouted forth, a Kool.

"I don't mind."

The cigarette in one side of her mouth, Debbie asked, "You want one?" She tapped out another.

Jill took it. "Thanks." It was as good a time as any to start. Not that she had never smoked one before—but from now on, she was going to do it regularly.

Debbie lit both cigarettes with her silver Zippo. The smoke felt good in Jill's throat. They were cruising at highway speed now. She was beginning to relax.

Celia had never let her smoke, since it would have stunk up the trailer. Jill was glad Celia was alive, but as long as her aunt stayed in Sherman, Jill would never see her. She could never have stayed in Sherman herself, and doubted she would ever return.

Debbie turned on the headlights. The dashboard beamed to life. Outside, it was getting dark. Jill rolled her window down a crack, so the smoke would be sucked outside. The air rushed by noisily, and the breeze coming in gave her a chill.

"So," said Debbie, "did you come from back there? That town?"

"Oh, no." She took a drag from the Kool. "That's just where the last guy dropped me off."

"You mean, he actually lived there?" Debbie gave a look of mock astonishment. "I'll be!"

"I guess."

"Where are you from, then?"

"Rock Springs."

"Jesus! You know how to pick the winning towns, don't you!" She laughed, and muttered, "Rock Springs. My, my." She clucked her tongue. The car shifted itself into automatic overdrive.

Jill found out Debbie was a federal bank examiner, based in Omaha. She and other members of her staff pored over banks' financial documents, checking them for "technical errors." She said Jill would be surprised at how screwed up some of the nation's banks were. Jill decided Debbie had to be good at what she did, to be in such an important position at such a young age, and a woman at that. But when it came down to it, Jill didn't really care. She was just along for the ride, and small talk had to be made.

Jill realized she was already far away from Sherman. She had made it. She had escaped. In the inside pocket of her jacket, she still had Maggie's envelope stuffed with hundred-dollar bills. She had nothing to worry about; everything was going to be OK.

"You're a runaway, aren't you, Sue?" asked Debbie. But before Jill could answer, she said, "No, I'm sorry, I'm sorry, I take that back. I don't want to know one way or the other. I don't want to know. But sometimes a clean break is the best thing all around. And I should know. I often think that if I'd have stayed in my hometown of Waxahachie, I—"

"Wax-a-what-y?"

"Waxahachie. It's in Texas, trust me. Anyhow, if I'd have stayed there one more day, I truly think I would have been stuck there the rest of my life." She finished off her cigarette and stubbed it out in the ashtray. "I wouldn't be here right now. And you wouldn't have got a ride!"

Jill laughed. The scowl had fallen away from her face. Her own cigarette was half finished. "But you got out," she said. "You made it."

"Yeah, that's right. I made it. I wouldn't have made nothing in Waxahachie. I went back later, you know, but I had to make that break first."

Just like a yuppie, Jill thought, she thinks she knows everything.

Jill hoped her own "break" would be forever, that she would never go back to Sherman.

Only one thing could ever make her go back, but the prospect itself scared her to death. She had gone back to Maggie's trailer and figured out what Curtis had done. He had released the souls of Sam, Mr. Prenez, Kraig, and anyone else who had been killed by the lake, by giving up his own. Stink Lake would have snatched the souls of everyone in Sherman if Curtis hadn't sacrificed himself. It was the same thing Wolf had done forty years earlier. When Maggie had removed the sugar bowl Friday afternoon, she had set free Wolf's soul, to go wherever it was supposed to go. Now, Curtis was watching over the lake, protecting the town from the ever-present threat of the curse. His own soul would be imprisoned there until someone, someday, found his sugar bowl and took it out of the water.

Jill was the only one who knew. She was the only one who could do it, but she wondered if she loved Curtis enough—as much as Maggie had loved Wolf—to go back sometime and release his soul.

"Son of a bitch!"

Jill started; she had been drifting off, her head leaning against the cool, smooth window. She looked over at Debbie, who was messing with her rearview mirror and looking disgruntled. "What is it?" asked Jill.

"This jerk's got his brights on behind us. He's bugging the hell out of me."

Jill looked over her shoulder, out the back window. All she could see was a blinding pair of headlights. The car was nearly tailgating them. "Shine them back in his face," she said groggily.

Debbie grabbed the rearview mirror and moved it around, from side to side, reflecting the headlights at the correct angles to make sure the driver behind her got the message.

The other car dimmed its lights back to normal and started to back off.

No longer blinded, Jill tried to get a glimpse of the car in Debbie's taillights before it fell back into the darkness. She could only tell it was a small foreign car, but it dropped back too quickly for her to tell exactly what make it was.

What if it's Curtis in the Porsche? she wondered. What do I do if he . . . if *it* comes after me? Jill squinted her eyes and once more tried to determine what kind of car it was. She found herself biting her nails.

"Slow down," Jill said in a cautious whisper.

"Huh?"

"Slow down and let it pass us."

Going up the next hill, Debbie let the car lose some speed. Jill watched closely as the headlights of the other car approached. For a moment it looked as if it might crash right into them, until the other car's engine roared into a higher gear and swerved around them. Jill's eyes followed it as it sped past, back into their lane, and disappeared into the distance.

It hadn't been a Porsche, but a Mazda. Jill sighed with relief.

It was craziness to think the zombie Curtis had become might be trying to follow her. If it had no consciousness and no soul, surely it could never drive a car. Jill wondered how long it would last, if it would eat, if it knew anything about survival. Most likely, it would get hit by a car while trying to cross the street. But even if it did learn how to survive, someone would come across it and get it into a sanitarium, and lock it up in a rubber room forever. No matter what, Jill was certain she would never meet up with it again.

"Why are you so uptight?" asked Debbie.

"I'm just tired, I guess. I couldn't get any sleep with those bright lights shining in. For a while I thought they might follow us all the way to Omaha."

"Slim chance of that! Go ahead now, go to sleep."

Jill turned back around and leaned once more against the window, propping her head against her hands. She knew she'd never get any rest now. Whenever she closed her eyes, she found Curtis right there, staring back at her.